DEATH
AND THE
MAD HEROINE

DEATH
AND THE
MAD HEROINE

S. F. X. Dean

Walker and Company
New York

First published in the United States of America
in 1985 by the Walker Publishing Company, Inc.

Published simultaneously in Canada by John Wiley & Sons
Canada, Limited, Rexdale, Ontario.

Library of Congress Cataloging in Publication Data

Dean, S. F. X.
    Death and the mad heroine.

    I. Title.
PS3554.E1734D4   1985   813'.54   84-25632

ISBN 0-8027-5612-3

Book Design by Teresa M. Carboni

Printed in the United States of America

10 9 8 7 6 5 4 3 2 1

This one is for

CHUCK AND LOUISE

Sure as the most certain sure [him] *plumb in the*
uprights [her]
   well entretied, braced in the beams,
Stout as a horse [choose one each]
     —affectionate, haughty, electrical [me]
I and this mystery, here we stand.

                        W. W. [FS]

Death and this mad heroine
Meet once . . .

Dylan Thomas

Prelude 1

NEIL KELLY, *a professor visiting the campus of his college in Oldhampton, Massachusetts, for the first time in two years, stands outside Morecomb Hall and considers. It is eight o'clock of a showery Monday morning in late April, but the light in his old office is on and someone is in there typing. They've given his office to a madman. No one works at this hour on a Monday morning.*

Neil had wanted to pick up a book and use the phone, leaving a note for his temporary tenant to explain the intrusion. He has even fingered out already from his pocket bunch the key stamped MH-11, which he never relinquished when he went on leave simply because it seemed too final.

Now he puts the key away with a shrug and enters the deep Romanesque archway of the old brick building.

The temporary occupant inside is typing furiously, as he has been all night. He is unshaven, his eyes are blood-streaked with fatigue, and he is snarling, almost sobbing at the unknown, but hated person who will eventually receive his letter.

Dear Though Unknown Department Chairman, Chairwoman, or Chairchild:

Every college campus is a mad town in miniature, and this backwater of the Massachusetts commonwealth is no exception. There is no real democracy, but they are very hot to teach the theory of democracy. There is scarcely any literacy, but the best books abound. They languish, to be sure, in the fun house of a library, which has witnessed mayhem (I am told) and covetousness and lust (I am sure) and the rest of the dirty side of the human soul at least as much as it has been lit by the hard gemlike flames of intellects alight. Logic and grammar mildew with neglect whilst semiotics and electronics have much-roomed (I meant to write "mushroomed" but why tamper with divine inspiration?) and, if rhetoric survives from the grand trivium that education once balanced on, it ekes out a shamed living in the admissions office, its tropes in tatters, its schemes all software.

Trustees who have no wish to understand the curriculum raise money and give marching orders to a President who cannot teach, and he in his turn gives some of the money and all of the responsibility to a Dean he dandles on his knee and whose mouth he moves by means of secret controls. The lips of the President never stop smiling, and the faculty are thus instructed, as from Delphi or the burning bush, as to their destinies. Each member of that dropsical body styling itself in the local idiom The Faculty nourishes a shamed dream of personal excellence soured by a private grudge against an institution brutally insensitive to true worth, and in spare moments memorandizes colleagues for their lack of something called community spirit. Lost ships hooting forlornly to other lost ships in an eternal fog of obscured purpose.

I am a citizen of this particular mad town, called Old Hampton, for two years now near their close. I was brought here as a partial (sic!) replacement for a senior professor who has taken himself off to romantic foreign places to write best-selling books about seventeenth-century poets of arguable merit and to earn a laughable reputation as an amateur detective. You think I am inventing this, but it is all too painfully true. This academic thinwit has intruded himself, Wimsey-wise, into homicidal situations left and right, and various gullible policemen have praised his uncanny resemblance to a deep thinker. I labour under his sign; the door of this, my temporary office, still has his name on it, Professor Neil Kelly. Beneath the nameplate of this pseudosleuth—white capitals engraved in black plastic, to give you the flavour of the institutional style here at Old Hampton College—I am permitted, as temporary inmate, to add my own name, Visiting Assistant Professor Dewi Morgan-Evans, hand-printed on a three-by-five note card of striking design.

*In six weeks my tenure as the Great Man's substitute
will end. He will return (on clouds of glory? with a flourish
of trumpets? who knows?) and I shall find myself extracted back into the floating job market whence I came,
a market at this moment in time limp as a damp stamp.
(This is not really a job application, but an insincere love
letter to the world. I take my metaphors from the stock
at hand. This is called research.) I shall be out of job,
out of house (his, Kelly's, of course, to make my abysmal
substitute's role as contingent and abased as possible),
out of this neurotic seat of New England pretentiousness
and, if you know what's what, into your department,
teaching almost any damned literature from Chaucer,
Spenser, and Shakespeare to Miller, Wilder, and Mailer.
But in the perfect world, in the sane town I sincerely
believe your campus to be, to teach Dylan Thomas and
the Welsh poets, about whom, goddammit, I know more
than anyone else alive or dead.*

*Yours dead or alive, cordially, furred with sleep from
an all-night vigil at the shrine of St. Olivetti, at 8:00
A.M. of a morning with the great crooked white sun
just easing its sharp edges over the black sea limit
beyond Boston to blare day on this inland, dry-docked,
deadlocked, daft town,*

Dewi Morgan-Evans
Visiting Assistant Professor of English Literature,
temporary.

*The puffy, dark-eyed, rumpled man smiles grimly reading this
mock application over, sighs, and puts it on top of the pile to
the left of his battered typewriter. Murphy will understand and
get a smile out of it when she reads it.*

*With that off his chest, and slumped under the weariness of
an all-night bout of typing and sulking (he has quarreled with
his wife, whom he adores), he vows to inscribe one more le-
gitimate letter of application for a real job to an actual chairman somewhere. It will be his one hundred and twelfth. He is
up to the letter C in the* Dictionary of American Colleges and
Junior Colleges, *and he groans to find that the next listing is*

3

for a Chillington College in Arkansas, a state he cannot even imagine, let alone locate geographically.

It is for Murphy he labors. Murphy, his wife of just one year. Today is their anniversary, and so why did they have their worst quarrel ever on its eve, last night, when some daemon in him got him shouting, and some independent spirit resident in her told him to go to hell? It was somehow linked, he knew, with the ache of love he carried in his chest for her and the swelling nausea of self-disgust and responsibility when he imagines he will not find a job.

Murphy is unable to walk normally because of a childhood accident, which left one leg shorter than the other and only stiffly articulated from the hip. Dewi loves her as purely as he loves Welsh poetry, which is saying a great deal, more than he would have thought possible. To him she is not his crippled wife, a burden to be borne, a cross to be lugged, but a divine gift, a grace in flesh in his arms. Her mind is a field of flowers, endlessly changing color. She writes small poems for him and hides them in his socks and under his cup. He is short and fat and his lips pout and he is balding before his time, and he looks altogether like a ripe baby left in the sun to swell. But he is a champion typist, and he has that rarest of academic possessions, a first-class mind. He really does know more about Dylan Thomas than anyone else in the world. His students always begin by laughing at him but, unless they are intellectual thugs, end by listening to him very carefully and carrying his music with them when they leave. He is the sort of man who will someday single-handedly edit a new edition of the dictionary. But this hung over morning he is simply bored, exhausted, cranky, bitter, self-pitying, and ashamed.

1

DEWI SAT BACK aching luxuriously in the swivel chair of his detested, unmet, absent host and looked around him morosely. He made a mental note that before final exams, he should remove the pictures he had added to the room. There were four of them, three framed cartoons clipped from old newspapers, yellow and brittle with age, and one drawing cut from an English magazine and matted.

The cartoon directly over the desk showed a handsome, Latinate Pierrot, standing costumed in his performance clown suit, billowing white cotton with enormous polka dots, on the sands of Bournemouth beach, being asked by a thin lady in a hat, "How much would you charge to sing 'Never Been Kissed in the Same Place Twice' into mother's ear trumpet?" The jolly entertainer was said to be Dewi's father in caricature.

The clipping pinned to the wall above the typing table depicted four forgotten statesmen of Westminster arm in arm bawling some music hall nonsense, knees up, all dressed in the dotted suits and ruffs of Pierrots. And the one against the books on the top shelf of the bookcase was a sketch of Powell and Baines's Glad Cadets: Bournemouth, 1927, the seven men dressed in what looked like waiters' garb and the one woman wearing a beaded dress and fringed shawl, long white stockings and Mary Jane black patent leather shoes. She was Dewi's mother, Marjorie.

His father had been a famous Pierrot then, a devilishly handsome, black-eyed feature singer with the Glad Cadets, and also eventually with The White Coons, the Gay Hussars, and half a dozen other of the troupes that formed, dissolved, reformed, and migrated over the beach circuit of England's vaudeville on the sands. Some uncertain time in the summer of 1924 or 1925, Marjorie Evans, an ambitious, bony girl of exiguous talents as a singer, but with a brassy look about her and a common, comic face that somehow made the audience feel that their sister from Bradford was singing the funny songs, had joined the troupe. Within weeks she and Powys Morgan, him with his nickelodeon Sheik-of-Araby eyes the girls were mostly mad for, had formed the Morgan-Evans duet, famous eventually for "Ta-Ra-Ra-Boom-der-é" and the astonishingly popular "Never Been Kissed in the Same Place Twice."

That sunny duo was given credit for both the first prizes won that season by the Glad Cadets in the competition between the Bournemouth and Margate troupes. To be fair, though, Ganesh Francis Xavier Rahman, a Pakistani who had been converted to Christianity and taught the banjo by an Irish Jesuit from Boston in the city of Goa where they both felt the need for music and friendship (and whose ethnicity was ingeniously disguised by blackface makeup, wogs being unwanted in Bournemouth) was a favorite in the warm-ups, challenged only by Sid Dunn doing his imitation of a queer ballet dancer who badly had to go (saved for the late evening shows, when the mums, who loved it, could laugh to splitting without the kids there to wonder).

The second blue ribbon and cup seemed reason enough to Morgan and Evans for them to get married that October, that and the simplification of their domestic strategies by now permitting them to occupy one room legally.

Later (much later, after Powys had left Marjorie and gone off to Ireland to convince Yeats that the Abbey Theatre needed his new Irish play, and got himself shot by an Irish actor in some contretemps in a pub, an event that soured him on Irish theater and politics permanently . . .

and then come back and then gone off again in pursuit of one Queenie Thompson of the Adler and Sutton Pierrots, she to spurn him as an unwelcome detour on her road to the silver screen as the lovely and beloved Merle Oberon—as he always proudly referred to her afterward, as though being turned down by film royalty was cause for mortal pride . . .

and then returned to Bournemouth once again to charm his way back into Marjorie's affections and earnings), they produced, swiftly and astonishingly, Dewi, the baby that Marjorie had finally assumed, after fifteen years of off and on cohabiting, would never arrive.

"We should have tried you there years ago," said Powys to Marjorie at the sing-along and send-off the Glad Cadets gave the tiny family in the dressing tent in September 1939. To which the lanky, brazen lass replied, holding the infant at arm's length and looking askance, "Remember the rule, soldier, never in the same place twice."

For the soldier jokes had crept in, and the second war, never to be repeated, arrived by another miracle, and proved to be as great an attraction to Powys as Queenie Thompson or William Butler Yeats. The young men, even Ganesh Francis Xavier, now welcome, swapped their banjos and ruffs for other gear and soft shoed off. The beaches closed and sprouted barbed wire, and when the war was finished and the barbed wire came down, they all discovered the Pierrot craze was finished too. Percy Motherwell, lead tenor returned an RAF wing commander, decorated and one-eyed, with a future in uniform as doorman at the Russell Square Hotel. Ganesh Francis X. Rahman stayed on in India to become a hero of the Pakistani independence movement. Powys Morgan died doing a camp show somewhere in North Africa when an Italian shell mysteriously found its target. The tribute spoken for him, to a genuinely saddened audience who associated Powys with Bournemouth and bank holidays and peace, included the dubious claim that if he had been able to choose his way of going, Powys Morgan would have wanted to pass on singing his heart out on the sands for our lads. Marjorie vanished into London, last seen hooked up with Sid Dunn, the seedy hoofer who had always wanted her in his hangdog way.

Dewi's good uncle (the one required in every proper family), Thomas Evans, M.P., minor bureaucrat, junior minister twice, churchgoer, and childless widower, had somehow fetched up his nephew out of the stew of loose ends the boy's silly mother had made of their life. Cheerfully surrendered to brother Thomas for a one-time payoff of two hundred pounds, Dewi was carted off to Wales, first to Llangelynnin, then to Fairbourne in Meirionnydd, schooled, and taught a kind of Christianity. This last, encountered for the first time at the age of seven, astonished him more than anything else in its absolute

7

reversal of everything his casual show biz mother had taken for granted, from a nip of whiskey when he was fretful to an occasional new uncle sleeping over when one awoke in the mornings.

This newest, straightest uncle became the permanent one. He was the second minister from the left being lampooned in the ancient political cartoon depicting some forgotten coalition of party rebels as idiot Pierrots. The cartoon had meant more to Thomas than any other political memento in that it infuriated him past speech, and it had taken Dewi years to learn why: Thomas Evans had taken his own feverish youthful fling at seaside entertaining during the summer in 1928, in blazer and boater, at St. Leonard's on Sea. The young baritone had been so paralyzed with stage fright on his first appearance before a seated audience who had paid two pence each for their chairs that he had bolted offstage behind the wooden pitch and vomited and wept wordlessly, listening to the rowdy jeers from the front. In his moment of panic, he had managed to stammer only the shameful words, "I can't sing, I tell you, I can't sing," before running off. The master of ceremonies, an old pro who had seen and survived every kind of disaster in his time, rushed onto the tiny stage telling the audience about a fat man he had just seen fall off the pier who kept shouting, "I can't swim, I can't swim."

"So I shouts back at him, I shouts, 'Well, I can't play the piano, but you don't hear me boasting about it, do you?'"

All those scraps and bits and torn fragments of family history Dewi Morgan-Evans had assembled from the memories and scrapbooks and letters of forty years, filled out by one horrible evening following Dewi's graduation from Oxford, when his unbending Uncle Thomas, first tipsy on champagne, then maudlin on port, wept through a recitation of his own humiliating failure in the theater before falling dead asleep muttering pitifully, "I *can* sing, you know. In school I won prizes for it. I can sing, you'll tell them that, Dewi, won't you?"

And now the seaside child who had been dry-cleaned and pressed by the Methodists of Wales and the aesthetes of Oxford sat in a small college town in American loathing himself because he had no job prospects and he had let his worn nerves make him scream at the face of his beloved.

8

He squinted at the fourth of his pictures, the magazine cutout of a Michael Ayrton drawing of Dylan Thomas. Not the cherubic Welsh singer of the Augustus John portrait, beloved of anthologists, but the bleary, stubbled, stubby drunk who had killed himself with booze at thirty-nine. This was Dewi's icon. His patron saint, this alcoholic bard who had decayed so fast from chief boy of summer to mildewed barfly. When he prayed now it was only to Dylan, to intercede for all Welshmen who still believed the true faith, that poetry is a state of grace and language the sacrament.

"If there's a job going around that you know about up there in your quiet hullaballoo of singing saints, I'm not averse to standing still for it," he growled to the picture. "You might tell some of your powerful pals that. If you're out of purgatory yet, you boor barmy bastard, and if you're not, God have mercy on your soul, you must be parched."

A soft-knuckled knocking on the frame of the open door behind him jangled his frayed nerves and set his teeth on edge. It was, he knew with weary certainty, the timid knock of William Fulton, freshman student, who had attached himself to Professor Morgan-Evans like a bat-eyed succubus.

For once, he swore inside himself, he would not yield to the sad boy's importuning for more attention, more tutoring, greater patience with his overdue paper, and his inability ever to be satisfied with one more hour of tortured discussion. Dewi spoke without turning and without ungritting his teeth.

"Go away, William. I do not see students on Monday."

The answer seemed as amused as offended. "I'm afraid it's not William. It's . . ."

God, Fulton's father. The boy had hinted this. I will not turn, I will not turn. Fuck off, Fulton's army colonel father.

"Look, I know this might seem rude, but if you're William's father . . . You really caught me at an impossible . . ." He didn't look like an army colonel, now that Dewi braced himself and turned to confront the intrusion. It looked considerably unthreatening, rather like a middle-aged academic of the sort Dewi had just been maligning in his fictional letter.

It smiled reassuringly and spoke. "I'm afraid it's the landlord."

If it was intended as a witticism, it passed through and beyond the blankly weary Dewi without visible effect.

The visitor tried again. It appeared to him that the young professor at the desk was in a fog. He looked as though he had not shaved yet, and his clothes were rumpled. In the close office, even with the door ajar, he smelled faintly rancid.

"I'm Neil Kelly."

It took a heartbeat for the name to register. Oh God. Dewi's embarrassment, surprise, chagrin, and residue of undischarged bitterness at his life flooded up, sinking his last remnants of decorum. He screeched exactly as he had screeched at Murphy the evening before.

"Goddammit, couldn't you even wait until June?" It had burst out of him involuntarily, and when he heard what he was saying he was aghast, sick even. The heat of his flush made him break out into a sweat. He looked exactly like what he was, a man whose last reserves of personal dignity had snapped. "Oh, I say, what a shitty thing to have said."

He rose with what tatters of manners he could summon and offered his visitor a hand. "How do you do, Professor Kelly. Please come in. I'm Dewi Morgan-Evans." With that he burst into tears. The final indignity. Dear God, he thought, I'm going mad.

"I was going to ask if I might use the phone," the visitor said mildly. Neil Kelly didn't need a clinical report signed by two psychiatrists to grasp the elementary fact that the young man clutching his hand and blubbering was balanced precariously at the edge of a nervous breakdown, and he hoped that a light tone would keep things afloat for now.

"The phone." Dewi snuffled and drew himself up. "Of course. The phone is over there, no the men moved it, it's here, under my jacket." He waved his guest over to the instrument and blinked away a fresh cascade of smiling tears.

"Thank you. I am sorry for this early interruption. I never actually expected anyone to be on campus this early." Was the young man listening, or drowning? "I still have a key, you see, so I was going to use the phone, then leave you a note explaining the intrusion. We're rather casual around her—usually—about other peoples' offices."

10

His explanation sounded lame to his own ears. Did this forlorn man think he was skulking around checking up to see if his pictures were still in place? Come to think of that—he gave a swift glance at the wall above the desk—where was his print of Tung-fang So stealing the peaches of longevity from the Taoist queen's garden? Cartoons of clowns? Was that Dylan Thomas in his boozing suit?

". . . whilst you make your phone call," Dewi Morgan-Evans was saying.

Neil realized that he hadn't heard him, but smiled reassuringly, and added a footnote to his explanation.

"My friend is going to pick me up here as soon as I pick up a book. It's a wedding gift. For another friend. I'm sorry, that's all boring and irrelevant." To his astonishment, Morgan-Evans was nodding absently and repeating "I see, I see," as he sat down, for all the world as though they were about to begin a long narration. But, as if realizing, he jumped up, said, "Oh, yes," made gestures indicating either that he had to go to the men's room anyway or that he was about to have an autistic seizure, checked his fly, wiped his nose with his fingers, picked up his jacket, tossed it onto the chair, said "Sorry, you see, there's the phone," raised his eyebrows twice, grinned ruefully, held both hands out flat in an umpire's "safe" sign, tucked in a stray shirttail, and puffed out his cheeks as he edged through the door and shut it behind him.

It was worse than he had thought. Neil studied the door with quiet dismay for half a minute, as if he expected it to open again for another dumb show by the young man with the musical accent. He was not disappointed. As he watched, the door eased open a crack and the blind hand of Dewi Morgan-Evans reached in and fished around. Neil reached over and put the tweed jacket from the chair into it. From behind the quickly slammed door came a muffled explanation involving the Coke machine and thirty-five cents.

Neil thought a minute before dialing and took the time to look more closely around his old office. Tung-fang was sneaking off with his sly expression and the queen's peaches from a perch under the windowsill. The books from the top shelf of his bookcase had been removed and piled neatly in the corner, and the shelf now contained a row of books whose authors were, with few exceptions, strangers to him: Alun Lewis, Glyn Jones, Idris Davies, Edward Thomas, Henry Vaughan . . . He sighed for the specialization that made the best work of men in the same trade all but unknown to each other. Damn, the book he wanted wasn't here. That meant it was in the study at the house. He reached a decision. Taking a two-volume set of *The Spectator* from the second shelf, he put the books on the desk and dialed his call.

Or tried to. When he had moved out of this office some two years previously, for what had originally been planned as a six-month sabbatic, his phone had been a standard black dial model from the phone company. You dialed nine to reach an off-campus line, then your number. But the instrument sitting on his table was a beige handset of starwars design with fifteen buttons on its idiot face, including sharps, flats, stars, and chevrons. And something remarkably like a Greek gamma. It gave out no dial tone, and when Neil punched the nine button, it still did nothing. Had he been aways so long that he had forgotten how to make a phone call?

With a combination of simmering irritation and embarrassment he went to the door and looked out for Morgan-Evans. That red-faced fellow was sucking from a can of Coke and poured a generous bit down his chest in his hurry to speak while drinking.

"That was fast enough."

"I haven't called yet." Was there a way to say it that might sound less moronic? "I've forgotten how to dial. Have they changed the system?"

"Oh, Christ. Yes, they changed everything. We all had to go to training seminars. You can get conference calls on the bugger, or do any number of things no one in one's right mind would want to do. You can even dial the computer if you want to talk to it."

"Ah, the gamma."

"Right. And, oh, Christ, you can put it on do-not-disturb, see, and that's what I did, so it gives out a busy signal beep to anyone who calls. You set it on pound thirty-two and it does that. I've had it on that all night."

"Do you get many calls at night here?"

Dewi blushed furiously. "Ah, it's a domestic bit of stuff. My wife and I had a fight last night, and I've been here for twelve hours straight, you see . . . ah, just let me show you how to take it off busy. See, just punch pound five, then nine for outside. They call the sharp 'pound.' I've no idea why."

Neil said, "Look, Morgan-Evans, obviously I could not have barged in at a worse time—when I complete this call I shall buy you a cup of coffee to make up in part for all this—" he gestured around the room helplessly.

The Welshman looked round-eyed again at that and scurried out the door.

Neil ran through the prescribed sequence and heard the phone ringing finally at the other end.

Vic Foster answered on the third ring. "Neil? You ready already? Listen, can I pick you up in maybe twenty-five minutes? We've got a little homemaker's emergency here involving a jar of jam and the dishwasher drain. Things are a little sticky right now."

"Listen, Vic. I want to postpone our trip to Williamstown. Something has come up."

"You were the guy with the hots for Japanese calligraphy, not me. If you want to plan to try again next week, make sure you tell me before Wednesday, though, because . . ."

Neil cut him off, thinking it's nice to know who your real friends are, you can break a date made a week ago without any explanations and they don't ask for details.

"We'll see. Thanks, Vic. Good luck with the jam, et cetera."

He hung up and took a deep breath. Maybe it was a good idea to sit and chat with young Professor Morgan-Evans and maybe not, but his professional conscience would nag him for a long time if he didn't try. The man was close to blowing his stack, and if a little talk could bring him back from the edge of fury, then maybe a morning of studying a unique collection of Tokugawa calligraphy was well lost.

He opened the door and invited Dewi Morgan-Evans back into his office. "My turn. Come in, please. I thought we might chat for a few minutes until the dining commons opens, then go get some coffee. Or tea or whatever."

"It's coffee. I've become addicted to it." Dewi entered awkardly, not wanting to claim the good chair again, but unwilling to take the tutorial chair either. Neil saved him the decision by turning the student's chair around and straddling it.

"Sit down where you were, please. It's your office, at least for the next six weeks, as you've already pointed out."

"Oh, I say, that was—oh, God."

"I think we've reasonably established that it's not me you're pissed off at, not really, so tell me, if it's not a state secret, at whom are you? Pissed off."

Dewi slumped brokenly into the desk chair and scrubbed his hand across his face.

"Actually, I was thinking of shooting the president and dean and setting fire to the administration building."

Prelude 2

THE TOWN OUTSIDE *the room where the two teachers sit uneasily facing each other is not, to surface appearances at least, a mad town, as the furious Welshman has just described it.*

Oldhampton sits in the easy valley of the Connecticut River, once lush with tobacco farms, now ringed with malls and plumed with colleges. You could paddle your canoe down the river from near its source to its debouchment above Long Island and stop for a drink eleven times at an institution of higher drinking and learning. Midway you would take a dram or a pint at a college with the same name as its town, although they are distinguished in that the town is one word, Oldhampton, and the college two. Both have been there more than two hundred years.

Fragility and fertility dance in the outdoors in April in the valley. New buds and tender trees and mud-rich acres of bottomland still harvested for corn and onions and the world's tenderest, best asparagus. The naked weather this morning has become a thin slant of rain, and from the upper window of the red brick hall where they sit the campus is becoming starred with flowering umbrellas. The hope of spring is still under constraint from the last spite of winter, the rain is cold and uninviting.

Nothing except spring comes so warily among people in this place as friendship. The two men sit for a moment that is as long and as fateful as a week. One of them watches the rain slice weakly against the window. One scratches his stubble of beard and realizes suddenly that he smells.

2

"ERASMUS, YOU KNOW, used to pray to Socrates."

"I didn't know that. I have a terrible pong, I apologize."

"True." Both. "There's a reference to it in an essay there by Addison. Number 213 in the first volume. Addison is praising the Dutchman for being 'an unbigotted Roman-catholic.'"

Dewi picked up the leather-bound volume and turned to the essay. "I'm a bigoted backslid Methodist myself." He read the passage. "Hah, he really did." He handed the book to Neil. Instead of taking it, Neil indicated the companion volume. "It's a gift. For taking such good care of my office. And getting me that marvelous twenty-first-century telephone." He fended off the younger man's frowning embarrassment at the gift with the irony. "It's nothing special, just an old 1826 edition I got at the league of Women Voters' book sale for two dollars years ago. I'd like you to have it. One doesn't meet many men who pray to famous alcoholics."

"You heard me then, did you?" Dewi growled, rubbing his neck, and settling for putting the two books on the edge of the desk between them.

"Yes, afraid so. Praying to his nibs," Neil indicated Dylan's picture with his thumb. "That's what brought Erasmus and his Greek friend to mind."

Dewi inclined his head toward the little picture. "He called himself 'captain of the second eleven,' you know, but he was much, much better than that. If good poems aren't good works, to hell with it," he said in a sequitur whose logic was almost entirely obscure.

"That's a fine theological dogma, but somehow it seems an inadequate ethical justification for murdering the president and the dean. When you stop to think about it."

Dewi laughed spontaneously for the first time. "I suppose so." He found it difficult to cut the laugh off now he'd started. "But I thought it might clear my head, like a good nosebleed." Neil laughed along with him, glad to see him easy now. "I'm afraid I have to add that I caught sight of my own name in that letter sitting on top of your pile there. I agree about the standards of institutional taste around here—the plastic nameplates on the doors—but I thought 'thinwit' and—'pseudosleuth' was it?—were a bit hard on what's his name." They were both laughing full out now.

Dewi sponged off his face with his cuff. " 'Road company Peter Wimsey,' did I put that in? I was going to." He went off into another gale of merriment. "Christ, I'm getting gaga. I'll be hysterical if we keep this up. I was hoping to amuse Murphy—my wife. The letter's a joke, you see." He sprayed spit through his attempt to stop giggling. "Christ, I'm sorry. Again."

"I like to think of myself as Captain Cat," Neil said in a hollow voice.

"Captain Cat in *Under Milk Wood*?" Dewi lit up. "Oh that's grand. Keeping an eye on Willy Nilly delivering the mail, eh?"

"Can't have Mr. Pugh ordering *Lives of the Great Poisoners* behind Mrs. Pugh's back, eh?" They shared a laugh at the literary joke. Neil felt the need to keep the easy talk going. "Have you discovered yet that we have a section of Oldhampton called 'Milkwood'? Originally Milliken's Wood, I guess, but that got lost over two centuries."

"No, I never heard of that." Dewi tried to sound fascinated, but dropped it. "I have a copy of it signed by himself. It's true," Dewi added quickly, as though the miracle of it was too much for belief without confirmation. "I found it in a shop for two dollars. Rather like your finding Addison and Steele at the Women's League sale. I'm not going to give it to you, though," he blurted, miming panic.

Neil knew that the hysterical edge had drained from Dewi Morgan-Evans's laughter and talk now, and it was more like talking with a tired drunk past caring about decorum.

"I hear you're a splendid teacher. May I call you Dewi?"

Dewi calmed, sniffed suspiciously. "Sure. Are you sure you didn't catch sight of some of my own song of self-praise in the letter on top of the pile there?" He had been realizing slowly that the letter, with its damning sarcasm about Neil Kelly prominently on display, might well have been read while Neil phoned.

"No, I heard it from an admirer of yours, the very dean you were apparently thinking of doing in."

"What, my own intended victim?" Dewi looked thoughtful and dismayed. "I'd better give him time to get it into the written record before I off him entirely, hadn't I?"

"Dean Calder told me that he'd attended the reading you gave in the department's Victorian Evenings series. He thought your reading of *The Wreck of the Deutschland* was 'a brilliant tour de force.' Direct quote."

Dewi groaned. "It was something. I never saw so many eyes glaze over so fast."

"Fred Calder is the author of a much-neglected book on the period of German history in which that event took place. I rather think he thought you were tossing him a bouquet."

"Dear God. Now I'll *have* to kill him. I was making a point about Gerard Manley Hopkins's vision of English patriotism."

"You know that and I know that, but does the dean have to know that?"

They both smiled broadly at the donnish joke, the atmosphere between them relaxed now, two cronies talking shop in off-hours.

Neil took up his hollow voice again. "So there's little need in his case at least for plotting 'alone in the hissing laboratory of your wishes . . . et cetera.'"

Dewi took up the dialogue from Dylan's play. "'Yes,'" he said, his eyes dancing with delight, "'poisoning can be lovely, too.'"

"I was First Voice in the college production years ago," Neil said. "I remember six or seven lines of all that now."

Dewi crowed with delight. "*I* was First Voice in our production at Oxford. Isn't that an astonishing coincidence? Not when you stop to think about it, I suppose." He subsided in some embarrassment at his own effusion.

There was a short embarrassed silence and another one of his irrepressible comments, this one a question, broke the surface.

18

"Why *are* you back on campus six weeks early?" Once he had asked it he simmered with shame at the baldness and rudeness of it, hanging in the air.

"To host an engagement party for an old friend. Dick Colrane, over in the sociology department. Do you know him?" Dewi cocked a baleful eye. "A sociologist, is it? Not bloody likely. Those daft birds . . ." he let the summary evaluation trail off.

Neil grimaced. "It tells you how old I'm getting. Dick was my student when I first taught here, and now he's about to be made department chairman over there in Pell Hall. Do you know enough campus politics to know that Purlie is stepping down? Apparently he's in the line of apostolic succession when our leader resigns the presidency to go to the Ford Foundation next fall."

"I make a poor American, at best, you see. You have been back on campus, what, one day? And you know all the gossip and all the political shifts pending. I met President Allen once, at a tea, and except for that I have never laid eyes on him. I'm afraid the campus newspaper is incomprehensible to me."

Neil laughed and assured him that it was to everyone.

Dewi was not consoled. "And my sole contact with the Ford Foundation was an attempt to find out how to file for a grant. The seventeen pages of response they sent me were so complicated that I chucked them all into the basket there. So put it down that amongst my other faults I'm a failure at the great American indoor sport of getting grants."

Neil pretended to jot a note as he tsk'd. "Homicidal mania. Not very good at swinging grants. It gets worse and worse. Next you'll be confessing lack of attendance at faculty meetings."

Dewi bristled. "I went to one. Honestly. Froze my blood, that did. I scarpered at the first intermission. Add it to the list, I'm afraid." He sighed and put out his lower lip to blow a breath of air up his face. "Christ, no wonder I'm jobless and hopeless. Past forty and still untenured and unemployed. I'm the most obvious counterfeit of an American academic one could imagine. I saw all these chummy politics and old boy networking at Oxford and I said to myself, not for me. I'll go to America, I thought cunningly, and be a free man. Is this the last delusion of Europe? I couldn't be a citizen of Wales—have you seen the bloke who styles himself the Prince of Wales? Charley boy. Christ on a crutch. And I wasn't about to become a true-blue Brit. So here he is, neither fish nor fowl nor good red herring. Declared his independence from the Lords of the Common Room, he did. Proud little bugger he was. But it's really the same drill here, isn't it? Cor, I haven't half ballsed it up. Poor Murph."

Neil felt genuinely sorry for the man, but he knew that with the load of self-pity Dewi was carrying around, he didn't need more from a senior professor snug in a tenured chair. A brilliant mind and a pure heart were far from being the best equipment for surviving and prospering in academia, whatever the laity thought. He decided to change the subject, even at the risk of rearousing the man's hostility.

"I wonder if you'd consider it a great imposition if I were to ask to visit our house to get a book from the living room."

Dewi smiled, then laughed and hiccuped. "I daresay you ask that full of foreboding lest you set me off ranting again and calling you a backwater Gervase Fen. I'd be delighted. You can meet Murphy. She thinks *you're* 'a fascinating character.' Direct quote."

As he spoke he scooped the bogus letter of application from the top of the pile and folded it into his pocket, slipped into his jacket, picked up the two leather-bound volumes of *The Spectator* and looked at them with a mixture of pleasure and perplexity. "I say, sir . . ."

Neil put up a silencing hand. "Please, they're yours. And call me Neil. What with my former students rouding into middle age, I have enough reminders of my encroaching senility."

Neil hadn't planned to mention the other thing yet, but he could see that the subject might be welcome. He indicated the office with a wave. "It's not a bad place for tutorials, I've always thought."

"I wish I could pretend I'd had better, but that view of the flowering dogwood must be rather spectacular in May."

Neil agreed. It had always been his favorite time, term end approaching, students generally over their winter term funk, and the purple-and-white glory against his window in the afternoon sun.

"You wouldn't by any chance be interested in staying on another year, would you, if I can convince the dean to extend my leave?"

The Welshman paled. "Don't joke."

"No joke. I wasn't going to bring it up until I talked with your boss, but in view of that—" he indicated the pile of letters.

"That's only the tip of the frozen continent beneath the water. I can't really believe what you just said." He blinked rapidly. "You did say what you just said, didn't you?"

"I'm quite serious." Neil scratched his nose and looked out of the window again. "There's a, ah—woman in England I'm rather—well. And I thought that if— But if you—"

Dewi was as embarrassed as his visitor. "No, no, really. I say. If *I*, did you say? Will it help to convince you what dire straits I am in if I tell you that yesterday I had a letter of reply from a Bob Appleby College in South Carolina, a Baptist basketball institute to which I apparently wrote while unconscious, and they wanted to know if, as a 'Welshperson'—and there is a word I had never hoped to see in print—as a Welshperson I qualify as 'Third World.' I haven't the foggiest, of course, what the question even means, but I thought the enquiry so alarming, those Southern fundamentalists so hemmed in by Supreme Court decisions that they were flailing about trying to qualify for federal assistance by hiring Welshpersons, that I knew I had reached some nadir in my job quest. Oh my. Oh, I say, this isn't some terrific American leg-pull, is it, because I'm getting quite excited? You think I actually might be able to stay on here at Old Hampton this coming year? I must calm down. My voice sounds higher to me. This is the drowning syndrome one hears of, isn't it? The whole life racing past one's consciousness. Do make me shut up."

Neil shrugged. "The people in the department really like you. Although, to be honest, some of them think you're too shy to be a successful teacher. Survival of the Fittest is the rule, you know. Weak to the Wall, that sort of thing." He glanced at his companion to see if a little old-fashioned British irony helped. "Maybe it's the way you Third World types adapt, but you actually seem to fit in reasonably well. And not entirely without reason, Dewi Morgan-Evans. I did happen to read your article in the *PMLA* on David Jones. I think I now understand the *Anathemata* for the first time, really."

"That's awfully decent of you." Dewi beamed. He had wondered if anybody at all had read that essay.

Neil continued, knowing that his listener was only half listening now, savoring his praise. "Between you and me and the new gymnasium over there beyond the maple tree—dear, it does stick up, doesn't it?—I might never actually return to OH at all. I'm at an in-between place, I suppose. Near the end of my teaching career in any case, and with a book so successful that it pays me more than my TIAA pension will anyway."

He left the thought he had begun unfinished. "Let's just say that we should consider the possibility further after you have talked it over with your wife and I've met with Fred and done the necessary."

The two men left the office as if they'd known each other much longer than an hour. To Neil it seemed an hour well spent.

Dewi was already beginning to shift his thinking to home and wondering if Murphy would be mollified or made even madder by his bringing home their landlord at nine o'clock in the morning. Please God she wouldn't let her Irish temper loose before he could tell her what delicious things Neil had proposed.

They decided to skip coffee at the dining commons on campus in favor of breakfast at their house. Ha ha.

Neil was perfectly aware in his companion's nervous good humor that he was being taken home as a sort of hostage. And he knew that if the younger man had indeed quarreled with his wife the evening before to the extent that he had stormed out and stayed in his office all night with the phone set on "busy," the abandoned young wife in question might not be all that sweetly pleased to see the chum who had apparently brought her husband home rumpled and red-eyed in the morning.

They chatted about the inconsequential things new friends do. Dewi told him with charming diffidence about the book he was writing on the young Dylan Thomas.

"Do you have a working title?"

"Well, yes, actually. 'The Only Tenor, Nimble and Crocus.'" He glanced rather fearfully at his senior. One's titles sometimes struck others as insufferably pretentious. "Does that strike you as awfully—you know . . . ?"

"No, I think it's grand. He called himself that, didn't he? The only tenor in a mob of sopranos, or something like that?" Dewi glowed with pleasure. "Yes, yes, exactly so." Encouraged, he rambled on loquaciously and, for a man exhausted and unsure of his forthcoming welcome, amusingly.

Neil listened with the sure sense that Dewi needed this unwinding. He had started out on this morning's walk partly just to revisit the campus he genuinely loved and partly to see the newly constructed, soon-to-be-unveiled gymnasium his friend Vic Foster had warned him about, a glass and white steel trapezoid they were now passing, housing an enormous pool, a bleachered basketball court, and even a wing where undergraduates could learn to manipulate all the latest weight-training paraphernalia. Dewi merely shuddered when Neil asked him genially if he had visited the establishment yet and said, "They keep announcing that it will open as part of commencement week's events. Perhaps they won't be able to find the key. Isn't it monstrous, like a greenhouse gone mad?"

The two-hundred-year-old college had come to dial-access computers, weight-training rooms, and coed saunas. Between them, the two men exchanged ironic speculations about where OH might go in the next two centuries. Their guesses at what spage-age education might eventually come to were equally wild and grim, but each man warmed to the other's bedrock conviction that unless fine teachers who held the language as their last patriotism continued to teach the bewildered young how to think logically and to respect originality, the idea of education was sunk.

The streets around the college were beginning to fill with the morning traffic of workers, clerks, teachers, and students who preferred to drive from one of the dozen enclaves of housing around the edge of town into the center rather than walk. The college paths were less empty now, near nine o'clock, as students in vivid rain gear sprinted to their first classes of the day.

"It's strange," Dewi said, watching Neil checking his observations against his memories and deciding nothing much had changed in his hometown, "they're not at all different," indicating the students with a sideways jerk of his head, "and the college could well be in Kent or Surrey. Yet the whole context is different. I still feel like an alien. Will I always, do you think?"

It seemed as much an appeal for reassurance as a genuine question.

"Probably." He waited the time it took to walk four steps. "I still do."

He got the expected grudging laugh.

Neil went on. "We're the intellectuals, they're—most of them—here only incidentally, on the way somewhere else, not because they really crave what we have to offer. If we catch them just right we influence, perhaps even change the way they think. If not, not. The trick is, my Welsh friend, to keep from getting the idea that we're the odd men out. They are. Them and their fathers. Sorry if that sounds monkish, or as though I thought of myself as part of some saving remnant, but there it is."

"Gosh, no," Dewi said. Neil was struck by the boyish delight he had sparked in his companion. "That's what I've always thought. But I was beginning to think it was just me. Thanks for the confirmation."

A junky Volvo with an exhaust problem cut them off as they started to cross Spring Street. Its bumper sticker encouraged the reader to save the whales.

Dewi raised his eyebrows as they exchanged a wordless comment on selective do-goodism.

"The bank is having a bumper sticker slogan contest for Oldhampton. Murphy says I must enter."

"I Brake for Poets, that sort of thing?"

"I suppose so. She has submitted about seven. The first prize is a thousand-dollar shopping spree downtown, and she says we can at last get some new clothes. Is everyone else always broke?" It was a rhetorical question, asked in a bemused, offhand way, and Neil let it go.

Neil started to read bumper stickers. You Can't Embrace a Child with Nuclear Arms. Awkward. I'd Rather Be Dancing. Or walking, he thought. It's Great to Be Polish—this one on upside down.

"You don't suppose they'd like It's Great to Be Welsh for a town slogan, do you?" Dewi asked him. "Actually, I wouldn't mind at all winning the thing. But I tell Murph her entries are all too literary. Or literate, whatever. Oldhampton: A Town Full of History, Mindful of the Future, for example. Her best one is Oldhampton—A Glad Diversity and a Common Center. Eh?" He cocked an eye, glancing over shyly for approval, proud.

"Rather good. More than just clever. I suppose it depends on who's doing the judging."

"The president of the bank and his cronies in the Rotary Club, I suppose. I know the chief of police is a judge, because they made a big point of it in the ads. Murph stuck in two safety slogans for him."

Neil laughed aloud. "Scalli? His own car used to have a sticker that said If Guns Are Outlawed, Only Outlaws Will Have Guns on the front and Mafia Staff Car, Keepa You Hands Off on the back."

"There's glad diversity," Dewi said as a gaggle of students passed them. Two were wearing punk hair dye jobs in green and red; two, both female, were wrapped around one another with their hands down into each other's back pocket, and one wore an Edwardian outfit complete with bowler and walking stick.

"And that's only the tip of the lunatic iceberg."

As they turned into Milken Street they passed a shaven-head person of indeterminate gender lying spread-eagled among the crocuses on the lawn of the Wesleyan Methodist Church, singing the Budweiser commercial, a look of wet bliss on the upturned face, the orange cheesecloth robe plastered to the skinny frame.

Dewi made a Wildean moue of distaste. "That's why I left the Methodists," he said with a shudder, "all that exhibitionism."

By the time they had reached the short street where Neil's small brown house with its modest white porch stood, they had begun to understand each other's grunts and oblique jokes. Friendship lives in such shorthand, and that is another thing computers are incapable of.

Prelude 3

THE MORNING HAD brightened briefly, but now again down pelts the naked weather. The two men walk up the path quickly through the cold shower, ducking under the straggling hawthorn bush that overhangs the walk. Each is uneasy because he thinks the other imagines the house is not really his at the moment.

The fatter, littler man says, "Ah, you killer," to a black-and-white cat who trots across their path carrying a fresh chickadee.

They shelter on the porch gratefully while the key is produced from above the doorframe. In Oldhampton the provisions against burglarious intrusion are likely to be primitive and predictable. The door is held open for the owner by the tenant. Both enter the familiar hall.

The younger man cocks his head listening a moment, then calls out, "It's me. I've brought a visitor."

He cranes his neck up the front stairway and repeats his call. There is no answer, only the kind of dull echo that says nobody home.

3

THE BIKE HAD gone out of control on a simple stretch of straight
farm road with a gentle grade to it, just below Teakettle Hill.
In that southwestern corner of Oldhampton, farms of assorted
small sizes, most of them owned by hobbyists growing corn
or truck vegetables for the weekend market on the common,
scattered themselves around the wetlands and the single piece
of commercial property, a fulsome piece of property used as
a storage dump by the local chemical company, DVR Chemical.

DVR's main plant was four miles away, in Granfield, but it
probably qualified as Oldhampton's most hated and best loved
taxpayer. It gave jobs to some eleven hundred locals, but it
also was responsible for that storage dump, which some
claimed was threatening to pollute the entire local water supply.

The woman who had been laboriously pumping her rickety
Columbia bicycle sprawled in the hard dirt beside the blacktop
road and cursed with the fluency of a farm girl. Her busted
bike had landed across her, and she was trying to get it off her
without ripping her pants, which were jammed in the chain.

"Jesus God almighty."

Perhaps it was a prayer. In any case, it worked, after being
accompanied by a hellacious yank which tore a chunk out of
her red corduroy pants. "Will someone get this goddam freak-
ing thing off me so I can stand up?" she screamed in exas-
peration, heaving the bicycle away from herself.

Considered abstractly, she made a furiously handsome sight.
She had a wild shock of dark red hair, held together by a knitted
green headband, a homely, wonderful face with a blunt
snubbed nose, and a fine, square, lively, sexy body. Except
for her right hip, which was out of line, and her right leg, which
was not quite matched to its mate.

She executed a maneuver she had obviously practiced, flipped herself onto her stomach, did two fast push-ups, jumped up onto her bent left leg, then straightened herself, clutching her hip and adding a few curses to the total before breaking into a smile and crowing aloud, "Way to go, Murph, you idiot. Now what the hell are you going to do?"

The smile made the ordinary Irish peasant face radiant, or perhaps it was only the contrast with the black scowl of wrath it had worn when she was tangled in her bicycle on the ground. A woman whose moods would never be hard to read.

The right leg gave way when she tried to stand fully on it and she promptly sat down hard. "Shit." She ripped her headband off and threw it on the ground. While she was down there, she reached over and hauled the bike back to her and looked at the chain, which was now off the front gear. It was too taut to stretch back on by hand and it wasn't the class of bike to have a tool kit attached.

She took a smashed peanut butter sandwich from the pocket of her zippered windbreaker and unwrapped it and ate it. She knew she was going to have to sit there until someone with a car came along and gave her a lift back to the house. Great wedding anniversary. Damn Dewi, this was all his fault. She didn't even have a pencil she could write with if she had to sit here for an hour. Where the hell were all the Polish farmers on their tractors who were always driving ten miles an hour up the road ahead of her when she wanted to pass? A good strong Polish farmer who didn't think wisecracks were social currency would be goddam welcome. She chewed her sandwich glumly and waited.

Two kids in a pickup truck whirled down the road and gave her a big wave and yelled something apparently hilarious as they sped by. Did they think she was bird-watching or something?

She flipped herself up onto her feet again and yelled, "Hey, you jerks," at them, but they were out of sight by then. Her smile lit her face again as she saw a blue-and-white police car coming along. She waved both hands and yelled, "Hey, you guys, hey."

The patrol car skidded to a stop twenty yards past her, then backed up with a squeal of tires. A youthful cop leaned out the window.

"You Okay? You hurt?"

"Yeah. I mean I need a lift. My bike broke. I—"

"Jesus, lady," the driver yelled over his partner at her. "Wait here. We thought those two hiho's hit you. That's my pickup they stole. Stay here, we'll be back or send someone to help you out." They roared off, this time with the siren going, one of them talking into the radio unit.

She puffed out her cheeks and waved good-bye to them with a slow flap of the hand. Great. If you're going to have an accident, Murph, have it in the middle of a crime wave. Stay here. Well, I had been planning to flap my goddam wings and fly away, but, okay, just because you asked so nicely I will. Stay right here. Not move one goddam inch. She wished she had made two sandwiches.

She sat down again, deliberately this time. Her hip ached and she realized her jaw had a long scratch on it, oozing blood. Damn. She checked her pants to see if the cuff could be sewed and her leg locked on her. The same thing it had done to cause the accident. The black Irish look came back. She threw a rock at a bluejay, but it didn't help. Damn. She sat propped against her left hand, right leg stuck out stiffly and sent up a shower of prayer curses for someone to come along and get her out of this ridiculous posture and place. Anyone. Damn leg, damn bike. Damn Dewi.

A green Plymouth came bumping carefully along the pot-holed road and pulled up in front of her.

"You come here often?" The driver with the bar-scene witticism was a Newman-handsome man in his forties, just a touch of adorable silver around the ears, black hair, and a smile to win a thousand hearts. Shit. Him. Not hers.

"I'm fine, thanks."

"You don't look fine."

"I'm just waiting for the police car to come back." She added heavy emphasis on the words, then added quickly, "They told me not to leave the scene of the accident."

"You could be here all day."

He was right, it was the cops' car they had stolen. She could be sitting here till noon. And it was starting to rain coldly. Of all the damn people in Oldhampton, why did it have to be him who stopped?

"Nah. Really, I'm fine. I'm doing some bird-watching while I wait."

"You've got blood on your face."

"Just a scratch. Really. No kidding."

He sighed, rebuffed, and backed his car up fifty yards and drove up to her again. "Morning, miss, had an accident? Can I help?"

She dimpled and did her Shirley Temple imitation, finger to cheek, voice high enough to be inaudible to all but trained dogs and eardrums tuned to squeaky frequencies. "Why don't you fuck off, you funny man, or I'll report you to the cops?"

He laughed and got out of his car. "I've got it now. You're Catherine Murphy's little sister, aren't you?"

"I'm Dan Murphy's daughter." She stared at him with her darkest practiced look. Shit, why did he have to be such a nice guy? A little grossness or lechery or maybe a hint of superiority at least would have been welcome, but as he leaned over her to offer a hand up, all she could think of was what a nice guy he was.

"I'm Dick Colrane. I guess you already know that, from the way you're acting. I'm on my way to the college, won't you let me give you a lift? I think you've hurt yourself." He held out both hands now. "As you might remember, I know a little about that."

"My father didn't shoot you."

"I never said he did. C'mon, let me give you a hand into the car. I think the bike will almost fit in the trunk." Without waiting for a reply he picked up the old Columbia, held it out at arm's length and shook his head, and jammed it into the trunk. The front wheel stuck out, but it would do.

He came back and made another try, smiling. "Listen, just let me drive you home. I won't say a word."

"Well, he didn't. You might as well know, I'm writing an article about it for a book." As she said it she thought, and I might as well get in out of the rain at least, and reached for his extended hand.

"Goddam." He let go of her and let her fall right back on her sore butt in the dirt. With an angry flurry he yanked the bent bike from the trunk of the Plymouth and hurled it back beside the road.

"You must be as dumb as your sister. Well, I hope the damn cops come for you some time next week. Lots of luck." His face contorted with bitter rage, his movements jerky with suppressed energy, he slammed back into his car and roared off. Despite her shock at finding herself sitting in the dirt again, Murphy couldn't help watching to see if he limped as badly as she did.

"Lots of luck to you, too, Dickie Colrane, you all-American prick bastard," she screamed after him, tears streaking her face. She hammered her fist into the dirt and shrieked maniacally at the bluejay, who had returned to mock her. "Shut up you, too, you stupid son of a bitch." For lack of a rock in reach she crumpled her green headband and hurled it at the offending bird. It missed and hung harmlessly from the end of a branch out of reach.

When the blue and white returned for her, she was stretched out flat on her stomach bawling into her arms, her husband's stupidity, her idiotic hip, her crumpled bicycle, and her half-awake night all combining against her. At first the two young cops thought she was unconscious or dead, and had instant thoughts of dismissal for cause, leaving an injured woman on the road. But when she lifted her bloody, tear-stained face and smiled, it was as if the sun had come out.

"You two clowns certainly took your sweet goddam time," Dan Murphy's daughter Margaret Mary said, wiping her chin.

The two men sat sipping tepid instant coffee, which Dewi had hastily slopped together in the kitchen, hoping he could get it back into the front room before Neil came out and saw that Murphy had left last night's dishes piled in the sink.

Neil went on explaining about his reasons for coming to the house for the book, filling the time by justifying his intrusion while the anxious Dewi peered around him up the street out the side window.

"And since Dick is a sociologist with a special interest in Russia, I know the book will mean a lot to him. Kosorin wrote it after he escaped from Petropavlovsk prison in 1920, from the notes he kept there on scraps of newsprint."

"Yes, I see."

"He had been accused of trying to murder Lenin, but he swore to me in 1947 that the charge was trumped up. He had been in the Kerensky inner circle, of course, but if you had known him you'd find it hard to imagine him as an assassin."

"Lenin, eh? Yes, I daresay."

"I understand there are only some dozen copies of this edition known to exist. You see, he signed it and wrote a phrase from St. Augustine's *Confessions* on the flyleaf, 'God grant to men to see in a small thing ideas common to things great and small.'"

"You don't suppose she's run off, do you? Oh, I say, that was stupid. Sorry." Dewi looked out the window again.

"Really, I'm sure she just went on some early morning errands."

Dewi flushed with embarrassment. "We haven't a car. If she went, she went on her bike, and she's not supposed to. Bit of a bad hip, y'know." He had the characteristic British need for understating difficulty.

Neil rose. "I should probably be going anyway. I've got to get over to the faculty club before ten to see the steward. I plan to give a little party for Dick and Jill as soon as the announcement about their engagement is official, and if you know Garabedian, the club steward, you knew he's a tyrant. I know from experience the only time to see him is early morning."

"But you can't do that." Dewi looked stricken.

"What, rent the club for an evening? Oh, it's pretty commonly done."

"Exactly. What am I thinking of? My dear fellow, I've been to the faculty club. Once. Common, I should think so. I've been in railway waiting rooms in northern Wales with more style. No, no, you must have your party for your friend here. It is your house. Really, I insist." Now that he had let his concern about Murphy escape his mind for a moment, he was all solicitude for his guest's plans.

"Actually, it's the college's house, you know. One of the advantages of faculty tenure is a free house. The disadvantage of that is that when one moves out after thirty years, one has

32

no equity in the real estate market, where my friends tell me prices have now reached insane levels."

"All the more reason you should have your party for Colrane here." Dewi had the social bit in his teeth now, and would hear no objections. "I really do owe you for your admirable equanimity and generous good humor in the face of my outburst earlier this morning. Please. Murphy will love it. She actually adores parties, but, finances being what they are—we are not just broke this week, you see, we are always broke—I daresay you recall what it was like starting out—oh, I say, Neil, you'd be doing us a great favor, actually. I'm not offering to pay for it, you understand, just to have it here. Murph and I can retire upstairs for the evening if you insist, and just crouch on the landing, peering down through the banisters at the quality. Cor, gimme a look in, Gov, eh?"

"Are you sure?" Neil like the idea, and Dewi was precisely correct about the ambience of the faculty club. "I promise you, it won't cost you a cent, and both of you can stay down here with the grown-ups. We'll devise some way of having you sing or something to pay for your supper. All Welshmen sing, don't they?"

"I do a lovely dirty lyrics version of 'Who Threw the Overalls in Mrs. Murphy's Chowder' or a medley of old Welsh hymns woven around the theme, 'Jesus Wants Me for a Sunbeam in the Garden of Love,' also with dirty lyrics. You can have your pick."

When the blue-and-white patrol car pulled up in the driveway and the two cops gingerly assisted Murphy, stiff-legged and bloodstained, up the stairs, they were greeted at the door by two laughing, hand-shaking old pals.

Dewi's first comment was as spontaneous as it was unfortunate. He said, "What was it this time, Murph, drunk and disorderly in a public place again?"

"I'll kill you for that, you fat Welsh son of a bitch," his wife said, jerking out of the grasp of her helpers and limping into the house.

She turned to study Neil Kelly contemptuously and gave him the full benefit of her maddest glare. "And tell your chum here," she snarled at her husband, "that we aren't at home to visitors today. And happy anniversary to you, too."

33

The door slammed behind her, leaving the two embarrassed men and the policemen on the porch.

Neil took the opportunity to squeeze Dewi's shoulder reassuringly and leave without comment. As he walked up the path he could hear one of the cops explaining to Dewi that Mrs. Morgan-Evans, when asked to describe the truck thieves, had come up with a perfect, if superfluous, description of the truck itself, a 1980 Subaru Brat, blue with white stripe, four-wheel drive and roll bar, but only remembered that the boys had been wearing John Deere tractor hats, which had been in the cab of the truck anyway.

"Those little suckers rammed a utility pole up on 116 with my truck and beat it through the housing project over into the high school. Four hundred little bastards just like them there, fat chance."

Neil thought that perhaps he'd better go see Garabedian at the faculty club, all things considered.

Prelude 4

*EACH PART OF us has a life of its own in its working, and our
bodies are the world's own habitat. Without us to act it's a
mindless hill that might as well be a cinder in space.*

*Understand the feet and you understand that it was the feet
first made the gesture we call walking. The shining long bones
of the shin, the cunning knees, the upstanding thigh—all these
have their own connections with the world.*

*Grasp this: the hand knows holding, throwing, touching, and
the special skills the thumb added—strangling, shooting.*

*This great union, the body, banks at the brain. Trust brain
for cross-references, inside connections, data; but it's really
only a clearing house for action.*

*Feet, hands, joints, eyes, tongue all know what they are
doing best if they can do it before thinking intervenes and con-
fuses act with intention. They go into the unexpected with a
five-hundred-million-year-old past, grew up going on, know
their job instinctively. A few bodies in each million go by a
slower pulse, which quickens them. Certain feet move faster,
some legs pump stronger, a few throats sing higher, eyes see
farther, and the beneficiaries of these endowments are sometimes heroes.*

*Take away that comparative edge, alter the shape of the
singer's larynx, dim the hitter's eye, shatter the dancer's knee,
and nothing else in them is ever the same, because the formerly
living, unique thing is then dead. You can kill a man, you can
change a whole world, just by killing a knee.*

4

IN THE YEAR 1960, there was a rumor that finally made print in the sports pages of the Sunday *New York Times*. The New York Giants of the National Football League, according to that rumor, were maneuvering to make an unknown youngster from some preppy college up in western Massachusetts their first pick in the NFL draft.

The phones rang off the hook for days in the Giants' offices as season ticket holders, already angry because Lombardi had left for Green Bay, jammed the lines trying either to get a denial or to cancel their tickets. They may have been divided among themselves as to whether they wanted to draft Billy Cannon of LSU or trade first-draft rights to L.A. for Del Shofner and change, but they *knew* they didn't want some fairy from—where?—Old Hampton College—quarterbacking the Giants.

But the hard men who ran the Giants' front office and made the money and the moves, especially their new, slick, slim, fast-talking coach, Allie Sherman, an old quarterback, also knew what they wanted. Their heart's desire was precisely that tall youngster from Old Hampton, whose name was Dickie Colrane.

The Springfield papers knew him, and had first called him Cool Colrane. But except for the town weeklies between Amherst and Chicopee, that was nearly the limit of his fame. Even the Boston papers didn't catch on until the middle of the year. The Boston College coach, speaking at a CYO Sports Night in St. Mark's parish hall in Dorchester answered a question by saying, "Listen, if I was an NFL scout, the first kid I'd grab would be that quarterback they've got out at Old Hampton, Colrane. That kid will make them forget Baugh, I'm not kidding."

A B.C. alumnus, working as a stringer covering high school sports for the Boston *Globe,* smelled a story and got himself on the interstate west after the talk as soon as the coach told him that the man to see out there was John Venuti. The story he got seemed more appropriate to the *Times* than the *Globe*, so he sold it to the *Times* for eighty-dollars cash and a shot at a job reporting college sports in New England.

John Venuti had played tackle for Fordham in the days when Fordham was a football factory and you could play sixty minutes, offense and defense, in the line, weighing 186. If you were tough enough. After Fordham he played off and on for the Providence Steamrollers, the Père Marquettes (who sort of floated around), the Boston Yanks, and the Brooklyn football Dodgers. Once, as a favor to a friend who had a hundred-dollar bet on the game, he played a night game for the Charlestown Townies in the old Boston Park League after playing an afternoon game for the Yanks. He never even took off his jock, just changed his shirt and his name. He fulfilled a long-standing ambition at the same time by playing under the name Francis D'Assisi Valentino, for his mother's and his sister's patron saints, respectively. He played relaxed until halfway through the first period, when the guy opposite him, a longshoreman from Southie with a big mouth, asked him if Francis was really a sissy. John smiled and knocked him on his ass. When the longshoreman got up, Francis of Assisi knocked him on his ass again, even though the play had been over for half a minute. Then John, and St. Francis and Rudolph Valentino took turns doing it for the rest of the night. The Townies won big.

John Venuti was a survivor from the rough, tough dark ages of pro football. When he had to quit because the legs that had been spring steel turned slowly to cement, the friend he had done that favor for got him a job. Since the friend was by then the biggest contractor in Massachusetts, and had a son named Francis at Old Hampton (where he played a little gentleman's soccer, like any WASP), he took the opportunity to donate and build the college's new stadium, an attractive, modest shell seating twenty thousand. John Venuti got his job at Old Hampton because his friend owned the stadium.

When he coached Dickie Colrane in his sophomore year, John called his old Fordham buddy Vince Lombardi, then coach of the New York Giants, and told him what he had. Since he had never touted another football prospect in his life, and since no one knew him to tell a lie about anything, Lombardi listened carefully and sent a couple of his wide people up to Massachusetts to find Old Hampton College and Dickie Colrane.

The plan to draft Dickie somewhere down around the seventh round was actually made then. They were worried that Conerly couldn't hold up much longer and George Shaw didn't look all that great in practice. When Lombardi moved to Wisconsin later that year, he convinced his new bosses there that they should cut ahead of the Giants in the draft and nail Colrane.

So by the time Dickie Colrane played his senior year, a dozen people in the football scouting business had traveled up to Old Hampton with stopwatches to check him out, and there was no longer any possibility of sneaking him by under wraps until a late round. Not with the new league calling itself the AFL already sniffing around for maverick talent.

One scouting report said that Colrane had the best peripheral vision they had ever seen. "Apparently he can see the field side to side. His second and third receivers are just as clear to him as his primaries."

One said that Colrane was the coolest kid he had watched. The Old Hampton football team didn't have what you'd call a great offensive line in the best of years, and they appreciated the skill with which Colrane, given about 2.5 seconds to drop back and throw, made his decision and acted. "And he don't flinch," the report added, with the last word underlined. They couldn't know it, but that was partly because John Venuti, aka St. Francis of Assisi, had devoted many late afternoon hours to squatting down, then charging straight at Dickie Colrane as he prepared to pass the ball. A couple of times he even accidentally forgot to put on the brakes and knocked the slim youngster right on his ass. All he got for his apology was a wintry smile, and he stopped it completely the first time the target developed a sudden, quick step to the side that left his coach clawing grass.

Colrane was tough. He had the best reflexes anyone had seen. He was as strong as he needed to be to throw a football sixty-five yards accurately. The reports piled up. And he was patient. Every rating sheet added a comment about his patience, that unteachable ability to wait until the last millisecond before acting. The Dallas Cowboys report said, "he almost looks lazier than Meredith out there, but more patient at the strategic game, using three plays to set up one, shaping his calls to his sense of the entire design of the game in his mind. And he has a nice tactical flair for pouncing on an opponent's mistake and improvising intelligently."

Around the NFL, Dickie Colrane graded out very, very high. Perhaps the highest grade was given to him for the fact that he played no other sports. At Oldhampton High School he had played everything they offered with equal success, but when he turned eighteen he decided that football would be his only game.

The OH basketball coach wept bitterly. The baseball coach, whose only dependable pitcher threw a forty-mile-an-hour fastball, sat in the Horse moaning and bitching about Venuti putting the kid in a chastity belt. But the simple truth was, Dickie Colrane had dedicated his life to football, and the ability to narrow his vision down to a single focus when he chose to was just another superlative skill that came naturally.

His teachers were almost as hostile to football as his college's rival coaches. Stanley Dorfmann, who taught comparative literature, begged him to take the application for a Rhodes scholarship. Stanley had gone to Oxford and had waited twelve years to have a student he thought worthy to follow him there. Neil had seconded the suggestion. Dickie's senior advisor, a political scientist, who had served with modest distinction in the Truman State Department under Acheson, and knew a dramatic winning style when he saw one, urged him to take the law boards and think about politics. His sociology professor, James Purlie, who was later to become his father-in-law, persuaded him to think seriously about doing graduate work in sociology if—just if, mind you—things didn't work out as he hoped in his sports career. Dickie had written a senior thesis on early revolutionary movements in Russia under Nicholas I, and it won the Phi Beta Kappa prize that year. Since he was dating Professor Purlie's daughter Jill at the time, he promised solemnly that yes, he would surely think about sociology when the time came. The average life expectancy as an active quarterback in the NFL is only about five years, but Dickie contemplated Conerly still throwing for the Giants after twenty years, Blanda down in Houston, looking as though he could play forever, and privately saw no reason why he could not play ball until he was forty-five. He had never been hurt in his life.

But he was never to play even a day of professional football. After what happened just two weeks before the NFL draft that year, the Giants decided they could squeeze another year out of Charley Conerly (they were wrong, he was injured in the first game, against the Rams) and Dickie Colrane's name faded from everyone's memory as a football player. It became instead the center of a teasing mystery in Oldhampton which was still unsolved.

On an April morning in 1960, while he was taking his morning ride on the ten-mile circuit from the campus to Hatfield Center and back, on the long slope behind Teakettle, Dickie Colrane was shot exactly in the knee joint of his left leg.

The knee joint is an intricate piece of engineering. It is actually two joints, one for flexing and extending, the other for rotation. The patella itself, the kneecap, has on its back surface six well-defined facets, each of which makes contact with the condyles, the knuckles, of the upper leg bone, the femur, in a different position. Where the lower leg is connected with the upper, just behind the patella, it has its own independent rotation on the upper bone between the cartilages within the joint and the tibia, the lower leg bone. During flexion or extension a different set of cartilage connections operate.

After surgery Dickie Colrane no longer had a proper knee-cap, or good rotation, or good flexion in his left leg. He had what is called a limp. He was thus no longer a desirable football property for the New York Giants or anyone else. Which is how he happened to wipe his mind clean of what had filled it for four years, grit his perfect teeth, and enroll in the Graduate School of Arts and Sciences of Harvard University in the Department of Social Relations to become a sociologist.

The bullet had been a .22 caliber. It had shattered itself as well as the knee, and since it had been soft and heavy for its length to begin with, as the bullet used in hunting small game usually is, it was, when they retrieved it surgically, roughly the shape of a cigar butt after someone had ground his bootheel on it.

Actually, there isn't just one standard .22 caliber ammunition, there are several. The .218 Bee and the .220 Swift and several others in between are just called twenty-twos. The Bee has only about two-thirds the muzzle velocity of the Swift, although both have a weight of under fifty grains. A .22 Zipper weighs fifty-six grains and has a three thousand fps muzzle velocity, and will still be traveling over twenty-five hundred fps after a hundred yards.

The bullet they dug out of Dickie Colrane's leg was an ordinary .22 short with only a twenty-nine-grain weight, designed to be fired at a muzzle velocity of just above one thousand. If it had traveled anything like a hundred yards before hitting him, its energy would have been nearly negligible, less than fifty foot-pounds. So one thing they knew, from the damage the shot did, was that it had come from very close range.

The land all along Teakettle slope and back up into the elbow of the valley had once been cleared, drained, and farmed. That was before New England farmers in their thousands starting hearing stories about the fresh, black, easy soil of the Ohio Valley, and one by one looked up on some spring day from lifting boulders to add to their stone walls, dropped everything, and moved out.

By the end of the nineteenth century the farmhouses had crumbled or been cannibalized for timbers to build elsewhere. The fallen-in cellar holes grew over, with dense fern growths to mark the places fire had finished the deconstruction, and the cleared acreage turned back into woodlands and wetlands.

Some corn had always been grown, in scattered acreages throughout the area, seventy acres here, two and a half acres there, six somewhere else, in an irregular, crazy quilt pattern. It was simple to grow, and there was always a demand in the Boston and Springfield markets for the sweet butter-and-sugar corn of the valley. More than one college professor kept in touch with the land by planting ten acres in corn and teaching his TV-hooked, car-crazy kids to harvest the heavy crop and sell off the family's surplus in the Saturday market on the town common.

Squirrels thrive on the edges of the cornfields. Hunters flourish where squirrels thrive. Most city people have never tasted squirrel, which is, arguably, as sweet as rabbit, but even if the hunter leaves the meat, the pelts are marketable and the animal is so swift that the game is a modest challenge. If the hunter is lazy, the stupidity of the squirrel helps him. A hunter who's in no mood to go stalking a small, racing prey able quick as a flash to reach the opposite side of a limb for cover, knows that he can have a good, lazy morning of hunting by just picking a spot near any tree with a squirrel nest in it, or one marked by a clutter of cuttings dropped from their feeding, and squat there until a squirrel pops out, then nail him with a .22. And the beauty part, as they say down at the Gulf Station, is that if you stay sitting there, not even bothering to remove the first victim, after a minute or so another animal will stick its head out, then venture out to eat or forage. Just as though there had been no shot, as though there were no corpse right there under the tree. With a little patience and luck a hunter who's a half-way decent shot can pot four, five, even six squirrels in a morning without moving anything but his trigger finger.

Dickie Colrane had been coasting down Teakettle slope when, near the bottom, going southwest toward Hatfield, two things happened. He extended his left leg fully while he looked down to check his right toe clip, which had come loose. At that precise second a squirrel darted across the road, directly in front of him. He caught just a glimpse of it out of the corner of his eye. Then the third thing happened, which he did not see and which was never explained. A shot came from the scrub woods across the road to his left and a twenty-nine grain bullet of twenty-two caliber tore a path through the rear surface of the patella of Dickie Colrane's left leg, demolishing itself and sending fragments ripping through portions of the transverse ligament, the coronary ligaments, and the synovial membrane, and ricocheting ruinously between the knuckle of the thigh and the upper end of the shinbone facing it.

The doctor on duty in the emergency room of the Cooley-Dickinson Hospital had done battlefield surgery in Korea, and so had seen worse knees. But that historical fact did not endow him with the skill to repair what he found so that the knee would ever rotate, flex, or extend again with its original brilliance. He knew that the patient would live, but that the knee was dead. He did the best he could and turned over to the state police sergeant waiting outside the operating room the fragments he had removed along with a thimbleful of bone splinters from the wound.

The evidence that someone had been squatting in the woods just south of the road, maybe only twenty feet in, and potting squirrels, was pretty plain. Three dead animals were still lying there uncollected. Every indication was that an animal had been spooked, had darted away across the road and—one chance in ten million—the unknown hunter had tried a snap shot and missed his target, but hit the famous bicyclist.

Stupid was what they called it down at the Gulf Station, and in the Horse, over and over. Stupid and one in ten million. The phrases wore thin with repetition. Dumb son of a bitch. Dumb fucker. It's people like that give guns a bad name. Of all the . . . There really wasn't much more that could be said.

That April morning was also the last one on which Dan Murphy was seen in Oldhampton. And since Dan was a little crazy, in a generally harmless way, and owned two or three guns, like everyone else, and was a famous champion of squirrel stew, popular opinion tended to congeal around the notion, gradually the sad conviction, that Dan had done it, seen what he'd done, and cleared out, probably to New Hampshire where he came from. If he had needed any extra incentive to go, it was probably provided by the additional facts that his gun license hadn't been renewed for two years and that a lot of people remembered that when he was fifteen years younger, but still old enough to know better, he'd shot Jess Dillon's holstein cow in the udder with a .22 Savage.

Even his older daughter, Catherine, accepted the obvious with a sick heart. She had dated Dickie Colrane for almost a year in high school, and she was too ashamed for a month even to go into Manley's Market for the weekly grocery order.

His daughter Margaret Mary refused to accept the obvious. She marched herself into Manley's looking everyone in the eye and not backing off from one halfhearted "good morning" or "hello." Margaret Murphy knew what she knew by faith, and she believed that often evidence was slow to catch up with truth. Faith respects its own power, takes the heart's aims for granted, and expects results. Hope follows as a large, plain matter to the true believer; it can be breathed like good air, promises rain. Love is the root. Whatever the tree looks like, understand staying and nourishing. A five-foot-one-inch red-haired woman with a heroine's heart who loved her foolish, feckless, abused father is a force to be reckoned with.

Prelude 5

THEY SIT BITTERLY sipping their coffee, as though it were acid, neither speaking, the two of them waiting for some accident or incident to prime the pump of their marriage's deep well again, so that their separate good news might not be spoiled by the other's thickheadedness.

The little, fierce red-haired woman has decided that she'll not only write the article she was planning about her father, she'll write a whole goddam book. She knew it the second Dick Colrane dropped her on her hurt tail by the side of the road. She has in an envelope propped on her mantel a check for thirty-five dollars, the first money she has ever earned by writing. A publisher in Burlington, Vermont, has paid it to her for a fifteen-hundred-word outline she submitted in response to an ad in the New York Review of Books. *There is to be an anthology of unsolved New England mysteries, and Margaret Mary Morgan-Evans, who for shyness' sake has used the pen name, Monica Stark (a name she thinks makes her sound tall and thin), wrote a précis of her father's disappearance. She can now write a full chapter, not to exceed ten thousand words, and she stands to earn three hundred and fifty dollars and one percent of the royalties from the sale of the anthology. When the check arrived in yesterday's mail she was ecstatic; the money would be an anniversary present for her husband, whom she adores.*

But she knows now that she will write her own book; nothing else will suffice. She will find out who paid her father, Dan Murphy, for disappearing after the Colrane shooting, or frightened him into disappearing. No other explanation will fit in her mind; she is convinced that Dan Murphy, on some dumb cluck errand in that dying patch of woods the local people call

Milkwood, saw the shooting accident and was bribed or scared off. And she suddenly knows how she will start her research. She had gone with her hitching leg, pedaling eccentrically, cruising down Teakettle Road past Milkwood to start by finding the exact place where the shooting had occurred. But she had come a cropper, her leg locked and her pants cuff jammed in the chain, some three hundred and fifty yards north of the actual site. Now, she vowed to herself, straining the lukewarm coffee through the tiny gap in her front teeth noisily (a sound she knew got on Dewi's nerves) she would start her research right here in this room. She had decided to give a party, and somehow—God knows how—invite all the people who had any connection with the event.

The small, tight-faced, black-haired Welshman she is married to sits behind his scowl and wants to murder her for that idiotic noise she makes with her coffee, waiting for her to realize she is doing it and apologize, thus breaking the ice for larger apologies to come from both. Of course he was the one who walked out last night. The first time that ever happened. Granted, she started it, calling him a wee dark devil from ten generations of ignorant miners, jumped up by an Oxford education to thinking he was God's gift to America. That and other things he hoped she now realizes were a bit thick. Little fat slob, for example.

He thinks, ah, you shanty Irish farm bitch, just wait until I tell you what I have to tell you. God's gift indeed. Didn't the dean himself, that fine old scholar, him of the famous book about German history in the nineteenth century, find my reading of Hopkins irresistible? Don't I have the theater in my blood, with my fine Welsh flair for the dramatic, and I a smashing teacher to boot, a legend in my own time for all practical purposes.

His lips curl with an inner amusement he cannot quite conceal. He is contemplating her discomfort, tasting it already, savoring it. Vengeance is indeed sweet, but he will linger in its neighborhood only a minute or two before passing through to the open fields of magnanimity, forgiving her for her harsh words already nearly forgotten.

She sees his imminent smile and thinks, ah, here it

comes. The quip to save his ugly face, then the apology he knows in his black heart he owes me. Left me alone on the eve of our anniversary, did he, the bastard? Let's see what quality of secondhand poetry he can pump up his groveling with.

5

"SHALL I TELL you now who it was you insulted on our door-step?"

"The police carry your wife home half-conscious, bleeding and bruised in a road accident, and that's the first word out of your mouth? Who *I* insulted?"

"A scratch on the jaw is hardly mortal injury. It didn't even keep your mouth shut. I wasn't going to mention what you did to our bike."

"*Our* bike is it now? Who fixed it when you wiped out the only two gears left on it? Who paid a quarter at a tag sale for a decent seat, so that *we* could actually sit down on it and not pedal it around with a length of pipe sticking up *our* arse?"

He decided to rise above her petty particularity. "I'm thinking of buying a car in any case." Look at her eyes pop.

"You're drunk in the morning. Not with my thirty-five hard-earned dollars you're not making any down payment on any car. You saw my envelope, didn't you? You knew all about it all along, didn't you, you nosy bastard?"

"Knew what? You're screaming, and there's no need."

"I'll scream as much as I want to. My ad in *NYRB* that I answered."

"You. One of those ads for lonely sincere F to exchange sonnets with a tubercular M poet in Spokane, Washington, or Arkansas or somewhere? You answered one of those? And now your androgynous lumberjack lover has sent you the bus fare to join him in his wilderness idyll? Go, go, you idjit."

"Personal ad my foot." She grabbed the check from the shelf above the fireplace and waved it furiously at him. "What do you call that, eh?" She wished she had been able to think of a better way of saying that. "Don't you touch it, you son of a bitch, it's mine, I earned it by writing. Writing." She crowed the word at him, then stuck out her tongue for good measure. "And I'm going to write a whole book, not just a chapter. I'm going to write a best-seller, goddam you. And what's more, when our absentee landlord, Neil Kelly, shows up here in June to reclaim this house and his stupid job, am I going to greet him with cries of resentment and secret pins stuck in his picture to cause him migraines? Like hell I am. I'm going to get him to teach me how to solve mysteries. Me." She pounded herself on the chest painfully. That was always happening. "With my goddam gimpy leg and everything." She whacked herself on the bad hip with the same fist. It settled properly in its socket and she could move it again. That was always happening, too. She must remember which self-punishment worked and which just stung.

Her husband started to laugh, his babyish, round face under the shock of dark hair turned red with mirth.

"Don't you laugh at me, you bugger," Murphy screeched at him, "*I'm* a writer, and I have proof." She held the check over her head and struck a pose.

"And don't you yell at me, you Mick terrorist, *I'm* a professor, and I expect I'll be one for another year at least, and how do you like that?"

He waved his fist over his head in a triumphant circle. A six footer who had just kicked the winning goal for Wales in the World Cup. Yes, by God.

"You mean they want to hire you back again?"

"You mean someone is paying you to write about the famous case of missing Dan Murphy?"

"You first." Margaret was as astonished as he had ever hoped she'd be. "We have a job?"

"I said we did, didn't I? Yes. I think. Now wait," he added, as they embraced and danced and never remembered to notice who had made the first move. "I *think*. Neil Kelly doesn't want to come back for a year. He's got some dolly in England he's wanting to cuddle up to, and so he asked me—"

The dance broke off with a terrific suddenness.

"You don't mean, you bastard—"

"I do, I do. He wants me to stay on. Says I'm doing hell's own beauty of a job here. Slathers of praise. Praise to waste. I'm a hit. Ta-ra-ra-**boom**-der-é . . ." he started to waltz her around the living room, singing the song that made Morgan and Evans famous.

She stuck a flat hand into his stomach and pushed him off. "Do you mean, you thick comedian, that that was *him* I insulted on the front doorstep just before?"

He cocked an elbow on the mantel and smoothed a nonexistent mustache with a languid finger.

"Well, one told you, didn't one, I mean, when one was trying to be reasonable and you were, what, being so *idiotically*—" he pronounced each syllable venomously, "Irish and inattentive. And, well, Irish."

She smacked herself in the forehead with her palm and plunked down into the sofa. "Jesus. Now how am I going to get the man to teach me how to solve a mystery? You bastard, Dewi," she wailed, "this is all your fault."

"And a happy anniversary to you, too, Margaret Mary. And many more of them, if I may say so."

"Your present is better than mine," she sniffled. "I was going to give you twenty out of the check to buy an L. L. Bean chamois shirt."

In each lovers' argument and reconciliation, there is one moment in which one heart breaks with new love. That was Dewi's. He had coveted an L. L. Bean chamois shirt in fire engine red ever since he had seen one advertised in a catalogue of Neil's that had come to their door. It represented the good life, the life of American ease, rugged, but not stressful. It was a late drinks in front of the fireplace shirt, a leisured lover's shirt. He went to her and lifted her up and hugged her.

"Nothing could be grander than that. I'll take it. I don't care if the job falls through and we starve on the roads, walking west toward California. I want that damn shirt like nothing else on earth but you."

"Oh, Dewi. I'm so proud of you, getting rehired." She wept and hugged him.

"It's not sure yet, you understand."

"Of course it's not sure, but I'm sure. Oh, Dewi, you're really a wonderful teacher, and a wonderful husband, and I'm a bitch to yell at you, and . . ."

50

"It's all my fault, it is. Ah, Murph, happy anniversary. Do I need a shower very badly?"

She sniffed the air above his shoulder. "Yes. Very."

"Well, then, let's both go take one. I'll scrub the blood off you while you tell me all about your famous accident, and you can sponge all the dew off me and we shall both smell like cawl and buttermilk and cowbreath and Welsh cakes, like the people in the story."

They did. And it was better than the people in the story.

Later, lying together on the bed, his first class still an hour away, each thought those thoughts married lovers do after anger has been transformed to the breath and body of communion.

He remembered with a blaze of feeling the first time he saw her. She had been selling used clothing at a tag sale on the town common for the benefit of the high school choral society. He had simply wanted her. He was not generally a passionate man, nor was he a womanizer. He had reached forty without a wife, and with only one involvement serious enough so that her family started hinting about a wedding, which ruined everything for both of them. But seeing Margaret Mary Murphy taking three dollars from a woman for a black coat and giving her two coins change in return, he simply knew, at some level of himself where he had never known what wanting was before, that he wanted her.

His initial rush of assurance, which had flooded through him like heat, immediately abandoned him, and he found himself standing in front of her holding a belt in his hand asking her the price.

"Whatever you want to give, for belts."

"Would—would one dollar be enough?"

"Too much. You know, ten cents or maybe a quarter. If you want to contribute a dollar to the fund, fine, but belts always go for, you know—"

He was rooted to the spot, trying to think of a reply. "Actually, I mean, actually, no. I'm afraid I've never been to one of these—" he gestured vaguely around him, "before. Before today."

"I see." She left him to sell a red sweater to a girl with a baby in a corduroy carrier on her stomach.

He stood in the exact spot, the belt, which he noticed for the first time was about fifty inches long, dangling from his hand.

"It's a little big, isn't it? Are you planning to cut it down?"

"Huh?" Dewi heard himself say it and hated the moron who uttered the empty grunt.

At least she finally looked at him, and her smile lit up her face. "Are you trying to pick me up?"

"Thirty-two. I've been getting a bit—you know, fat, I suppose from sitting in an office all—" He realized that she hadn't asked him that. "Oh, yes. Yes, I suppose I am."

"In that case you can pay a buck for the belt. Hell, it'll be worth that just as a souvenir. Thirty-two, did you say? You're a little feller, aren't you?"

Before he could protest or stand straighter, so that he might appear taller than five-five, she added, "I like small, tight-bodied men. I bet you don't know who said that."

She was gone again, but failed to persuade a teenage boy that the pin-striped navy vest he was trying on was exactly what his wardrobe needed.

When she returned—and it occurred to him that she had returned, for no apparent reason except that he was standing there—he said, "You're correct. I don't. Who?"

She laughed and poked him hard in the stomach with two fingers. "Last month's playmate in *Playboy*. My girlfriend showed it to me, because it's something I said once, and it's kind of a joke between us. You should exercise or diet, you are getting fat. Don't you Englishmen have stoutness exercises that you do? I read that in *Winnie the Pooh*."

She had played into his hands. Literary allusion put him at ease; it was like receiving a fix of courage.

"I'm not English, actually. I mean, I daresay, I sound English to you, but I'm Welsh."

"Welsh? Like Richard Burton? But you're a little dark feller. I thought you were all, you know, like Burton, big bruisers, or white-thighed, blond giants, all that."

A man who was trying to get her attention to buy a flowered shirt growled and went over to another woman wearing a change apron. Dewi was strangely encouraged.

"No, no. Few blonds at all, and no giants except in stories. As for Burton, he is not a true Welshman at all. He was made up special to order, for the overseas trade. We're mostly miners, you know. If you've read your Lawrence you remember the armies of small dark men swarming from the mine shafts at dawn and dark, an ancient race of men from the bowels of the black earth."

"I only read Lawrence for the dirty parts. Would you like to read him to me—the clean parts about your ancient race—sometime?"

"I'd do it now if I had a book in my hand."

"I'm not pig ignorant, you know. I went to college for almost two years. I write—" suddenly she felt shy talking to this foreigner she barely had to look up to, with his rumble of a voice like soft music—"I write poems." She had never said that to anyone else and she hadn't the faintest goddam notion why she had just told him, of all people. She could see two women looking for someone to wait on them.

"Look," she said, putting her hand on Dewi's arm, "at this rate the chorale is never going to get to France. This is supposed to be a benefit to raise money for their trip to France, so I better sell, sell, sell. Invite me out."

"Would you like to go out?" He indicated the larger world with the hand not holding the belt.

"Sure. Yes, I would. Now give me something meaningful for the belt—no, not a whole buck, dummy. You're going to need your folding money if I'm your date. I eat like a horse."

He gave her the first coin he found in his pocket, which was a five-cent piece, but neither of them noticed. Clutching his immense belt, he wandered across the common, until he realized that he didn't know her name or address.

She was ready for him when he edged back into her work area.

"Right here, under the maple, seven tonight. I'm Margaret Mary Murphy."

"Murphy. I shall always call you Murphy. My name is Dewi, spelled D E W I Morgan-Evans."

She winked at him. "See ya, Dewi."

"I hoped you were named Fiona, did you know that? Did I ever tell you that? The first time I set eyes on you, I hoped you were named Fiona."

She had been remembering their actual wedding, a hodge-podge ceremony of Catholic bits and pantheistic bits, whatever the priest, who was a trendy ecumenist of pronounced anti-Vatican views, had permitted them to bootleg in. Dewi had treated the whole thing as a delicious conspiracy to organize his religious views, which were diffuse at best, and cooperated madly, beaming fellowship on the poor priest, who had never made a convert and felt sure Dewi was a hot prospect.

"You've always wanted to do that to a Fiona, have you?"

"Well, yes, logically. Certainly the first time I saw you—"

She clouted him with a pillow and hugged him close to her.

He had come to Old Hampton to fill a vacancy, available at the last minute because he had been let go at the last minute by a college in New York where they told him the soft money budget had been embezzled by the department chairman, which meant there were no funds to pay him to teach freshmen to write compositions. He had expected no more of a blessing from it than a one-year job, a stopover on his way somewhere else, perhaps Canada. He had heard that Canada was dead keen on accents like his. He had also heard that the winter temperature reached thirty below zero Fahrenheit there. Now, by a small series of miracles, he was a married man, he appeared a sure bet to have a continuing job, and Murphy truly loved him. He felt grateful to the universe, and he wondered if that made much sense. Good God, he was praying.

"I'm going to find out what happened to my father, you know, Dew, I mean it."

Dear Murph and her fantasy of playing detective. He listened to her comfortably, feeling a small rush of pity for her. She had had to live here in Oldhampton, where it was universally assumed, he knew, that Dan Murphy had shot this Colrane fellow, who appeared to be such a great friend of Kelly's, and ended his sports career. He guessed that there would be a hard core of local football enthusiasts who'd never forgive that, would treat it as a personal loss of glory. At home in Meirionnydd just one lad had made a name for himself playing for the FA Cup, in goal for Arsenal—not even a Welsh club, mind you—and the cocky citizens of that pimple on the backside of nowhere two miles from Tywynn had boasted of it for years, finally erecting a sign at the entrance to their pip-squeak village announcing that it was the home of Will Waldo, champion footballer. It must still be hard for Murph, and the realization that she still felt ashamed sometimes made him fierce in her defense.

"You do it, Murph."

"You don't mind, then?"

"I think of my own mother sometimes, where she went, what she did, and I hope she turned out fine." He realized that was true as he said it, and his own melancholy in the moment amazed him.

Murphy was sitting up, naked and freckled and rosy, all plans. "You've got to explain to Kelly that I didn't know it was him, you know. God." She slumped down and pulled the covers over her head, remembering.

Dewi laughed and reached for her, but she slapped his hand away and leaped out of the bed.

"You called him 'your chum,' you know. 'And tell your chum here,' you said, et cetera. And I believe," he added with dreamy mildness, "that you announced that you intended to kill his pal, the Welsh son of a bitch with him."

She glared, but dressed. "Then use your Celtic charms on him and explain it away."

Dewi crossed inside, and produced his trump card. "Why don't we have a small party here, and invite him? Wouldn't that be a nice gesture while he's in town? Let him know we have nothing to hide, that we haven't gouged the walls or anything?"

"Are you serious? Could we?" She grimaced. It was her own idea, but now the cost of it made her shudder. "Can we afford it?"

"We can and we shall. As a matter of fact," he grunted, getting into his trousers, "he was the one who suggested it,

55

and he is the one who will foot the bill. Kelly will play and Kelly will pay, it's only right.''

While she found him a decent shirt and he raced through his final preparations for teaching his class, he told her the full story of Neil's suggestion of an engagement party for Dickie Colrane, saving the man's name till the end.

Murphy indicated her shock by sitting slowly down on the floor and wailing. ''Jesus, Dickie? He's mad at me, too. For some goddam reason the minute I said I was writing about the shooting, he dropped me on my ass.''

Dewi was on top of the world. He looked down at her from that superior advantage. ''Well, you're just going to have to break this habit you've developed lately of alienating everyone in town, aren't you? I noticed that the two peelers who drove you home in their patrol car weren't all that thrilled to have your company, to judge by their relief when they left you off. You really must be more amiable, Murphy. A mystery writer needs all the friends she can get.''

With a blithe sweep of his arm and a delicate wave of his fingertips he wafted out the door to work. The last thing he heard was his gentle wife, from her seat on the floor, cursing his ancestry and mouthing rhetorical questions. Such as: ''Who says I'm not amiable, you bastard? I've got more friends in this town than you have in the entire Western hemisphere, you toad, who says I don't?''

Prelude 6

NEIL KELLY FINDS that now, back in his hometown, its everyday history and problems are immediately familiar, as though he had never left. As though he has not been ignoring them entirely for two years. He supposes wryly that, despite Frost's famous definition of home as the place where, when you go there, they have to let you in, this is what home really means: some part of you never leaves at all.

He sits in Vic and Liz Foster's living room at his ease in sock feet, reading the Oldhampton weekly newspaper. His oldest friends on the faculty, the Fosters, have insisted on his staying in their guest room during his week in town. He feels completely at home.

It seems to him, skimming the news, that every article listed for the warrant of this year's town meeting has been there in some form for years past. The mothers of primary school children want a set of traffic lights at the Stockade and Northampton roads intersection. A record shop in the center of town wants to install video games, but neighboring merchants are protesting, fearful of adolescent troublemakers clustering in the spot. A new proposal for additional downtown parking will be presented to the Selectmen, the tenth in ten years. Whatever a leach plume is, some engineers from the university have found one seeping from the DVR Chemical storage lot in Milkwood and threatening to contaminate the groundwater with toxins. The fire department is resisting women fire fighters, but wants to reestablish the custom of having a Dalmatian as station mascot, over the protests of an animal protection group.

Except for the chemical pollution question, nothing new there. But come to think of it, hadn't there been a protest way back in 1960, when Dick Colrane was shot from the DVR land, about the stored chemicals poisoning the ground there even then?

Neil sighs. *Plus ça change . . . The rest of the paper is lots of* la même chose.

6

THE PERSON AT the door was Mrs. Morgan-Evans, blushing furiously through her freckles.

"I came to invite you back to your own house. I didn't know that was you with my husband."

"Mrs. Morgan-Evans. Come in, please."

"Murphy, please. Dewi calls me that, and I like it." She entered the small front hall and laughed ruefully. "Or you can call me Monica Stark if you like. That's the pen name I picked out. But I think I'll junk it," she added hastily. "Dewi says it sounds like an S-M hooker."

They went together into the living room, where, because she had learned what helped her sit gracefully and what didn't, Murphy chose the straight-backed oak chair by the front window.

She apologized again, but Neil waved it away with a dismissive comment about those certain moments in every household when the outsider has no business being there, and apologized himself. He asked her about the Band Aid on her jaw, and she blushed again and described her fall from the bike, adding an explanation of how her leg tended to lock under certain kinds of stress.

"I'm not exactly handicapped, but it's just a goddam nuisance every once in a while."

"Dewi told me you lack a car."

"Yeah. Well—" she shrugged philosophically. "We're a little broke usually."

Neil wondered how to say the next thing inoffensively. "You and Dewi would be welcome to use my old Volvo, the ancient blue job I left in the garage. The problem is, they don't know what the problem is, but it's busted."

Murphy smiled a nice calculating smile. Cars were her duck soup. "I kind of wondered about that nice little car, just sitting

59

there. A problem a garage man couldn't solve, or just your-self?"

Neil almost laughed; the assumptions other people make. "If I pretended for five minutes that I know anything more about my car than how to stop it after I start it, you'd spot me for a phony immediately. No, I took it down to College Town Motors, they sold it to me in the first place. But they fiddled with it and frowned at it and told me my problem was an in-soluble mystery. Some help. So I put it in the garage and left it there; I was leaving for England in a few weeks then any-way."

"Buddy Ruger?" Murphy was all scorn "That moron down at College Town? We were in the same auto mechanics class in high school, and Buddy couldn't pass a quiz on changing spark plugs. Describe the problem." All business now.

Neil raised his hands, groping for words to describe some-thing he didn't understand. "It suddenly started using oil by the quart. The gallon. From no problem at all to needing a quart every five hundred miles. They couldn't find any leaks—and they made me look in there to see, along with them—and they gave it a compression check that showed all the cylinders had the manufacturer's recommended per-square-inch speci-fications. No place for the oil to go, but it was going." He finished helplessly. "Are you an automobile mechanic?"

She snorted. "Compared with Buddy Ruger, I'm an engi-neer. Did they really tell you that? No place for the oil to go? Jesus. Some people." She smiled and offered her hand to shake. "I'll make you a deal. I'll fix your car for you if you'll tell me how to go about tracing my father—not step-by-step or anything, just in general what I should do."

Her grin, chipped tooth and all, made her freckled face hand-some. Neil suspected he was being hustled, but she was putting her skills on the line, and the least he could do was wager a few hours of conversation against the chance to get his old friend the Volvo back.

"Deal," he said, shaking hands. "I'll pay for any new parts if you discover I need them."

"You bet you will," she said cheerfully. "I'll look at it later today. When can you talk with me about how to do the research for my book?"

He liked her optimism. "One hour after my car is fixed."

It was fixed by five o'clock that evening.

Murph described her trip down to College Town Motors glee-fully, especially the part where she showed her old classmate the difference between oil rings and compression rings on a piston.

"You were losing oil through your oil rings into your cyl-inders, even though your compression rings still gave you a good tight reading." She added an admission that made her blush. "I was really afraid you had worn valve guide seals, and I would have had to pull the head to get at it. Your oil was being burned with your fuel. Are you impressed?"

Neil sat down and ordered coffee. He should have known she would know what she was doing. Now he had to try to explain to this gleeful young woman that solving the kind of mystery she had was a good deal more guesswork and patience than inside knowledge.

He lectured her for an hour, flat out. She was not a notetaker, she was a total absorption listener.

His theme was the impossibility of writing anything, any-thing at all.

"Writing is an unnatural act. Perhaps the most unnatural act in the human repertoire. Singing, dancing, nursing, and fighting were all there in the arboreal home when humans left. Where we went after leaving the tree was to the library. If you intend to write—anything, even the most trivial story of crime and detection—you are performing another step in our long walk away from the tree. Now, do you really want to take on that responsibility?"

"I have to." She didn't blink; it was a statement of fact.

Neil sighed. He wasn't discouraging her one whit. "A sort of *roman à clef*, then?"

"I only had two years of college, no foreign languages."

"A true story, with the names changed and the characters only slightly veiled?"

"If I have to. You know, to avoid getting sued."

He felt his usual mixture of admiration and pity for anyone about to undertake the unnatural practice he had just been describing. But he knows that there is finally no advice, no counsel however sage, no warning he can administer that will avert the ultimate act. When someone, particularly a woman, announces that she has thrown aside shame and normal human reticence to the point where it can be admitted publicly that she is expecting a book, it is already too late.

He knows that there are dark places where one can go in search of those whose advertised skills include terminating books. Some poor souls meet in taverns and practice a kind of group abortion, talking each other's germinal books to a withered death. And there are the notorious MFA programs, the summer writing workshops in Vermont or Colorado, the shameful probings between friends in shade-drawn bedrooms, and there are plenty of awful fragments hidden in trunks or dresser drawers to be discovered by a horrified nephew only years afterward.

Neil has personally known half a dozen otherwise respectable and respected professors of literature (a group peculiarly, perhaps genetically, susceptible to the problem) who have mistakenly tried to imitate what they have only vaguely understood, and who have either ended their own books untimely or, in a desperate clumsy effort to do what seemed the right thing at the time, have published their own books and blighted countless lives besides their own.

With nothing but loathing for the undertaking, and knowing that he has wasted precious time trying to forestall the inevitable, he began.

"First you will need a metaphor."

"I thought first you needed a mystery."

"A common misconception." He saw no point in mincing words. "No, first the metaphor, then the mystery."

"Why?"

"Actually—" (he is hearing the old phrase in his head as he first heard it at nineteen—her blunt question reminds him of himself then) "Aristotle explained it nicely. 'Metaphors,' he said, 'are a kind of riddle.'"

She looked at him dully, wondering whether she was thick or Kelly was not quite what he was cracked up to be. Riddle indeed.

"Isn't a riddle a mystery?"

"The Japanese would say a koan—that is, a riddle or mystery with no *rational* solution." He emphasized the adjective and raised a finger to underscore the point.

"But—" she was outraged at what she perceived as a flagrant self-contradiction, and she wanted to put it as nicely as she could. "But *you* said that every mystery must have a rational solution." She blinked at her own temerity at contradicting the greath sleuth, but held her ground.

Neil looked both aloof and offended. What a pesky pupil. "I can't have said that, I haven't come to that yet."

"You said it in a newspaper interview two years ago, in the *New York Times*. When you solved that awful murder here in Oldhampton—I'm sorry, I don't know how to refer to it without hurting you." She flushed. The murdered girl in that notorious case had been Neil Kelly's fiancée.

He glossed over her embarrassment; it had happened before. "I don't recall the occasion, but I might well have said it."

"You did. I memorized it. You said, 'a pattern can always be discerned.' That was your phrase exactly. 'Unless it was a random crime,' you said, 'like a mugging, or something done on impulse—unmotivated in the strict sense of planned,' you said, 'then we could always detect a pattern, and at the center of the pattern, no matter how fantastic, we would always find the criminal.'"

Neil's face showed that he was remembering. "Ah, the famous interview in which, rather offhandedly, I compared criminal detection with literary research. I'll show you my fan mail from police chiefs all across America sometime on that remark." He groaned and then laughed. "One of them wrote to me with the address: Son of SFX Van Dusen, Oldhampton, Massachusetts, a rather sarcastic literary reference, I'm afraid, to a fictional detective from Harvard once known to mystery buffs as 'The Thinking Machine.' I thought that showed a nice touch of informed malice, but I did regret that the local post office had no hesitation in delivering it to me here."

"The Murphy Version."

Her mentor looked mildly askance at her non sequitur. She hurried to explain.

"That's my title."

He smiled as though she had said something wonderful. She was a better pupil than he had been thinking. "And that is your metaphor. If it is also your title, so much the better. That is the mystery that one cannot truly solve, but must enter into in order to solve the other one, the discernible one. Have you made a list?"

For the first time, her face darkened. Inside her, her heart sank. What list?

He spent the next twenty minutes explaining that if there was to be *a* version called the Murphy Version, then there would first have to be many Murphy versions, hypotheses.

"And," he had concluded flatly, "then you pray for luck. No mystery gets solved without some."

She had worked on her list since. With some bouts of sleep and a meal or two, about twenty-four hours. The sheet of paper in her hand was headed "Versions" in response to his suggestion. Versions of what people and the police believed actually happened, followed by a list of versions Neil Kelly had told her to call "What Ifs"—versions purely hypothetical, but plausible and possible, to be eliminated one by one until one couldn't be eliminated. The first list had just one explanation on it, the second, despite her best efforts to be ingenious, just two.

The police version and the generally accepted Oldhampton version coincided in their few particulars. Dickie Colrane had been shot by Dan Murphy in a dumb accident while Murphy was squirrel hunting down below Teakettle Hill and Dickie Colrane rode his bike into the line of fire. Dan Murphy had seen the fallen bicyclist, and either thought he had killed someone or knew he had badly injured someone, and, fearing the law, had lit out for places unknown.

The other list began with Murphy's own favorite version, although Neil Kelly had warned her against trying to solve a puzzle with a fixed mind, for then the only evidence she would accept would be what fit her preconceived notion. Dan Murphy, in version one, had been squirrel hunting, but had seen someone coming, and had hidden himself in the trees. He saw another hunter sitting south of the road take a shot at a running squirrel and hit Dickie Colrane. Then he had either been frightened off or bought off—Margaret Mary was willing to concede the possibility of the payoff, she knew her weak father.

The second explanation was that Dan Murphy had seen someone try to murder the man on the bicycle—perhaps had seen him briefly run out and stand over the stunned rider, mistakenly assume he was dead, and come back into the woods. Afraid for his own life, also believing Dickie dead, Dan Murphy had fled in a panic. He had never returned because he could never be sure that some evidence—the dead squirrels he had left, perhaps—would tie him to the scene and the killer would seek him out for silencing.

After this second version the page was blank, and reading over what she had written, she admitted ruefully to herself that both explanations were only slightly modified versions of one idea—that her father had been a witness to the shooting, but had not done it, whatever else base or cowardly he had done afterward. If either was correct, then the most urgent question became the identity of the other person. Or persons. She wrote the words "or persons" down and underlined them as part of her reminder to herself to keep an open mind.

When she took her notes to Neil Kelly later that day at Vic Foster's house, as he had requested, she realized how exiguous her scenario was.

In reply to his first question she could only say, "Well, first of all, what if my father only *saw* the shooting, but didn't do it?"

Neil nodded. "Then?"

"Then—" she flushed through her freckles and felt idiotic, but pressed on, swallowing, "he either ran away because he was afraid of getting involved, or maybe the person or persons who did the shooting paid him something to go away and forget he ever saw anything."

Neil considered her hypothesis. "And why would he stay away for this long—over twenty years?"

"Pa was a pretty famous coward. I think everyone knew that. Mama was about twice the man he was. She always said there was a weak strain in the Murphys. One of his brothers was a wino and one was some kind of a petty thief who beat up a ten-year-old girl and got sent to prison in Thomaston, Maine." She clenched her jaw, as if daring him to say the obvious, then said it herself. "Now you know why I thought about changing my name to Smith or something, but then I decided that I by God would be a Murphy and let a few people know we had some good qualities, too. Even Pa did, if you didn't scare him. He just scared easy, that's all, but is that a crime?"

Neil pursed his lips and shook his head. "No indeed. If it were, most of us would be in jail. Archie Ammons says, 'Bravery runs in my family,' and I suspect the real heroes among us are a tiny minority."

"Well, what do you think, is that possible? That my father was a witness, but not the actual shooter?"

"Oh, yes, it's clearly possible. And we might amplify his reasons for staying away to include someone in town here sending him a bit of payoff monthly or annually. But if some version of your scenario is correct, then the task becomes identifying the other person, doesn't it?"

She found out in the next half hour that she was going to have to confront some people she would just as soon not even see at a distance. In for a penny, in for a pound. She hitched up her bad leg, got on her feet, and headed out to do what had to be done.

He stopped her long enough to say, "Now that I've found you actually did find and fix the mysterious ailment in my car, I have great faith in you for this, you know."

She turned and smiled gratefully.

"And, if it's not to embarrassing to both of us, I'd like to consider it *our* car until I leave." He paused, enjoying her frank pleasure at the prospect of having transport. "And when I leave, it would be a favor to me if you and Dewi would buy it off me for one dollar. Ask him, will you?"

Prelude 7

WHEN HIS UNANTICIPATED, *unwanted visitor left him—funny woman, to come to his office like any student, to wait in the hall until the two students ahead of her had explained their problems with the term paper and received their instruction about what to do next—Dick Colrane sits back and considers his options.*

Margaret Mary Murphy, with her chipped, crooked teeth and her Irish music hall face, was obviously to be taken more seriously than her appearance suggested. He thought of a badger, those sharp little teeth that would not let go once they got into something.

She had come, no apology, to let him know that she had begun writing a book. That she intended to satisfy her own curiosity about what had become of her father and if possible to identify the person or persons who had actually shot young Dickie Colrane that April day twenty-three years ago.

He thinks of her anger, that her family name is so casually treated by the town as permanently blemished by the event. And her passionate avowal that she will dig the whole thing up again, whether he likes it or not.

He thinks of her final question, one that he realizes has just occurred to her as she asks it. Why doesn't he want her, or anybody for that matter, to write about the shooting? He's a successful man now, and the accident is a long time in the past; why can't he accept her need to open the whole thing up again and once and for all find out why her father disappeared that day?

She left without an answer. He knows the answer, but he could not give it to her.

They had called him potentially the greatest quarterback in the history of the game. They had measured him by every index, and they had praised his arm, his eye, his legs, his reflexes, his cool, his intelligence, his tactical sense, and above all they had talked and written about his patience. He waits, they wrote. Like an animal in the wild, he knows how to reserve his energy, his stroke, for the precise last deadly moment. And then to go for the jugular. "He never hurries," they had written in Time *magazine, "because he knows he was born to win, and those against him to lose."* Newsweek *had named him the Smiling Assassin.*

As he thinks about that now, he feels his muscles tense. He's been waiting a long time.

7

BERYL HOMEYER HADN'T wanted to take the woebegone nephew landed at her doorstep by the death of her sister and brother-in-law. She and Kurt Homeyer had been married for ten years without children, and she had been increasingly embittered by her shameful barrenness, then learned to accept it. The bitterness had been made poisonous when she had conceived a boy child, then lost it in the fifth month, a stunted fetus that would have been only half a child if he had lived. Kurt, stolid and prayerful at first, had patted her clumsily in her hospital bed and then watched her like a mournful hawk afterward, never daring to ask each month if there was any sign of another child in her, kneeling and bawling like a baby with his Lutheran pastor, a thin, scholarly clergyman who was horribly embarrassed by such pastoral tasks. As the years went by Kurt had drunk more and cursed her. The farm went from shabby to rundown. Then Lane and Kyle got themselves killed in a four-car crash out on Interstate 95, and when the paperwork was finished, nine-year-old Dickie Colrane was theirs. All but his name. To be sure of that, Kyle had left his insurance to raise the boy—on condition his name remain Colrane.

A few years after they took the boy, Kurt, whose surprising willingness to adopt Dickie had shocked his wife, slashed his leg in a tangle with a disk harrow. The cut was as casually treated as any injury Kurt ever got (his preferred first aid for all field accidents had always been to urinate on the wound, then wrap it up until the day's work was done, then go in the house and wash it off and bandage it). The treatment was not particularly effective for a deep gash with manure in it richly reproducing its bacteria content, and after a long, maniacal bout with fever and a leg swollen to four times its normal thickness, then emergency amputation, he died in Cooley-Dickinson Hospital.

Beryl did no public mourning. Grim and thin-lipped, her skin increasingly drawn like parchment over the bones of her face, she drew the stringy, sallow child to her and their terrible mutual need for love fed each other.

From her poured all the frustrated, undemanded love a romantic girlhood and late marriage had generated, then repressed. The skinny boy, whose own parents had been genial, easygoing, partying schoolchildren suddenly forced to get married, felt first the dark awe in the woman, then the simple grace of her devotion. To her he could do no wrong, and in the sun of her adoration he grew out of his sunken-eyed childhood into a strapping, popular, all-around boy everyone wanted for a friend. He drew on Beryl as a spendthrift draws an unlimited allowance. He was neither grateful to her nor ungrateful. As he came to realize that he was a kind of king in his town and school, that there were other boys and, increasingly, girls who would give him all the unstinted admiration and flattery he ever got at home, he spent less and less time at home, spoke less and less to his foster mother, and thought less and less about her feelings.

By the time he went to Old Hampton College on the town scholarship, given annually to the outstanding boy at the public high school, his aunt had been left entirely to the holidays. Her parched life, which had flowered not for her husband, and not for any cause or belief, but only for him, pinched down to a drawn-out bitter loneliness. The farm grew over, the barns fell in, and except for a few chickens, she kept nothing.

There were those in town who said it was disgusting that Dickie just ignored his aunt after all she had done for him, but they were few, and tended to be old farmers who didn't care about his athletic feats, but remembered Kurt Homeyer as a decent sort of fellow and thought that the adopted boy should have taken over his responsibilities. Old country sentiments.

When Dickie had been shot, the reporter from the local newspaper who tried to get a statement out of Beryl Homeyer got only the repeated remark through the locked screen door, "If it happened, it was God's will for him, that's all. It was God's will for him."

70

She watched, mostly in the newspapers, as her adopted child recovered from his injury, went on to success as a professional scholar, and returned to the college to take a faculty position there, something her family could never have imagined for any one of them. She read in a clipping from a Cambridge, Massachusetts, paper a cousin had sent her enclosed in a Christmas card that in 1963 Richard Colrane, the famous college athlete of the fifties, had testified for Christ at a famous Rally for Christ at Boston Garden, preached by a world-renowned Gospel missionary, along with a group of others who called themselves "Scholars and Athletes for Christ." But she never spoke of him to anyone.

At sixty-five she had surprised everyone who had thought they knew her by advertising in the valley farm journal for a husband (a practice that was common among rural people long before *NYRB* personal ads were invented to bring city people together). She declared herself in thirty-five words to be a fit Christian woman with a run-down farm able to be built up again, and asking any farmer of good disposition and sober habits to come see her.

A Polish potato farmer from Hadley with a sensational record of drunkenness, who had once pushed his refrigerator on a dolly three miles up Route 9 to try to swap it for drink at the Aqua Vita Motel, was sent packing.

A German named Adolph Otter, who had come over from Hamburg at fifteen with Kurt and remained a bachelor all his life, decided that he was ready for marriage at seventy-one, put on an orange necktie and the suit he had bought to be buried in, drove his truck into the yard of Beryl's house, and made the match. They drove together to the Lutheran Church a month later for the ceremony, then spent the weekend at a Howard Johnson Motel in Holyoke, visiting Mountain Farms Amusement Park, solemnly riding the Whip, and listening to country and western music.

From that day forward Beryl Homeyer Otter shopped regularly, held her head up in town, and cooked regular meals for her Adolph, who grinned at everyone and patiently rebuilt her farm into something respectable.

Dick Colrane did not attend the wedding, but he sent his foster mother and her new husband a copy of his first book, a sociological study of kinship patterns in Puritan New England, which won a prize.

When Murphy sat in Beryl's overfurnished parlor to ask her about her memories of the time when Dickie was shot, she smiled shyly, her hand partly masking her new false teeth, and shook her head.

"I said it was the hand of God then, and I say it again now, missus."

Murphy seethed with resentment of her own lack of skill as an interviewer. There were probably all kinds of techniques for drawing people like this wild-looking old woman out. She plowed ahead with a doomed feeling.

"Have you always believed that my father, Dan Murphy, did that shooting, Mrs. Otter?"

The old woman drew in her cheeks. "Whoever pulled that trigger, missus, it was God's hand aimed the gun. Ask me now, I'd say it was the best thing could have happened to Richard. My nephew."

Murphy looked past the gray head to the glass-fronted gun case against the wall. Three rifles, not exactly gleaming, but looking useful, and a single-barrel shotgun lay on the racks.

"Did you shoot a gun when you were younger, Mrs. Otter?" She felt breathless asking the barefaced question.

"Pshaw. You trying to kid me? I could shoot when I was ten. What farm child couldn't? Shot a doe with a Savage .250 when I was younger than you, cross wind, forty-five yards."

"Does Mr. Otter shoot?"

"You ever meet a German didn't like guns?" The old woman rocked back and cackled hilariously, snapping her teeth shut just in time to avoid an accident. "Them barn rats I had just give up and ran off when Adolph started popping them."

Again Murphy felt her lack of skill. How did you keep a conversation like this going? She floundered around in her mind for anything to ask, knowing she was going to sound stupid no matter what came out.

"Did you know my father, Dan Murphy, Mrs. Otter?"

The old woman closed her hooded eyes and stared off at some private inner view. She opened them and stared at Murphy.

"He wasn't much, missus, I'm sorry to have to say." She pursed her lips as if she tasted bitterness and glanced away, then back at the girl seated across her parlor from her. "I heard he died anyway, so that's that, isn't it?"

Margaret Mary Murphy pounced on the statement. "Who told you he died? Where did you hear that? No one ever told me he died, and I'm his daughter." She slowed herself deliberately. Hold the speech, Murph, just ask your question.

Beryl Otter grunted and bit down on her new teeth, smiling insanely for a moment.

"Heard it, though. Somewhere up in New Hampshire, someone said. Someone."

"Just someone? Don't you remember who?"

"Someone," the old woman said again, vaguely. She grinned her teeth-firming mad grin again. "About the same time Adolph and me went to Holyoke, like."

Neil had not had a good day so far, and he sought out a quiet table at a newly opened restaurant on the upper end of Spring Street, hoping that his old friends would be at their noontime haunts and he would have an hour to himself.

It was a surprisingly pleasant pair of rooms with just eight tables, intelligently if not grandly set into the space behind a jewelry store. The menu had the usual college town quota of tofu and vegetarian dishes, but there was a decent array of opened wines on a rack to be sampled, and the fettuccine Alfredo was not likely to be treated exotically in a small kitchen. He sampled a Bulgarian Pinot Chardonnay, which had a nice dry bite to it, and ordered a half bottle.

The fettuccine was reasonably light and creamy, and the meal and his solitary reflection on the unexpected moments of his visit to date was going nicely. Then James Amazing Grace Robinson materialized in the door and lifted a hand in benediction.

"Brother Kelly. Heard you were in town, honoring our humble village school with your worldwide presence." He glided over to Neil's table and offered a hand to be slapped or shaken, as one wished.

J. A. G. Robinson was a dandy with a shiv in his shirt. A street fighter who wore silk, acted silky, and threw up a screen

73

of banter around his vicinity that was intended to persuade the unwary that he was a large, shiny, black idiot. Those who had been taken in by the act always wondered when they found blood on their suit how Jag Robinson had got the knife in so deftly, how he had removed their assumed advantage over him so quietly. Jag Robinson was an academic terrorist and the self-appointed guardian of all minorities everywhere.

Neil shook his hand drily. "James. Nice to see you."

The tall black shook his head mournfully. "I could have warned you about the fettuccine here. It's not what you would call the chef's special gift, pasta. Now the chops, the chops." He rolled his eyes and lifted his hands. He tilted the wine bottle to read the label. "A Chardonnay from the Black Sea? Hold on dere a minute, Mister Sommeliar, we got our own sea somewhere nobody done told old Jag about?" He broke himself up with a falsetto laugh.

Neil ate on. He and Jag Robinson had sparred off and on over the years without any clear-cut victory for either. Public performers were not Neil's first choice for close friends, and the man's permanent itch to make political hay of every trivial campus issue was just another academic monomania he could do without.

Jag Robinson leaned grandly down half his elegant length to whisper near Neil's ear. "We hear you thinking of not coming back, like."

Robinson had good sources, he'd say that for him.

"Really?" Neil poured himself another glass of the white wine.

"We hear," the whisperer added, glancing around with hugely magnified caution, "you thinking of handing your job slot over to that fat little Irishman, Scotchman, whatever he is that's warming your chair while you on leave."

"That right?" Neil knew the punch line would arrive soon, and he was willing to wait for Robinson's routine to reach its tiny climax.

"We—" the word was intoned this time, portentously, "have another position on that. I thought it was only fair to let you know, Professor Kelly, that it is now considered time for the Department of English Litt-richer in this here honky college to come on into the present century, join the brothers in welcoming one of Us into the fold, dig? And we all sing 'We Shall Overcome,' et cetera together next commencement day to signal the birth of a new era, how 'bout dat?''

Neil looked up at him. The bleak brown eyes were the message, not the foolish smile.

"Gotcha." No return smile, just full frontal eye contact. It was a conversational ploy he had learned from a policeman friend in London. Not argumentative, not submissive. Street talk, and the street man understood. Jag Robinson's eyes widened just a fraction.

"You keep the faith now, Brother Kelly," he said, exiting the small room grandly, sashaying right out the door.

Neil realized that Jag Robinson must have actually followed him in from the street for the exchange. He thought about Dewi and the job for a moment, then put that out of his mind to think about Dick Colrane. He still had a party to organize, and he wasn't making much progress. He also had to talk with Jill Purlie, and soon. It was she who had been responsible for his making this trip, and he felt an urgent need to check signals with her on her fiancé's state of mind about the pending marriage and many other things.

"I swear, Neil, she *must* have done it. Look, everything fits.''

Margaret Mary was leaning across the booth table where she and Dewi and Neil were having drinks in the Horse. At four in the afternoon the L-shaped room was still only sparsely occupied, and they had the whole lower, shorter arm of the room to themselves.

Neil sipped his Heineken and listened calmly to the excited young woman talking to him from just a foot away. Dewi drank his watery American beer, which he had convinced himself would slim him down dramatically if he imbibed enough of it. Murphy ignored the colorful mixed drink she had ordered in a moment of exotic feeling and talked and waved her hands.

Dewi growled at her brave assertion. "Some detective. Come off it, Murph, or you'll have your teacher here committing suicide. You talk to one half-cracked old woman and you've solved your case.''

She rounded on him furiously. "Is it my fault if all the facts fit with the first person I talk to?" She challenged Neil in turn. "Is it?"

He held up a calming hand. "It's possible—just barely possible, but hardly probable—that what fits is the facts, but more likely what fits is your hypothesis, nicely trimmed. Don't feel bad if that's the case; it happens in research all the time."

"Fact one," she held up a finger, daring them with her eyes to stop her. "She raised Dickie Colrane and he walked out on her, never even said thank you. Everyone in town knows that. She resented that. And she resented watching him grow up to be a champion athlete in the first place, since her own baby that would have been was nothing but an aborted freak. She wouldn't have minded his being some kind of scholar, because there was never any idea in her head that her son would have been anything like that."

She stopped to take a breath.

"I count eleven facts, three suppositions, and four conjectures in that," her husband said, taking a drink of his awful beer and making a mouth.

"But it's completely logical," she hissed angrily.

"So she shot him? Because she lost her own child about one hundred years before?" Dewi put his head down on his arms and muttered, "Christ on a pogo stick."

"You bet she did." Murphy was vehement again. "And Dan Murphy saw her. And listen, because this is the clincher. She paid him to go away. And," she poked her doubting husband awake with a brutal finger in the arm, "she sent him money regularly. She sold off her farm stock, didn't she? And she went into that long time of hiding in her house and doing penance or whatever it was to her until *something*—" she underscored the word with another poke, and Dewi backed away from her into the corner of the booth, rubbing his arm, "—released her from all her fears and she finally knew she wasn't ever going to be discovered. Then out she comes from her self-imposed incarceration and marries again." She concluded triumphantly, "And if that wasn't my father dying so's he couldn't blackmail her anymore, what was it?"

She thumped the table with the flat of her hand, daring the two of them to answer her rhetorical question.

Neil said, "Murphy, I want you to do one thing for me."

"Don't tell me to forget it, because I'm right, and I'm not going to forget it, I'm going to prove it."

"Will you, for the love of God and the sweet saints, woman, let the man tell you what he wants before you attack him and stab him to death with that lethal finger of yours?"

Neil had learned already to wait for the lulls in the rhythm of their hectic, practiced, happy quarreling and then speak again. "Interview one more of your suspects. Any one at all."

She took a swig of the red drink before her and held it off to regard it distastefully. "Who ordered this crap? Get me one of those good beers Neil has, not that diet swill that's making you fatter." She hitched herself over to Neil's side of the booth to let Dewi out, and he patiently went to the bar and got her a cold Heineken, from which he took a grateful long swig on the way back.

"Why?" She was still scowling, rather shattered that her brilliant in-one solution hadn't seemed to persuade anyone.

"Discovery. That's the point here, what all detection and all research is about. Discovery of the unknown. Sometimes what is discovered is useful. At worst it will let you see what you already know in a new light."

"And I'll tell you ahead of time," her husband said, setting her drink in front of her, "what you'll find. How's that for a bet?"

"Okay, you fat Welsh slob, I bet you ten dollars, Mr. Know-It-All. What will I find out?"

Dewi smiled beatifically at her. "The so-called facts will fit in the next interview, too. And the next after that. Yes, they will, you silly bitch. You don't believe me? Go. Do it. It's something like the principle where the work expands to fit the available time. All the evidence in research constantly expands to fill the available theory."

Her face burned with anger, her freckles standing out boldly on her cheeks and the bridge of her nose. "You both still think I'm twisting the facts to fit my own silly preconceived notions, don't you?" She resented their attitude, and as she sat there she could not keep from feeling increasingly that they were right and she was making an ass of herself. But she was damned if she'd let them know that.

"Murphy," Neil said slowly, trying to draw her attention away from her inner feelings of hurt, where it had obviously taken root, "what your learned husband says has a large truth in it. Everyone, in any field, who starts out nursing a hypothesis runs the risk of weaving a fantasy out of the rags of evidence that turn up. More than half—much more than half—the academic and popular cults in the world had their genesis in just that kind of innocently perverse fact-finding. Chariots of the gods, the newest cancer cure from wet tea bags, boy Hindus who are this year's true avatar of God, all that, and down to the systems gullible gamblers take with them to Las Vegas. There is in all of us a terrific will to believe, and it often succeeds even when we bar the door with every trick of logic we know."

She stared at him. "Beryl Otter was a crack shot, did I tell you that?"

They both sat staring back at her, sipping their drinks and waiting.

"Jesus." She slammed her hand on the table again. "All right, dammit, who?"

"Why don't you talk with the person Dick Colrane was closest to in those days," Neil suggested, "his coach."

"Venuti? I don't get it. What's he going to know?"

Dewi, at some risk to his health, smiled and patted her hand. "You won't know until you talk with him, will you, luv?"

Without another word Margaret Mary Murphy Morgan-Evans picked up her purse and walked out.

Dewi leaned back into the corner of the booth and blew a long breath out at the ceiling. "Ah, dear, there she goes. And just as I was about to propose a toast in slimmer's brew here to my new job prospects. Ahem, which, may I ask if, and so on . . . ?" Dewi was just a shade more anxious than he hoped he appeared.

The gloomy look that came over Neil Kelly's face did not improve his feelings.

"I was going to mention that when I had a chance," Neil said, making circles with his glass and avoiding looking at him. "To put it bluntly, my young friend, we have a problem."

Now Dewi was sweating large drops of pure pain. He had hoped for so much so suddenly. Was it all going to be washed out now by some bloody bureaucratic gimmick? He was all bravado.

"I swear to you, I'll attend faculty meetings until they force me to stay away. I'll apply for grants. I'll offer my kidneys for research. What's the bloody obstacle, then?"

"Brother Robinson."

"Who the bloody fucking hell is he?"

"Professor James Amazing Grace Robinson. Our resident gadfly on all matters Third World and Rightly Civil. He teaches American political history, and he is a very shrewd scholar, and he is chairman of the standing committee on minority recruitment. J.A.G. Robinson has informed the dean that the next appointment vacated in the English department must—I underscore the word 'must' because he did—I am told there was table pounding, fiery oratory, and other ostentatious oratorical devices—must go to a Third World person. Or we've got trouble. Right here in River City, as they say in the song."

"I don't know the damned song, but does it mean that if you leave the college they must hire a wog, even if I'm better qualified than he is?" Dewi wasn't bothering to moderate his tone, and the pub was getting busier. A few heads turned.

Neil waved genially to an old acquaintance who raised his eyebrows.

"Allowing for your colorful use of the vernacular, that's it. Jag Robinson's general theme was that Kelly and the visiting Irishman, as he prefers to call you, are not going to get away with any under-the-table deal."

"He called me an Irishman?" Dewi was livid. "I'll kill the black bastard. God, the ignorance of the man."

Neil spoke evenly. "He goes through this routine every time—and I mean each and every time—a faculty FTE slot opens up."

"That's another thing," Dewi groused. "Every time jobs are discussed around here, someone talks about FTEs. Would you mind telling me what the bloody hell an FTE is?"

"A full-time position or two half-time positions or any combination of fractions that make up a full-time equivalent. FTE. You represent, to the computer and the bursar, one FTE."

"Crap." Dewi stormed over to the bar, which was filling as the happy hour with half-price drinks waxed and drew in the drinkers. He came back with two whiskeys for himself and none at all for Neil.

"If you think I'm buying you a drink and you bringing me news like that, think again, Kelly." He downed the first drink. "And the next time anyone impugns my nationality and you fail to punch him in the snoot on my behalf, to hell with you." He downed the second.

A tall, thin ancient figure tottered toward them across the room. Neil whispered quickly to Dewi, "Treat him kindly. Famous bore, retired, college fixture, Thomas Paddington."

Dewi glared at the man's shetland jacket and leather elbow patches malevolently. Paddington put out his hand and announced himself.

"Thomas Paddington. I played for Amherst in 1940."

"Liar," said Dewi.

"I have the team photo in my study" Was this man mad?

"Faked," said Dewi.

"There are three men in this room who will support me."

"Bribed," said Dewi.

"What about *that*, what about that, eh?" the old gentleman shouted furiously, shaking before his stomach the small gold football hanging from his chain.

"You got it in a pawnshop," Dewi said mercilessly.

Thomas Paddington turned the color of calves' livers and made for the bar, tottering.

"That wasn't very nice," Neil said to his companion.

Dewi threw his hands into the air with delight and crowed. "I never thought I'd get a chance like that. This whole charade is stolen from a Dylan Thomas story, I swear to you, and stage directed for my benefit. Wonderful, wonderful. Feed me another famous college person and I'll devour him on the spot, I'll devour them all."

An angular faculty wife who put her cheek to Neil's and was cautiously introduced asked Dewi if he were a poet.

"A cornucopia of phalluses cascade on the vermilion palaces in arabesques and syrup rigadoons," he replied gravely.

She was ecstatic. "I told Melvin you were a poet. Will you give a reading at the OH Bookstore sometime? Everyone else does, I mean, that's the way it seems. You have such a beautiful voice."

He deepened it an octave. "Alas, dear madam, you have just heard my entire output. I put out little, and rarely. The rest, many volumes, to be sure, is as yet radiantly unworded in ambitious conjecture. I quote, of course."

"Of course," the lady said, smiling bravely.

"I'm leaving," Neil said.

"This is the most fun I've had in this poor excuse for a town," Dewi announced in his most sepulchral tone, "so I better leave too. And I expect you to comfort me, Kelly. Speak words of succor, you fucker."

Neil shouldered the street door from the bar open and let his morose friend pass through ahead of him. As much to take Dewi's mind off his own new difficulties, he stopped the Welshman on the porch and asked him, "Has it occurred to you that Murph might ruffle someone's feathers with her investigation for this book?"

Dewi squinted at him. "It has," he growled softly. He was only a quarter drunk. "But I know the two things are that important to her, first finding out if her dad was the idiot rogue everyone thinks, and then doing the book. She's brighter than you might think, Neil, and if she can actually finish and publish the whole story, she'll get a lot out of her system that's damned up behind that clown act of hers. Like you know who," he added forlornly. "Still."

"Still, yes, I realize I might just have to keep an extra eye on her shenanigans." He shrugged, and from the softness of his tone when he said it, Neil almost missed the significance of his next observation.

"When I think about Murph wanting to find out about her father, what became of him and all, I find myself thinking about my mother. Weird conventional things—do I look like her? Did she have a happy life after she chucked me? I hope so, I really do. Is she dead or alive? That one gives me goose bumps sometimes, that she might be propped up on pillows in a bed sitter in Finsbury somewhere, looking out the window at a dirty courtyard." He shrugged again. "Has it ever occurred to you, Professor Kelly, sir, that it's an insane world? I mean, have you ever noticed that this very theme might be suitable for say, works of literature, writings, as it were?"

"Why, no, Professor Morgan-Evans. What a keen insight."

"I don't know my own mother and 'A stranger has come to share my room in the house not right in the head, A girl mad as birds.'"

"Would that be your man Dylan?"

"The very man. There are days when I think he wrote my biography before I was born."

After he had left the newly melancholy Welshman, Neil Kelly placed a call to Thomas Bowie in London.

It was ten at night there, but Thomas was as likely to be at Scotland Yard as anywhere, and a message would soon reach him in any case.

Bowie and Neil had enjoyed a long adventure together in the past in the City, the commercial heart of London, a matter of death by bombing and detection by teamwork. The cynical, tough, autodidact from the London streets and the oblique pedant from New England's green and pleasant land had become good friends, and Neil had no hesitation in making his abrupt request when Thomas finally came on the line. Besides, it was an opportunity to ask indirectly about Dolly. She and Neil had mutually agreed before he left England that a week or so totally apart and out of touch would give them both a chance to reflect on their increasingly hectic love affair. Neil had only the smallest twinge of conscience about garnering secondhand intelligence, just in case Thomas had seen her anywhere. Surely there was no harm in knowing at least if she was looking well.

Thomas was sarcastically glad to hear from him. "You say the woman, this Marjorie Morgan-Evans or Evans-Morgan might be dead, or alive, might be in London somewhere or might be out of it, and might have a different name. No recent physical description, but you'd like me to find her and call you back. Is there anything else, you Yank aesthete?" The familiar drawl came over the line as if they had parted yesterday and were merely continuing an interrupted conversation.

"You're my man. Do it. The man she was last with was Sid Dunn, an old vaudeville dancer. This means a lot to a friend of mine, Thomas."

Bowie snorted and told him succinctly that the vast forces of the Met, most especially the super-brilliant men of C Division, their intelligence and reflexes honed by years of training and even special video cassettes imported from the Los Angeles Police Department—get that, will you?—to razor sharpness, were not at the beck and call of every chum with a thirty-year-old missing person report, but that on the other hand, he would get back to him as fast as he could.

Neil gave him Vic's number, and for good measure his own house's number, and told him the best times to call. That reminded him to get the time and charges for this call from the overseas operator. His friendship with the Fosters might not survive too many unpaid transatlantic calls.

Prelude 8

JOHN VENUTI IS bugged by Title IX. The first time he heard of it, he laughed out loud. Title IX no longer amuses him. He loathes it, he fears its capacity to destroy his sanity, he is dedicated to signing every petition he can find to repeal it. He does not think it a Good Thing. Many male athletic directors, especially those in their middle years and beyond—the Old Guard—share his feelings. When they get together at conferences they drink, chew, smoke, fart, and bitch about Title IX. It is the Magna Charta of women athletes in colleges and universities. Title IX lets women have a slice of the athletic budget, and even lets them play varsity sports.

"Volleyball, for Chrissakes," he had moaned when it had first become an issue to explain to the president of OH. "Basketball with no dribbling. Slow pitch softball. Beanbag."

It was one of his more explicit oral presentations.

Two years later, with women running in the Boston Marathon (something John Venuti had long desired to do, but had never done) and women's sports teams appearing on every other campus, and with a noisy group of newly admitted women students at Old Hampton calling themselves WONT STOP (Women On To Sports Teams Or Perish), John was told by the president to provide.

"Provide what?" he asked his drinking companion rhetorically at the VFW hall. Among his distinctions was being the only member of the OH faculty (in accord with serene tradition his proper title was Professor Venuti, although everyone in town called him Coach) to do his drinking at the VFW instead of the Horse. "You know what those broads need to be provided."

Nowadays the subject is rarely mentioned by his comrades-in-arms. Their buddy had lost, progress so-called had *triumphed, and the coach had been known to haul off and deck anyone who thought the subject was funny.*

"Women athaletes." He spit each time he said it. Women TV reporters made his saliva flow, too. And women professors. Not to mention women ministers (although he grudgingly enjoyed having the Protestants stuck with the problem) and women lawyers.

"What ever happened to all the women mothers, I wanna know," John Venuti says to himself as he sits in his basement office reading a piece in the Globe about women weight lifters.

The faculty senate, a body he despises without regard to race, sex, or religion, has just informed him by memorandum that it has voted unanimously to have the weight-training rooms in the new gym facility open to men and women, and therefore he is to create a position for a one-third FTE women's weight-training coach.

"Jesus. First they buy $231,000 worth of this Nautilus equipment that's not budgeted for, just because they have these rooms, and now I'm supposed to carve another slice off my budget for a goddam female iron pumper." He shouts to the walls, but they have heard him before and offer no defense. He balls up the paper and throws it at the door, where someone who apparently doesn't know the coach's moods is patiently knocking.

It is Margaret Mary Murphy Morgan-Evans.

8

"Sure, I knew Dan Murphy, what about it?"

"I'm his daughter."

"Which one are you?"

"Margaret. People sometimes call me just Murph or Murphy. My husband is a teacher here. Visiting," she added reluctantly.

Venuti looked off into space, his feet between her face and his. She studied the worn soles of his Keds patiently. "You know what my wife Jenny and me got?" He held up seven fingers. "Seven daughters. You at least kept your old man's name. Not one Venuti in the bunch. All married. One to a doctor, two of them to brothers who own a trucking outfit over in Springfield, one to a cop, one to the coach over at Classical, one's divorced—you like that? divorced?—and one to an ex-priest. How's that for a record? And the ex-priest is the only Italian in the bunch. And he goes by the name Billy. You like that? You meet him, he gives you a big hug and he says, 'Hi, my name is Billy.' An ex-priest. We got two grandchildren, both girls, out of the whole bunch, the cop and the coach over at Classical. You got any kids? Babies?"

"Not yet." Murph was beginning to wonder why she had come.

He looked at her disgustedly. "Not yet. That's what my girls say. Not yet, Pa. We're thinking about it. We're not quite ready yet." He sighed through a muffled epithet. "You kids, your generation? If you'll pardon my French, you stink. Family means nothing. Husbands are all a bunch of toe dancers."

Murph finally decided this would go on forever if she didn't prevent it.

"I came to talk about something else."

86

"Did you, little lady?" The fierce, square old face glowered at her. "Well, we're in my office, ain't we? So we'll talk about what I want to talk about."

He nodded in vigorous agreement with his own dictum and took a cigar, a twisted black Italian stogie, from a red, white, and green box and lit it, making plenty of smoke. The smell of those cigars had shortened many an unwanted interview. He clamped his teeth on it after he got it going, leaned back in his chair again, and put his Keds back up between them.

"Your father, Dan Murphy, was just an ordinary guy."

He looked around his feet at her, apparently to see if she was satisfied with his summary of the matter.

She was watching him, narrow-eyed against the smoke. Finally she stood up to see him better.

"I don't think he was responsible for shooting Dickie Colrane, and I'm writing a book about that."

John Venuti sighed again. "Tell me someone who's not writing a book about something and it'll be news. Guy was in here the other day he's writing a book about Wop sports legends. I'm supposed to tell him about people like Vince Lombardi that I knew, Robustelli, people like that. I said to him, who's gonna wanna read about a lot of Walyo athaletes? So he says all their Walyo grandchildren. He says there's a new ethnic pride sweeping everyone, and the Wops are getting back to the basic of being Wops just like the Jigs and the Jews and all the rest of them. He should tell my kids that. I tell you I got exactly one Italian son-in-law? Course he took a vow of celibacy, but that don't stop him from marrying my Angie. Only thing is, he's not sure he wants to bring kids into the world. I told him St. Joseph wasn't sure either, but they took care of it for him, so watch out. Why couldn't he marry some ex-nun? Those people are made for each other. Why'd he have to marry Angie?"

"My book is really about the shooting of Dickie Colrane."

"That so? You figure your father didn't do it, so someone else did, right? And you want to find out who, right?" He puffed at his stogie through clenched teeth, smiling for the first time.

Murphy told him what she thought. He listened without looking at her once. The phone rang and he lifted it, grunted into it, said, "That's a lotta garbage," and hung up. She finished with her exposition of the Murphy version.

Maddeningly, he pointed a finger at the phone and ignored what she had just said. "You know what that was? This Jigaboo James Bojangles Robinson we got here looking out for one third of the world. He's put himself in charge of hiring minorities left and right, and he tells me he just heard we need a new weights coach and the committee on hiring Jigs just decided it should be a woman of the black persuasion." He blew stogie smoke at the telephone. "The only black thing around here I did like was my old telephone. So they took it away and gimme this Debbie Reynolds model. Your father thought he was a fisherman."

Murphy was too confused by the man's logic and cigar stink to know if that was relevant or not. She decided to let him talk.

"He used to stand in those rubber boots in the Stockade River and whip those little flies out in the water, wait for the fish to jump up and play with him. That's not fishing. Some goddarn Scotchman invented that. Fishing's when you go out in a boat with six or eight guys and you take a case or two of beer, and you fish. You fish, you get it? You put bait on your hooks and you hang them out inna water and when the fish bite on 'em, you haul 'em in. None of this five-pound test line for a ten-pound blue darter. If you have to do it for a living, the way my old man did, that's another story, you use a net, you trawl, okay. But fishing? Your old man didn't know fishing from—" he glanced at her. John Venuti had strong principles about bad language in front of women. "—pardon my French, but he didn't know fishing from his own behind."

Murphy was getting mad.

"How do you ever teach anyone to play football?"

He stopped teetering in his desk chair to put his feet on the floor and say, "Whaddaya talking about?"

"I say I want to talk about my father and the day Dickie Colrane got shot and you rattle on for twenty minutes about your kids and fishing and every other goddam thing under the sun but that."

"Hey, watch your language, little lady, awright? We're talking about it, ain't we? Am I right?" John Venuti was genuinely puzzled by her attitude. What did she think they were doing? Here he was being Mr. Nice Guy. "I give you an interview and you say you're gonna tell me how to talk? I was talking before you were born, young lady. You're like your old man. He'd say one word every hour and think he was keeping the conversation going. He was a pain in the you-know-what, you want to know."

"Do you think he shot Dickie Colrane?"

"Do I think he shot Dickie Colrane? Do you? Does my Aunt Genevieve? Who cares? It was a long time ago. Who even remembers 1960? Do you? It's all dead and gone, past history. If you can even tell me who was the number one pick in pro football that year I'll give you a cigar."

Murphy smiled like a wolf. Neil Kelly had told her to do her homework first, and she had taken his advice. She had read every damn thing in the college library about 1960.

"Billy Cannon of LSU. The Rams got him." She looked him right in the eye. "Gimme my cigar."

The coach grunted another muffled curse and handed over a stogie from the red, white, and green box. Murph stuck it behind her ear jauntily.

"You want me to name the Giant's starting offensive team that year?"

"Too easy. Just tell me the quarterbacks, after Conerly got hurt."

"Another cigar?"

"You're on."

"Shaw and Grosscup."

He flipped her a stogie end over end. "Yeah, right. Couple of toe dancers. Think about that." He gazed past her off into some private memory space. "I guess you could say I've got an obsession about them people, them quarterbacks then. Dickie Colrane would've been first pick, you know that?" The rage that flooded his face suddenly almost frightened Murphy, even though she knew it was not directed at her. She had a quick intuitive sense of what it must have been like forty years ago to face this hulk of a man across the line of scrimmage in his prime, not this stogie-chomping caricature of an old bull athlete gone to fat. "He woulda been the first man picked. My ballplayer."

"Was he the best you ever coached?"

Venuti blew a screen of smoke. "He was, young lady, for his age, the best I ever *saw*. He was the reason we were undefeated that year. My only undefeated season, my only league championship. This ain't exactly the Big Ten you know, and winning the Valley Trophy ain't exactly like winning the Sugar Bowl, but I got it."

Together they looked over at the squad picture and the adjoining shelf with the Valley Cup on it. Venuti seemed to soften in his pride.

"Look, I come here instead of taking a job at Boston College. Nice Jebby school like Fordham. Just a dinky little commuter's school then, but Frank Leahy was coming in and a lot of things were going to change, including winning the Sugar Bowl from Tennessee, remember. No more of that old Gil Dobie single wing crapola, you'll pardon the expression, but modern football, like war. Good Catholic kids from tough towns like Everett and Brockton that the Jebs could teach a little ethics to and I could teach them blocking and tackling. Even as late as Holovak there I had a shot at the line coach job."

He squashed out his butt underfoot and kicked it sideways into the corner.

"But we came here instead, Jennie and me. Know why? Jennie's family. They're from Milan, see, very proud of being northerners. With Italians that's a big thing. So if we come here to this WASP heaven, I'm coaching a lot of snotty Protestant kids all want to be bankers and secretary of state. I'm on the faculty, right? *Professore* Venuti. You think that don't go over big with my goombas? We go over there for a visit, they treat me like I'm the president of Harvard. '*Professore* Venuti, my son-in-law from Old Hamptom College, in America.'"

He waved off the memory disgustedly. "Hey, so I get maybe two, three good athaletes a year. For coaches in this league, that's average. I really did have one kid, kind of a clumsy end, kept falling over his own feet after he'd catch the ball, good hands though, became an undersecretary of state. I saw him on TV talking to some Arab needed a shave. Then along comes Colrane, right out of the local high school. Nobody recruits him, he just shows up. If you know enough football to know about Billy Cannon, that jerk, then you know the papers and magazines went wild for Dickie Colrane. Cool Colrane. The Cobra. The Assassin. All that junk. My name for him was Shug. Only him and me knew that, but who cares now. Like Sugar Ray Robinson when he was a kid. Middleweight champ. Not this jamoke they call Sugar Ray now, makes commercials in a tuxedo. The moves he had. Colrane wouldn't of just been up there with Unitas and Baugh, he would've creamed their records. You had to see him to believe his arm."

Murphy knew that somehow she had got the floodgates open, and she leaned against the wall, her hip aching, trying not to gag on the pall of putrid cigar smoke gradually making the room a death trap, soaking it in.

The coach realized he was talking as he hadn't talked for years. He liked this spunky kid, but it was more than that. Listening to himself ramble and talk about Dickie Colrane and that fateful year, he realized that he didn't care about it anymore, coaching. Let them put women in charge of the whole goddam world if they wanted to. There was a real sense of lightness in his chest, and he knew that he had decided to retire. It felt good.

He lit another stogie. "Hope these don't bother you. I'll tell you one guy would've cheerfully shot Dickie right through the head, that was Paul Pettinger and his old man."

Murphy made her first note, writing the name down carefully.

"Paul came here the same year Dickie did. Some hotshot prep school in New Hampshire or New Jersey or someplace, all the passing records there, superstar athalete. His old man was president of some corporation made TVs, and they were an Old Hampton family. Old man went here, uncle went here, the usual garbage. Dickie takes the quarterback job away from Paul the first practice. Paul is going to be captain of the baseball and a star hockey player and run a little track, good enough to anchor the mile relay that set the school record. But he wants that QB job, see. That's what the old man wanted for him. So Paul sits on the bench for three years—remember, we couldn't play freshman then—and never even gets into a varsity game. The old man never did give a quarter to this place after that. I figure by starting Dickie ahead of Paul I mighta cost this joint a million, maybe more." He laughed gleefully and blew smoke at the telephone again.

"And I'm suppose to let some boogie behindhole from West Outfield come in here and tell me how to run my sports program?"

"Didn't you have another Division II all-American that same year? A lineman?"

He looked up quickly from retying his sneaker laces. "You really did your homework. Yeah. Guy named De Saulniers. Everyone called him Saul. Not big enough to play pro, but a tough kid. Went into acting or something after."

"I'll tell you something else I learned doing my homework, Coach." She watched the square, lined old face for signs of that same fury, which seemed to be flickering under the surface. "Mitchell De Saulniers is president of the Old Hampton College AGC—the Alumni Gay Council. You know about them? A group of alumni who have come out of the closet and want the college's policies to reflect more concern for homosexuals?"

The coach turned a dark purple. He turned his head and spat into the wastebasket. "Yeah. I hear from the AGC every once and a while. Another bunch of toe dancers. You don't wanna hear what I told them. Some things I won't say in front of any woman. They should go back in the coat closet."

"Mitch DeSaulniers and Dickie Colrane were roommates, weren't they?" That was the question she had been waiting to ask. She said a quick prayer for help.

"So?" Venuti shrugged.

Murphy had a blazing, intuitive sense that she was on the edge of something, but she hadn't the faintest idea what it was. She only wanted to keep popping questions until something arrived to fill in the outlines.

"Why did Paul Pettinger stay with football for four years if he knew from the beginning that he could never take the starting job away from Dick Colrane?" Where did that question surface from? Thank you, Saint Margaret.

"Maybe he thought Dickie would get hurt. It happens. Star player breaks his leg, substitute goes in, whips the behind off Amherst, fifty-two–zip. You see it inna movies alla time."

92

He was grinning at her, not answering the question. She kept rummaging in her mind. There was something there. Come on, for Jesus' sake, Saint Margaret, don't quit on me now.

"Maybe he just wanted to use it when he ran for Congress. Always looks good on the campaign literature. Football, Old Hampton College, yaketa yaketa . . ." Venuti's voice dripped sarcasm. Paul Pettinger had been a congressman. Murphy had her connection.

"Paul Pettinger was arrested, wasn't he, in Washington, for molesting a page boy or an aide of some kind in the Capitol?" She almost hooted, getting the connection. "From out west someplace—Iowa, Idaho, someplace like that. He pleaded nolo and resigned just before reelection time, right?"

"Hey, it's your homework. If it was in the papers, it's true, right?"

Margaret Mary pressed her advantage. She was by God getting the swing of this game, and she loved it. "Pettinger didn't spend those years sitting on the bench because he thought he'd ever get Colrane's job, did he? He stayed because he and someone else on that team were soul brothers, didn't he? You had yourself a couple of queer ballplayers, didn't you, Coach?"

John Venuti rubbed his hand across his mouth as if trying to erase the words that came to his lips. He spat a grain of black tobacco from the tip of his tongue viciously.

"Ballplayers is right. Here I am, right? I'm sixty-nine years old. They gotta rule now, you gotta retire at seventy, whether you need to or want to or not. They're getting together this testimonial for me for next year, I know all about it? You know what I decided just now, talking here with you, young lady? I'm gonna be off in the Bahamas or Disney World or someplace with Jennie when they spring it. All my old athaletes are supposed to come back for it. I'm the Amos Alonzo Stagg of Massachusetts. I go back to Bronko Nagurski, Mel Hein, people like that. Iron men. I'm the oldest living this and that. It's like I represent the Old Guard, see? Well, Miss Murphy, missus, whatever, if I got up at that banquet and told them what the Old Guard would think of their Title IX and their Black Power political athaletes that stick out their goddarn lower lip and complain to the NAACP every time you tell them to move their lazy black behinds, and their gay alumni, they'd lynch me, not give me any watch."

The sadness and rage in his face had made him livid again, and he had bitten right through his stogie. He looked at it and gently popped it onto the floor, crushed it with his foot, and kicked it aside.

One gnarled hand the size of a bunch of bananas pounded on his desktop, scattering papers. "I could tell them a lotta things that would make them rewrite their alumni magazine. Listen, if I'da gone to coach B.C. none of this stuff would of ever happened. You trying to tell me those Jesuits would've put up with any of this garbage?"

He sat silent after his outburst. The small, smoke-palled room seemed even smaller now to his visitor, trapped there by her own fascination and the force of his anger.

"You wanna write a book? Listen, your old man was all right. No goddarn world beater, but I never thought he was so stupid he'd shoot anyone across a road when he was aiming at a goddarn squirrel. You wanna write a book? Listen, *I* could've shot the guy. I could've strangled him with my bare hands. The priests say if you got murder in your heart for someone, you've already as good as killed him as far as your soul is concerned. Well, that's what I had in my heart for Dickie Colrane, murder.

"I'm telling you flat out, the best athalete I ever seen, let alone coached. Another Thorpe. My prize kid. On his way to the Giants, right? Gonna be right up there on TV with Gifford and Modjelewski and Katkavage and Huff, right? John Venuti's boy. Bullcrap. He was a sissy. Do you understand what I mean?" His massive, shaggy head was stretched toward her, the old veiny eyes staring as he jabbed at her idle notebook with a thick finger.

"Put that in your book. I think one of his boyfriends shot him, if you want to know. Maybe your old man got caught in the middle and took off. I think it was some kind of goddam sick triangle, like a fairies' soap opera, going on right on my own team, and I never tumbled to it until they were ready to graduate, that's how smart I was.

"I think Pettinger stuck around because him and De Saulniers and Colrane and God knows who else were playing their own private ball games in the rubdown room is what I think, and somebody got his fairy gizmo in an uproar because somebody he truly loved was sticking his in someone else and that was it. Now, shouldn't I be proud? I been here forty-one years, thanks to having an old friend who the college owes, and what have I got? I got Title IX, and I got some black hotshots who can't even tell time good enough to show up for practice before it's over, and I got their soul brothers telling me now I've got to hire some soul sisters, and I got a bunch of queer alumni who think they're all gay caballeros. And I haven't even got one grandson!" he shouted in final outrage.

"The doctor son-in-law got a vasectomy, one of them operations to keep you from being a father. Eighty-five thou a year he makes. I asked him, are you afraid you'll squirt out some of your famous brains if you have a smart kid, so you won't be so smart no more?"

He turned to his desk and lifted piles of papers with both hands. "Get out of here now, little lady. If I'm dead when you write your book—but only if I'm dead, or I swear I'll sue your rear end off—put in it that Dickie Colrane was the closest I'm ever gonna come to having a son. And put in it that I caught Paul Pettinger on his knees in front of him in the rubdown room November 6, 1959. What they call a date that'll live in infamy, right? You remember it the way you remember Pearl Harbor. All I said was, 'Okay, Shug, you can finish the season, but that's it! We never spoke to each other again, never."

He shuffled the papers into piles without seeing them. He was crying.

"I'm glad that pansy never got to the Giants. They'dve blamed me, right? So whoever done it did me a favor." He blinked and squeezed his eyes together hard, brushing his face brusquely with his big hand. "Do you even know what I mean? What these fags do to each other?"

"I'm a married woman, Coach, of course I know what you mean."

"What's that got to do with it?" he bellowed at her. "I'm married forty-three years, you think any of that stuff goes on between me and Jennie?" He wiped his nose with his fingers and wiped his hand on his pants. "Maybe that's the answer."

"To what?"

"To why some kid who's a fag ends up getting married. And not one of these fag marriages, to a girl. Did you know Colrane's getting married finally? To a girl?"

"So?"

"So maybe young people nowadays, young married people, do that stuff to each other instead of doing what God Almighty intended them to do. Cripes' sake, maybe even my own kids do it. It would explain why I only got two granddaughters, right? God help you people is all I can say. You and your generation. Now scram, you'll pardon my French. I gotta read brochures about weight-training equipment.

"You got your interview, right? Now you know the whole story. Look, I'm sorry about whatever happened to your old man, but that's all water over the dam now, right? Do you see what I mean? I think about it every so often, then I say to myself, John, forget it. It's not easy, I know that. I did the wrong thing, right? I know that. I saw them two there, and the first thing—the first goddarn thing—that flashed through my mind was 'there goes the League title and the Valley Cup.' The only other kid I had to play quarterback except those two was a sophomore who couldn't throw a rock through a pane of glass. I let Colrane play because I wanted that championship, see? I don't know if it's him or myself I don't forgive, but at least I can try to forget it, right?"

Out in the hall, sagging with relief against the wall, Murphy could hear the bull voice roaring over the phone to some hapless listener.

"What is this over two hundred thousand for this Nautilus bullshit? I'm supposed to cut into my sports budget so a lot of pansies can lift weights and rub suntan lotion on their muscles when they should be out on the track and playing ball?"

9

Vᴵᴄ ᴀɴᴅ Lɪᴢ Foster had not seen anywhere near as much of
their houseguest as they had hoped to, and now he was telling
them he'd just as soon meet some friends down at the Horse
if they were going to be having a neighborhood committee
meeting in their living room.

"Stay, Neil," Vic insisted. "You owe it to yourself. This is
still your town, isn't it? Listen, Liz was the one who dragged
me into this protest, but I have to admit I'm hooked."

His eyes truly did burn with the passion of a man with a
cause. He was sorting leaflets into piles on the coffee table,
but the sense of urgency in his voice was real.

"Listen, Neil, just let me say this much. You're our guest,
and I don't want to push. But if you care about Oldhampton,
you'll stay and hear what we have to say. So help me, this
town is in real trouble. Of course," he said with a throwawy
weariness, "if you're so into the jet set these days that your
own hometown doesn't mean all that much to you . . ."

Neil could still laugh at the deep suspicion many of his colleagues and old friends had that he was the intimate of countless jet set and media personalities. He had once, just once,
hitched a ride from New York to California with a talk show
host on whose show he had made a pleasant enough appearance, and the word had not only got around, it had multiplied
and magnified.

Liz was counting lapel buttons. They were supposed to get
a contribution of a dollar apiece for them, but there were at
least fifty unaccounted for. She knew she had given them to
the mailman and the girl who came to read the gas meter, but
had she really given away fifty? Bernice, who was treasurer
of the committee, would kill her. She turned to Neil. "Every
damned town in this state now has some version of this pol-

97

lution problem, but I honestly think ours will be one of the three or four worst when we get all the facts out. Milkwood is going to be another Love Canal, you wait and see. Or don't wait; help us now to stop that damned DVR crowd from poisoning us all."

Vic's speech was spilling over hers, begun before she had finished. "*If* our local politicians ever get off their duffs and act, we can still prevent a genuine tragedy here, Neil, I'm not exaggerating one iota. The state won't, and the goddam federal EPA is a dirty joke."

Liz cut him off. "Victor, leave the man alone. He's only in town for a week and he has other things on his mind. Just remember, Neil, one third of this town, the whole southern section, is lowland. The Conservation Commission has taken almost fifteen percent of it, to save the wetlands and what wildlife is left, but even though there are just a few farms left there, that is the aquifer recharge area for the whole town. And DVR Chemical is piling toxic debris right on that land. Are you going to tell me that the groundwater isn't getting poisoned?"

"Whoa." Neil held up both hands. "Really, I'm convinced. It sounds bad, and if you're right, it's going to get worse. I promise not to leave town without signing your petition for action by the Board of Health. If you'll tell me what those awful buttons stand for, I'll even wear one of those in the street. SPEW?" He grimaced.

"Stop Poisoning Everyone's Water. Plain enough? I'm glad you're disgusted. You're a fastidious man, so naturally you're revolted by the word SPEW on every lapel in town. Good. We want people not just intellectually, but viscerally involved. We chose it to be disgusting; so is toxic waste in our water supply."

"Please," Neil said, "don't cast me in the role of uncaring heavy. I really see your point, and if I were here full-time, I'd work for your committee. As it is, the best I can promise is to wear your button, give ten bucks to your committee . . ." which he did, handing it to Liz, who gave him no chance to change his mind ". . . and hope you succeed."

Liz was terribly fond of Neil, and she was really torn between her passionate devotion to the antipollution campaign and her sense of common decency about being a good hostess.

She kissed his cheek. "I'm going to let you go, but I warn you, you'll hear more from me about this mess before you leave. I swear, Neil, one year ago I didn't know DDT from rat poison, but I learned, and everyone in town is going to learn if I have anything to do with it. We've got 1, 1-di-chloroethane, we've got benzenes, and now we think we may have traces of aldicarb—my God, that's a nerve toxin, Neil—being pushed by the water table all over south Oldhampton . . ."

She realized that she had him by the lapel and restored his jacket to him, smoothing it down self-consciously. "Well, I said I'd let you go, but honestly, Neil . . ."

Vic came to cut him off at the door, waving the petition at him. "Are you still a registered voter in this town?"

Neil paused, taking out his pen. "I think so. Unless they cut me off the rolls for not voting the last two years. I know I'm still a legal resident."

"Close enough," Vic said. "Sign. Full name and address. It's a demand to the Selectmen that they instruct the Board of Health to close the Milkwood dump forthwith and get an application in for federal cleanup funds."

Neil signed the fourth page of the thick petition and left them to their organizing.

Vic called out the doorway after him. "Wear that SPEW button when you meet with George Purlie. He'll piss his pants. Ask *him* about the college's connection with DVR."

Walking down the path, Neil shook his head. He had almost forgotten what a thorny thicket, what a perpetual battleground any town in New England can be, especially an academic town. Town, gown, and their separate politics and passions, economics and morals constantly getting entangled.

In the early afternoon sunshine Oldhampton was very much the green garden he remembered. If there was pollution hidden in the ground a few miles from here, around the campus the scene was as charming and alive as any chamber of commerce could desire. The students had broken out their madras shorts and Frisbees, and everyone's pace was slower, everyone's voice less shrill for now.

He wondered at some deep place within himself if he really wanted to come back here with Dolly and settle back into his professorial existence. When his decade of routine had first been shattered two years before by the death of Pril Lacey, whom he had loved, he had rejected as impossible the idea of ever returning to OH. Then, in the green time of renewal and healing that two years had provided, part of it in the immense difference of the American Southwest, most in emerald Devon and lovely London, he had realized that his scholarship and his students still had a powerful pull for him.

Now again, on his home ground, he was not so sure. The astounding commercial success of his writing in the past two years had guaranteed that he could have the life he chose henceforth, and falling in love with a gifted professional woman, his editor, in England had provided only the happiest kind of complications.

Neil was in Oldhampton because Jill Purlie had begged him to come. She and he were the only ones who knew that. It had been no part of his spring plans, that first week in March when she had called and written, to leave Dolly and London for a week back at the college.

Her letter had come to his London publisher with an apology for not being a fan letter, if that's what letters to publishers usually were, and for being such a long, sad story.

Like Dick, Jill had been his student once. She had developed one of those mild crushes that some students seem inevitably to get while a favorite teacher takes the place of a temporarily disliked father. She had spent about the normal amount of over-time in his tutorial office, talking for fifteen minutes about her George Herbert paper, then forty minutes about Life, the dif-ficulties of Growing Up, and The Future. It was a future most college students project for themselves, automatically good and different from the dreary, poisoned parentally dominated past. She thought she would probably be an actress. Later a child psychologist, perhaps a designer.

She had been above average bright, and above average happy except for her bitterness toward her father. Her trust in Neil was total and her unhappiness about home was swamping her, so it all poured out—the monomania, perhaps the mild paranoia, of youth. Her father was trying to run her life, ruin her life, make her life miserable. Then she met Dick Colrane.

It was the heyday of his sports fame and campus glory. She grew radiant in love, confident and newly generous toward her poor father, whom she now saw as simply an unhappy widower, a middle-aged man with sore feet and a case of male menopause.

Her sad marriage to the wimp from Williams came later. Did Jill ever know, Neil wondered, that her father had once been denied a tenured appointment at Williams, and that he held a snarling hatred in his heart for that mellow, inoffensive if undistinguished place? On the basis of what little practical psychology he knew, Neil guessed that she probably had, although he didn't believe it was the basic motive for her choice of a husband after Dick left Oldhampton.

It was a poorly kept family secret that Jill had actually become allergic to her husband, a florist. After the marriage came apart in sneezes, sniffles, howls of outrage, and the usual battering arguments of divorce, Jill had visited Neil's office just once. Reduced to a woebegone state not unlike her freshman blues, she had sobbed out the whole tale of her wretchedness, her family's disgust with her (her father had remarried, to Selene Corey, a divorcée whom he had known in Washington, bringing her home triumphantly, like a florid trophy, no prior announcement, shocking the faculty wives used to managing such matters, the same week Jill had married the wimp), and her sincere wish that she were dead. He had listened, counseled, encouraged, urged her to get herself organized, said nothing either particularly profound or practical, and generally did what an experienced teacher does. She had never forgotten what to her was a momentous kindness that had saved her from suicidal impulses.

Her letter to him in England, read lying on the grass in Regent's Park one unseasonably warm March day, asked him, begged him, if it were humanly possible, to do something for Dick now like what he had done for her then. She wrote five pages about her happiness that they were together again, and her parallel misery that Dick seemed, with each passing day, to get more depressed and uninterested in his work.

The particulars had been convincing, and her voice on the phone when Neil called her later that week was on the edge of tears. She was genuinely afraid that Dick was having a mid-life crisis of faith in himself. He wasn't sure he wanted to accept the chairmanship, his last book had exhausted him without satisfying his original idea of what it would be, and he seemed, she struggled over the word, but got it out, *suicidal* sometimes.

That was the word that brought Neil back. He and Dick were never the closest of friends, but Dick was an admired younger colleague who had once been a student, and who had gone through his own personal hell at twenty-one with grace and style.

Too little mourning, too little grief. At the time Dick had been shot, a wise old Hungarian psychiatrist who had come to the campus as a refugee teacher in 1956 commented dryly of Dick's recovery that he was doing too little mourning, too little grief. He had shaken his head one day in the faculty club and sighed, and said to Neil that unless the boy grieved now for his lost, golden youth, he would find the need to grieve later, inevitably. Maybe, he had said, his eyes on another place and time, the need to kill, as well, a need that often becomes the need to be killed, to turn the undischarged rage against the self. He had shrugged sadly. "I have seen it happen may times. Dry eyes in childhood, terrible fires inside the self later, sometime unquenchable fires, tragic fires."

Neil suspected strongly that Dick was torn apart inside by the need to accept professional advancement from George Purlie while at the same time resenting the man's dictatorial bossiness. But was that enough of a schism in him to precipitate real tragedy?

George Purlie, if he was standing, looked at first glance as though he had dropped from a considerable height and landed flat on his feet. He was a broad-shouldered man with a barrel chest who should have been nearly six feet tall except that his legs were disproportionately short for the rest of his huge frame. And his feet were large, splayed, and flat. He remained seated whenever he could, and taught by lecturing from a platform across a desk.

He had as a schoolboy avoided all games and parties and concentrated his energies on developing his massive intelligence to give him a position of dominance among his peers. He had been a junior chess champion, a science fiction addict and expert long before video games, and a champion debater.

He had a booming voice, which he had cultivated from its first uneven appearance, and his mind was always described as cold, analytical, and passionate only for the satisfaction of being right.

His perplexed parents, both from families of small storekeepers, assumed that George's eighth-grade-prize essay on Alexander the Great indicated that he would make a good soldier. They sacrificed and sent him off to a military academy at fifteen. It was a place largely populated by the lazy sons of Southern capitalists and ambitious sons of German Midwestern farmers. He had endured the relentless hatred of his easygoing fellow cadets and the jealousy of the ambitious ones (both groups call him "Duck," an appellation he loathed), and had hung on to his sanity by a hair's breadth. He won every single award not for sports, graduated second in his class behind a languid athlete who could scarcely read (but who was the Cadet Corps colonel) and was then turned down for military service for assorted physical shortcomings, including a suspected heart murmur. But the army examination didn't, couldn't, reveal his greatest, most disabling handicap. George Purlie had absolutely no gift for making friends. He was to live out his whole life without grasping what that elusive thing was that other men found so easy and he simply could not begin to figure out. President Richard Nixon was his political ideal.

George had come to Old Hampton from Columbia in the fifties, after being politely told by Williams College that it could not use his talents. He was by then a man with a growing reputation as a social scientist and with political connections to McCarthyism. He had long since outlived that stigma to achieve a modest fame at OH as the only member of the faculty likely to be called down to Washington by the Reagan administration to consult for this or that federal agency. In the Nixon years he had actually turned down a post in Education, but had drafted a famous hundred-page white paper redesigning the goals of federal education support programs and social science funding. His own pet projects were, predictably, lushly funded in that period, and his articles and books welcome to conservative publishers.

Now the college trustees, Republicans to a man, bedeviled by rising costs, saw in George Purlie the president who might

103

take them finally far away from the spongy liberalism that had crept into the college in the seventies and back onto the high ground of conservative economic principles. After all, had he not, on a locally famous occasion, taken on a visiting speaker who had dared to attack the college's investment policies in South Africa, calling them "Neanderthal" and "brutally insensitive," and chewed the fellow to bits?

A friend who would, as each friend inevitably did, ask Jill Purlie if her father wasn't rather a difficult man to live with would always get the practiced, exasperated reply, "Daddy's just an old teddy bear."

George Purlie tamped tobacco into his pipe and sucked on it experimentally, added another pinch, packed that in, sucked again, and produced a lighter. He had all the inveterate pipe smoker's gestures and several of his own.

He glanced up at Neil as he puffed clouds of blue smoke into the air.

"That's a big decision, Neil. Too big to make impulsively?"

"That's why I'm putting it in terms of stages. I take an extra year now. My writing will support that, no problem. Then, if I still find myself reluctant to take up my teaching again, I'll retire."

The older man clamped the pipe in his strong teeth and leaned back in his chair, contemplated the ceiling. "I was counting on your being here in my first years as president, Neil."

"Me? Not in any adminstrative capacity, I hope. That would show worse judgment than I think you capable of, George."

"Why not? Oh, not the English department. God, I doubt if we'll be rid of your chairman there for another ten years. Didn't you ever think about being academic dean?"

"Once, for ten minutes. It made me deeply depressed," Neil grimaced.

George Purlie poked the air between them with his pipestem. "Look at it from my point of view. In a month Chip Allen goes off to the Ford Foundation and a crown of glory. Yours truly becomes the acting president of the college. That gives the trustees a year to go through all the folderol of setting up a national search committee, blah, blah, and screening every

104

dummy who can read an equal opportunity employment ad in the Education section of the Sunday *Times*. I know, and I trust you to know, that after the candidates have been duly invited and passed around from student ad hoc committee to faculty review board, and Jag Robinson and his ilk have jumped up and down for a week or two crying foul because only two black candidates are invited, and neither put on the shortlist, the trustees are going to discover that they have the best man already right here. Me." He poked himself in the stomach with the stem of his pipe.

Neil had been through dozens of faculty reviews and trustee committees, and he was perfectly aware that the general ethical level of academic politics was just about even with the Cook County Democratic machine. Purlie's summary was probably exactly right.

"And?" He fluttered his eyebrows, signaling George Purlie that if this joke had a punch line, he was waiting.

"And I'm going to turn Old Hampton College right around and take it to places where it has never been." He leaned forward and put his smoking paraphernalia aside to lean across the desk, his rumbling voice and his big shadowed eyes under the shaggy brows commanding attention.

"I want excellence for this place, Neil, not mediocrity. And that's what we've become, and you know it. Excellence." He stabbed the air with his finger. "Is that such a bad goal? They'll scream 'elitism' and they'll howl about antidemocratic ideals, but, by God, that Silber fellow at B.U. has it right about these kamikaze liberals—they've been on top too long, and they've diluted the whole purpose of higher education, which is to excel. To excel, Neil. Goddammit, how can I make this self-satisfied little place a beacon for every other American college if I don't have the best people around me?"

Neil clasped his hands comfortably across his middle and slumped in his chair in a fair imitation of undergraduate rudeness, his chin on his chest, looking at George Purlie up under his eyebrows.

"I think you just gave my decision to retire a big nudge, George. I haven't heard rhetoric that impassioned since Chip Allen announced he was going to raise eight million dollars to take this college into the computer age or die trying."

"Mock on, mock on, Voltaire," Purlie grunted, reclaiming his pipe and relaxing to attend to it. "I know this is only a preliminary skirmish between us on this matter, Kelly, and I'll be back at you again. I'm an inveterate optimist, I never quit when an idea seems right to me, and I'm hell's own worst loser if I don't get my own way."

"We all know that, George," Neil breathed softly, grinning. He was rather enjoying the feeling that he was looking over his own shoulder at himself gingerly trying out the freedom of not really caring any longer whether Old Hampton College, for which he'd given a lot of hard years' good work, flourished or floundered. Was he being disloyal? Don't you believe it, the shadowy self over his shoulder whispered, what you had, you gave, what you no longer have, you cannot give.

George Purlie changed the subject abruptly. "What's this party you're giving for Dick?"

"Nothing special. Alumni weekend, I thought an engagement party, with a few old friends in town, might be in order. A sort of early bachelor party."

"Good for you. Hell of a thing, those two finally getting together. Did you know that wimp Jilly married the first time, the florist from Williams?"

"I only knew she married and that it didn't work out." Neil also knew, from Jill, the violent breakup and a few screaming fights in public places, after which Jill had spent a few weeks resting at a ranch in New Mexico, close to or in a nervous breakdown, but all that scarcely seemed appropriate to add.

"The man was a fop. Soft as a grape." Purlie waved his smoking pipe disgustedly at the image before him in the air. "From Williams. No wonder, eh? Father owned some gigantic floral export business in Washington State. Well, I won't say his son was a pansy, exactly, but he had about as much backbone as a—a goddam tulip." He squeezed the air in his big, hairy hand as though he were crushing something fragile. "Every time I met him I wanted to swat him." He hooted. "Jilly developed an allergy to flowers. Really. Then to him. Every time he came into the room she couldn't breathe. Damndest case of hives you every saw. I suppose as her father I shouldn't laugh, but it struck me damn funny, I can tell you." He gargled and coughed, curtailing his amusement. "Well, they got a divorce and now she's doing what I told her twenty years ago she should have done, marry Dick Colrane."

"All's well, et cetera," Neil said.

"I hope, I hope, I hope, as Joe Penner used to say. She's goddam lucky Dick still wants her. Aw, come on, Neil, you're a man of the world, the bloom is somewhat off the rose at her age, and Dick Colrane, tenured professor at forty-two, about to take over this chair when I get my ass out of it and over to the president's office, brilliant scholar with a rising national reputation, is a pretty damn fine catch."

"I take it you approve of the party idea and you'll make an appearance, George."

"Hell yes. I don't party much, but Selene tells me that if I'm going to be president, it's back into black tie three nights a week, just like the old days when I was a rising young snot-nose trying to impress my betters and showing up for every damned sherry and cheese affair in town."

Neil rose and made for the door. "I've taken enough of your time. I hope you're not really planning on anything black-tie. It's just a few middle-aged folks having a drink together and getting maudlin about the good old days."

"Maybe I'll come and make a campaign speech, liven things up." Purlie said.

"Remember what we've talked about Neil. I'm going to need someone with savvy, someone with your kind of reputation for first-class thinking, to work with me restructuring and re-prioritizing this college of ours."

Neil paused before a signed portrait of President Eisenhower. "To George, with respect." Not bad. "I suspect, from the sly hints you've dropped, George, that you're going to need someone like yourself, a social scientist with brass balls and a basic love for managing people. Does that sound like gentle, affable, whimsical old Neil Kelly to you?"

"One, you're a humanist, and you're no more affable or cute than I am when it's a question of standards. Don't forget, we were on the curriculum reform committee together for three years, and I've watched you work over some of those dodoes who didn't do their homework. I intend to shape up the whole humanities division, Neil, and I'd rather do it with the daily advice of someone who might temper my sometimes rash judgments."

He rumbled a good-natured, self-deprecating chuckle that didn't fool Neil for one second. It was one of his familiar poses. Old reflective George.

"Deadwood, Neil, a load of it over there. Can the college afford a Van Rann with what?—fourteen students total in his three seminars? Classics program's a disgrace, might as well not exist as piss along embarrasssing the college. One senior thesis in classics in four years . . ."

He was in full spate now, and Neil realized that he had been doing his homework, that those casually tossed out numbers represented real counters he was planning to use when the war started in earnest. Was George Purlie really imagining that Neil would play the role of his hit man in pruning away budget from the humaities to sink into more computers?

"Dieter Wernecke has always argued that we can't have a decent classics program without decent library resources, George. When was the last time the college purchased any significant additions to our Greek or Latin collection?"

"Not the point, Neil, not the point at all."

Despite the chairman's doubly negative assertion, accompanied by another dismissive gesture through the hanging pall of smoke, Neil thought it was very much the point.

"Anglo-Saxon, for Christ's sake. Icelandic fairy tales and Sanskrit scriptures . . . We've got people sitting around this place who haven't been out in the sun for years, except to cash their checks. Are you going to defend Harold Sonnenberg, Neil?"

No one could defend Harold Sonnenberg, and Neil wasn't about to try. Harold was one of those pathetic academic anomalies who had been given tenure thirty years before, on the strength of the publicity for his book on sixteenth-century religious wars, after the king of Sweden had written him a fan letter. Harold had then promptly declined into chronic folly and personal eccentricity even beyond Old Hampton's elastic norms. His chief contributions to scholarship over the past ten years had been an endless succession of letters to the local press on every subject from the sexual suicide implicit in braless girls to the wisdom of public flogging as a deterrent to bicycle theft.

"The thing to do with Harold, I've always thought, George, was to make him academic dean. The real trivia would keep him too busy for anything else. George, there is really no use in your persisting. I'm not the man you want. The more we talk about it, the more I'm persuaded that I really ought to retire completely, right not. Somehow I've lost my gusto for all this."

"I give you fair warning, Neil. I never plan to lose." He smiled his feral smile again.

Neil eyed the door, but he thought he'd get some useful information for Liz Foster before he left. If anyone knew what was going on between the college and DVR Chemical, it would be George.

"One thing I meant to ask you, George. What's going on between the college and DVR? Some of our colleagues haven't been this stirred up since we offered an honorary degree to a Vietnamese dictator back in 1966."

George frowned ferociously and carefully knocked his pipe out into the huge glass ashtray beside him.

"Lot of children. Listen, take it from me, Neil, this will blow over like any other fashionable cause."

"As an outsider just walking into the argument, George, I think there's more to it than that. People seem pretty angry."

"Who, SPEW? I see that damned green button. If they would consider for five minutes that DVR, not this college, Neil, but DVR, is the biggest employer in this town, and the biggest taxpayer in the county, and if they'd grasp the elementary fact that this college *needs* to promote better community relations as part of our overall effort . . ."

George was slipping into presidential gear and was lecturing him, Neil realized with a weary resignation. Why had he even brought it up. He might have known he'd get a canned speech from the old fox.

". . . not an island, you know, Neil, but a piece of this larger community."

Dear God, John Donne, where are you when we need you?

". . . and you can tell this to Foster and that crowd, I know you two are thick, and if I'm not mistaken, you're staying with them."

He had indeed been following Neil's visit closely. And now he was priming the visitor to deliver his epistle to the disaffected. Well, Neil thought glumly, he had asked for it.

"The college traded—get that?—*traded* a piece of land virtually worthless to us back in 1955 to DVR. They needed some additional storage space, and we sure as God didn't need three hundred twenty acres in the south end of town three miles from the college. That damned old fool, Clarence Milliken, class of aught-nine had it in his family since God was a pup, so when he died without an heir he left it to us to build on. To build on, that was in the will. Christ, but we have some geniuses among our distinguished alumni. The college lawyers broke the will finally, not without some wire-pulling in Washington, and got us out from under that building provision. So we swapped the whole damned parcel, Milliken Wood in the deed but what everybody around here has always called Milkwood, half of it swamp, for a block of DVR common stock worth at the time sixty-eight thousand dollars. They wrote off half as a tax-deductible donation, we got it all, everyone was happy. I was the faculty trustee that year for my sins, and I sat on that committee next to Howard Klister, who was our chairman then, and watched him operate. Smooth as silk."

He swiveled in his chair to point his pipestem at one of the dense pack of side pictures on his side wall.

"Brilliant old bastard. Ran a four-man fast-food operation in Phoenix into an international franchising system worth two billion. The only billionaire who every called me by my first name. Taught me a lot, working with Howard."

He glanced back at Neil to make sure that old Howard had made an appropriate impression and aimed his pipestem across the desk to reinforce it. Seminar salesmanship, Neil thought. Probably intimidated the hell out of sassy seniors. He wondered if George had become entirely unconscious of his stagily absurd gestures.

"Howard Klister taught me something fundamental. Are you ready? The Marxists are right. Yes. Capitalism *is* a state of war, has to be. And a corporation—I'm saying any corpora-

110

tion, Neil, e.g., this college we both serve—a corporation is both a mystical body and a kind of regiment. A unit requiring discipline and generalship. 'Think of the Jesuits as the first corporation in the modern world,' Howard said to me, 'and you'll see what I mean.' You'll understand that, Neil, being Catholic yourself.''

Neil thought for a moment his friend was either going to bless himself or salute.

"Tactics? Howard was a master tactician. Strategy? I'm proud to say that Howard, when we swung this DVR deal together, said to me that my strategy for the college was ideal. Ideal." He bit his pipestem in a hard-jawed moment of self approval. "Fixed strategy plus flexible tactics equals success. Howard Klister."

"George, I saw *Patton*. Good movie, but I didn't get the sense he'd make a congenial colleague."

Purlie laughed with his head thrown back. "Don't let the candy asses get you down, Kelly. You know what I'm saying. You're a pretty good tactician yourself when it comes to academic infighting."

"Well, as one tactician to another, General, all I can say is, I'd dump that DVR stock if I were in a position to do so and oppose everything DVR is trying to do."

"That chunk of DVR common is now worth—are you ready?—mind you, it has split twice—$780,000 and climbing. You want classics books for the library? More scholarship students? Tell your liberal kamikaze friends that it all costs money and that's what the college investment program is all about. M-O-N-E-Y."

Neil was not quite sure how he had got into this as defender of a positon he didn't really hold, but even a neutral is entitled to clarify the issues.

"I don't think the objections are to the college making money, George. Just to DVR storing toxins on land where the groundwater is part of the water supply people have to drink."

"Tempest in a teapot, Neil, I promise you. A few dead trees? A what—ten percent drop in the squirrel and skunk population of south Oldhampton? People were chipping their teeth about this years and years ago, but right now it's a frenzy of self-righteous idiots, blowing a few spilled storage drums up into

111

a national crisis. If the Environmental Protection Agency hadn't been on TV every night for a month with that damn fool woman making an ass of herself in front of congressional committees, this town wouldn't even know how to spell pollution. Hey, it's called the industrial revolution, Neil, and some of our back-to-nature Henry Thoreaus who have taken up ecology as their new faith are all in heat about something that's been going on for two hundred years. It's piffle, Neil, I promise you. Listen, forget it. Before you go, though, tell me how your family is? Those daughters of yours still giving you gray hairs?"

Neil especially didn't want to get a "disappointed dads" support group routine. His daughters had each made a life different from anything he would have imagined, but he was convinced that was none of George's or anyone else's business. He dissembled with some general truths.

"They grow up, George," he concluded.

"I wish my one would. Gillian. Goddammit, Neil, she was a gifted, accomplished young lady. Should have had a career. Would have if she had married the right man, not that florist wimp from Williams."

Apparently George's question about Neil's daughters was just put to provide him with a segue to talk again about Jill. Neil watched him brush crumbs of tobacco worriedly from his stomach, as if surprised to see them there.

"I suppose I can be blamed, at least in part," the burly man said reflectively. "I should have made her drop that twerp the day he showed up, get back together with Dick right then. Jesus, you try to be a good-guy father and what does it get you? I blame myself, though."

He sighed and continued the pipe smoker's housekeeping on his desk and person. He examined the lining of his lower lip for another shred of tobacco, removed it, stared at it balefully, and snapped it into the wastebasket. "Forty-years-old, Neil, and she runs around wasting her time with this League of Women Voters crap. You'd think Selene would be a role model for her; at her age Selene was directing a bottling company in Delaware, big one, too. My God, what happens to them?"

"Free will, George. The same thing that happened to you and me and made our parents wonder if the world was going to hell in a hand basket when they considered our idiotic ways."

Purlie swept a handful of tobacco crumbs from his desk blotter and contemplated them for a moment before funneling them carefully back into his box. "Stuff's expensive. My own mix."

Unhappy people are all lonely; they can never simply say good-bye. Neil knew that George was unconsciously but deliberately keeping him there. He went to the door with a reminder about the party. Was the man really so afraid of being alone with himself?

"Neil . . ." The big man slumped, and he passed a hand over his face. It was at once a gesture of infinite weariness and shame.

"I have thought about killing myself. Would you have thought that about me, Neil?"

Neil was as startled by the truculent self-disgust in his tone as by the question itself, so unlikely coming from George. "It's been said that every intellectual contemplates suicide seriously at least once in his lifetime, George."

"Yeah, yeah, I know—the only philosophical question worth asking and all that nonsense that Frenchman wrote. But doesn't it strike you as totally out of character for me? Even to admit it, for that matter, eh?"

The pathos of the question, and the tiny break in the big man's rumbling voice on the last word, moved Neil to pity his colleague as nothing else might have. Why are academics as a class so blind to their own frailties? If there was any trait, Neil realized glumly, which separated them from actors, butchers, cab drivers—even poets—it was that characterisitic incapacity to hang on to any reality principle but good marks in school.

"Well, it surely was out of character, George, and it's well you resisted the temptation. I'd say Old Hampton is looking forward to having you as its new president, so where would the college be if you succumbed to fatigue now?"

The gratitude reflected in Purlie's improved posture and sly grin made him almost charming. Neil was reminded of the famous photograph of Robert Frost hamming it up during a standing ovation—his aw shucks, off-center smile, the big farmer's hand raised shyly, and the cagey eyes under the white bushy browns peering out, timing the act, almost daring anyone to withhold approval.

113

10

"WELL," JILL AMENDED her description with a rueful laugh, "a teddy bear with just a wee touch of megalomania."

Neil studied Jill Purlie as she chatted, sitting across from him. She was, at forty-two, plump and slightly buck-toothed, with big, perfect white teeth. Her blonde hair was ashen gray now, and her fair skin was starting to crepe at her throat. But she had energy and humor in her face, and she moved with the unselfconscious grace of a big woman at home in her body.

Neil had known her mother, George's first wife, only casually before her death from lung cancer when Jill was a teenager. Jill was now very much the image of her mother, but Neil could remember this confident woman as a plump, shy undergraduate, and George always grousing that he always wished she were a boy.

Her fiancé threw up his hands in mute disbelief at Jill's description of her father. Neil intervened to prevent George Purlie from becoming the real subject of their chat.

"Nothing unusual about that in our business, Dick, as you well know. There are enough power complexes and dictators manqué on any college campus to keep a Central American junta supplied with replacements indefinitely. Think of your old and beloved freshman advisor, R. C. F. Lockridge."

They were sitting in Neil's favorite booth in the Horse. It was nice having a local in which to hold court, considering that his own home was occupied, his office ditto, and the house where he had guest privileges was a hotbed of planning committees and proselytizing protesters.

Dick Colrane smiled and shook his head, remembering. "That crazy old bastard. How little undergraduates know. I don't know if I ever told you, Jilly, but when Arsie was my advisor, he'd get me in that Gothic office of his up on the top floor of Caverley, and he'd scream at me for everything I put on my elective card. Then he'd pull out his own prepared version of what I should really be studying and hammer away at me until I took it, shaking like a leaf. We were all supposed to major in classics, according to Arsie. Hebrew, Greek, and Latin were the only subjects he considered acceptable. The first time it happened I really thought, God, he's my advisor, I really have to study Hebrew. Then I found out what all his advisees did—I tore up his card and forged his signature on my own. I actually didn't know until I was on the faculty here that the dean's office was perfectly aware that all those cards were forged and that Arsie was nuts.''

It is easy to laugh at crazy old tyrants when they are dead. They all lifted a glass to R. C. F. Lockridge.

Dick suddenly choked and spit out some of his drink, laughing. "And Skink, remember Skink?"

His companions were caught up in his helpless giggles, remembering the mad Skink, an animal psychologist who had been thrown out of the college after a furor among the alumni who objected to his experiments teaching wild animals to commit suicide.

"Didn't he train pigeons to commit hara-kiri by diving into colored circles in the faculty club parking lot?"

"Better, he trained skunks to swim underwater. Skink's skunks, who will ever forget?"

"What about his famous movie screens with trapdoors in them, so he could teach animals to run in front of moving vehicles to get food? Squirrels, was it?"

They simmered their hilarity down, shaking their heads and biting their lips to get their dignity back.

Jill said through clenched teeth, "I often wondered what happened to all those poor things the psych department released in the woods after Skink made them psychotic?"

"All I know is," her fiancé said solemnly, "when he drove out of town they said there was a whole squadron of birds dive-bombing his car." He howled uncontrollably and started the whole booth shaking again.

"They're fine examples of what goes on behind the façade on any campus, in any small town," Neil said, still laughing.

"'Every campus is a town gone mad'—now where on earth did that pop into my head from? I know I saw it somewhere recently." He tried to recall. "A world gone mad?"

"One of your troubles has always been, Neil, that you forget nothing and sooner or later you start seeing connections between everything and everything else," Dick said.

"The curse of metaphor," Neil rolled his eyes up and recited the phrase melodramatically. "The word for religion comes from the same place in Latin, the fundamental hunch that everything *is* connected to everything else by design."

Jill was collecting her belongings from the seat. "All I know is, I'm entering A Town Gone Mad in the bumper sticker slogan contest. It fits these days. I see you've got your SPEW button, Neil. Did Liz also get your signature on our petition to the Selectmen about the DVR dump in Milkwood?"

"No fear. She also gave me a crash course in toxicology."

Jill was showing Dick her watch. "Look, I'm supposed to pick up Josie Westerman in Northampton for our meeting. Her car is kaput and I'm her ride."

She leaned over to kiss her fiancé and touch his face with her fingertips. "Dickie, be a sweetie and stay and talk with Neil, but I really have to run run run. I promised Liz. Neil, marvelous to see you." She kissed his cheek warmly. "You know how much it means. I'm really thrilled that you're throwing the party for us, and I'm really sorry it has to wait until next Monday. I love it—oh, has Dick asked you yet?" She glanced mischievously at Dick. "Have you? No? Oh, oh, I shouldn't have said that, I can tell. Well do, silly." She was talking a mile a minute, finding her bag, locating her glasses and getting out of the booth at the same time, then flying out the side door to the parking lot.

"Ask me what?" Neil glowered suspiciously at his companion, who was actually blushing.

"Now I know what 'sheepish' means. Do I look sheepish? I feel it. Thanks a whole lot, Jilly." He looked back at Neil. "We both want you to be the best man at our wedding. It's really the only present I want at all. Can you?"

Neil groaned inwardly. It would mean another transatlantic flight in September. He had just been deciding that one every two years was plenty.

116

Dick added hastily, "Look, Neil, if it's going to be a hassle, I understand, you know . . . I don't know what your plans are, but you do seem to keep pretty busy being a famous writer these days and so on. Hey, if you have to be in Hollywood or in Stockholm to get the Nobel Prize or anything, we'll understand."

His friend's mockery made it easy to fall back into genial rudeness, the preferred style of discourse for most colleague exchanges on any serious subject.

"Knock it off, Colrane. The local humor on the subject of my modest fame is wearing thin. No, really, I'd be honored, Dick. I do have to return to England, but I can easily get back. Mid-September? If you can put up with a best man who just flies in for the wedding, then disappears again the next day . . . I mean, I can't be here to iron your gloves or hold your head or any of those traditional chores."

"Thank God I'm too old to need to get drunk the night before. Or to wear gray gloves and frilled shirt, for that matter. We'll leave that to the twenty-year-olds. This deserves another drink, something special."

He strode over to the bar and came back with a dripping cold half bottle of champagne, untwisting the wire cap expertly, two tulip glasses tucked under his arm.

Neil extracted the fragile glasses gingerly and Dick popped the cork with a satisfyingly rich sigh.

"You're a good friend. To grown-up grooms and fly-by-night attendants!"

It was a velvety dry California wine, worth savoring quietly for a long moment without talk. They both drank, regarded the rise of golden bubbles from the mysterious petillant depths, and drank again. The most articulate men are reduced to silent exchanges of looks in some solemn moments.

Neil thought it would probably be best to get George Purlie back into the conversation again so that they could get him out again. When he had cut off Dick's bitter comments about his future father-in-law a few minutes before, he sensed that there was more to come, and if he was to have a central role in this marriage, he'd better know everything.

"I've just come from talking with George, actually."

"Let me guess, although it won't be a complete guess, since he has gone out of his way to drop hints to me in the apparent hope that I'll egg you on. He wants you to ride shotgun on his new administration, right?"

"I'm not sure I'd describe it that way, but on the other hand, maybe that's the perfect metaphor. He certainly would like to have me available to use as a cat's paw with the humanities faculty, which I gather he has in his sights."

"George is a lot of things, but subtle isn't one of them. Jilly calls it his Ozymandias complex. He'd like to stamp his initials on everything in the college. I predict that if they do make him president of OH, they'll end up with a forty-foot statue of him in a toga out on the east lawn."

Neil smiled wryly and sipped the cold champagne. "I suppose it goes with presidential ambitions on any level."

Dick said bitterly, "Yeah, but since George is just no good at straightforward friendship, he does tend to fall back constantly on manipulating people."

Neil was mildly startled to hear Dick say what he himself had been thinking earlier. It was clear that Dick's insight into George Purlie, like his own, originated in personal experience. He made a guess.

"Jill?"

Dick nodded and sipped his wine reflectively. "Jill. Me. His first wife, Jilly's mother . . ." he shrugged and repeated, "Me. Oh, I'm perfectly aware that he handpicked me to be his successor as department chairman when he moves out to the president's office. He began the maneuvering for that two years ago, lining up all the pins. I'd be too embarrassed to take it as a wedding present from my father-in-law, but, dammit, I've really earned it." He looked up from his contemplation of the wine. "Haven't I?" His voice was almost plaintive.

It was easy for Neil to reassure him on that count. "As you know, my friend, any campus is a battleground of petty personalities, and there is always plenty of sniping and backbiting. But I can honestly report that I haven't heard of anyone who doesn't think you deserve that chair, aside from the odd malcontent here or there. Robinson, that sort of professional spoiler."

118

Dick Colrane waved that ilk away as beneath comment. "Sometimes it gets to me. I don't have to stay here, you know, and I'm really torn about staying or taking an offer somewhere else. That's why I have to go down to New Haven this weekend, between you and me and the lamppost. I really promised those guys at Yale that I'd talk with them. They like the new book a lot."

Neil apologized for not having mentioned the book first. "I saw it displayed in the center of the window at the OH Bookstore, with the *New York Times* review cut out and mounted next to it. That can't hurt your reputation."

Dick bucked up and glowed modestly. A man can be brought back from the deepest melancholy by praise of his book.

"It's not your basic trendy solution to the modern malaise, which is what a lot of my colleagues in sociology seem to be writing these days, but it's getting its share of attention."

"Unless I'm mistaken, your studies for the last ten or fifteen years anticipated the whole trend back to the land around here—young professionals giving up urban technology for windmills, homesteading, the new consciousness of the land, all that."

"It was a long time coming, but I think it's not too late for the whole society to get itself converted and back in touch with its natural roots."

"'A born-again society'? Isn't that what the *Times* reviewer said you're preaching?"

"Good. I don't mind a bit." He put down his glass and reached into his inner jacket pocket, and took out a small leather-bound New Testament. "I won't say I'm a model convert myself, but you might know that years ago, when I was lying in the hospital with my knee in pieces and thinking about shooting myself in the head because I thought my life was over, I actually did get talked by my nurse into becoming a Christian. She was a plain, no-nonsense Baptist lady, and she talked about the Lord in exactly the same tone she talked about doctors and bedpans. While I was at Harvard—I admit, it isn't what happens to most people at Harvard—I joined a group of athletes and scholars for Christ who used to meet at Phillips Brooks House. And," he gestured with the peculiar helplessness of those talking about events in their own lives that still astonish them, "I accepted Christ and it changed my life, exactly the way that Baptist lady said it would. I stopped being bitter, and I wanted to live, not die, and I forgave whoever did this to me, and I set my mind on my future goals and I've never looked back. Well," he added darkly, "except for an occasional spot of awful backsliding, just every once in a blue moon, when I get filled with the old rage. It really is as though the devil had me by the throat then, and I have to get down on my knees and just pray." He repressed a shudder at the reality of the memory, Neil noticed, and abruptly changed the subject.

"You like that jazzy title, *The Social Ecology of Nineteenth-Century New England*? The publishers were holding out for *Wood Stoves and Windmills, Dowsers and Dunkers: New England Just Yesterday*."

"I know what a dowser is, but until I read the book, unless you explain the term to me, I don't know what a dunker is."

"It sounds like someone who finds lost doughnuts in your coffee with a piece of wet string, doesn't it? They were actually called Little Dunkers around here. A not terribly interesting sect of old German Protestants. They were all over Fairfield and South Oldhampton once. They believed in second baptism for men only. At the age of thirty each man had to be literally dunked. They'd actually tie a rope around the poor guy and lower him into a well for a few minutes to signify Jesus' descent into hell, pray over him, then haul him out. It seemed to become a kind of men-only stag night in the woods and the women protested. Anyway, it didn't catch on. One diary, it might just be a piece of old gossip, says they stuck a big farmer named Klaus Kittel down there once and the rope broke and poor old Klaus drowned. Anyway, most of them were run out to New York State by local pressure back around the Civil War."

Neil had, just the previous afternoon, seen a pamphlet in Murphy's jumbled files written by an old priest over in Fairfield that had rambled on about wells. Dick's anecdote reminded him of something.

"A Father Sullivan over in Fairfield wrote a pamphlet about miraculous wells . . . and something called 'The Devil's Well.' In your research did you ever come across anything by that name around here?"

"That old chestnut? Is someone still mentioning that? Hell, I guess it's one of the unsinkable superstitions of the valley. There are a lot of old wives' tales with wells in them. Miracles, witchcraft in the midnight woods . . . You'll find an entry in the index of my book about Devil's Well. There's not much but rumors to go on. I suspect some local lassie back in the last century dumped an unwanted infant in an abandoned well up in Milkwood and was found out. The rest is embroidery."

"We all do need those stories, don't we? I mean, the old wives' tales, the local myths attached to secret or sacred places . . . And don't think I find your personal religious experience bizarre. I like to think I'm a reasonably persistent Christian, I stay close to the sacraments of my Church. And it's perfectly obvious that you came out of that conversion experience a transformed man."

"Yes," Dick said gratefully. "Limping on one side, like Jacob himself after he had wrestled with the angel and found that his true name was Israel. You could say I found my true name was not athlete, but scholar."

They both lifted their glasses and toasted the truth silently.

"That is just one large class of reasons," Dick said sadly, "why George Purlie's vision of a completely rationalized society run by computers is such a bitter joke. It really is the devil's vision of humanity, and it runs counter to our deepest needs for mystery, for poetry, and for the experience of the sacred." He paused as if considering a larger point. "Besides, he rotates his shirts."

"What kind of thing is that to say about a man," Neil said laughing. "A terrible thing, surely."

"Literally true. Monday, blue striped; Tuesday, brown button-down; Wednesday, green striped . . . do you want to know the whole cycle?"

Neil thought back to what George had been wearing when they spoke. "Thursday, tattersall check?"

"Thursday, tattersall check, by God. I noticed it first when I was his student. My gift is my curse, I see patterns everywhere—the sociologist's curse, I suppose. But in his case it's pathological, I'm sure."

"A lot of people have regular habits, Dick. Aren't you being unduly hard on poor old George?"

"Regular is one thing. You're regular, that is, reasonably predictable. So am I. But George is regulated. That's inhuman. God knows how he produced Jill."

"She, I take it, does not rotate her dresses."

"Watch it, Kelly." He laughed at Neil's instant embarrassment at the unintended pun.

They rambled and chatted about a dozen things. Neil answered the inevitable questions about his life in England and his temptations to stay there and about his lovely editor, with whom he was in love. Dick made a passing reference to the events surrounding Pril Lacey's murder just over two years before, and then apologized with lively self-disgust for letting it come up.

Neil brushed aside his friend's confusion. "We've both had our troubles and we've both survived by the grace of God. Can I ask a favor of you that will dredge up some of your past sufferings for you, even if only briefly?"

Dick Colrane regarded him warily, but he was still angry at himself and felt he owed Neil more than a word of apology. "Ask."

"Will you talk to Margaret Morgan-Evans about that day— all of it—for just an hour or so? It would mean a lot to her."

Colrane's eyes glazed over with annoyance, and he read the wine label before replying. "Does she really want to talk to me? About her father?"

"Right."

"Doesn't she already know I have no idea if her father was responsible or not? That I didn't see anyone that day? If her old man picked that day to run off from his family, I don't see why . . ." He realized he was raising his voice and muted it. "I don't see why she needs to embroider it with some fantasy."

"Will you talk to her?" Neil ignored the diversion his friend had offered and stuck to his main point.

Dick Colrane rubbed his knee. "I wouldn't do it for anyone else. She came to my office, you know. I sent her away. But okay, for you."

Neil smiled sunnily. "Whew. The party I'm giving you is at her house."

"Wha—I thought you said at your house?"

"Same thing. She and her husband, who's teaching in my place, are living in my old house. So she'll be your hostess that evening."

Colrane gave him a dirty look. "Thanks for setting me up, pal."

"Do we still have a deal?"

"You clever bastard. Deal. Remind me not to play poker with you."

"As compensation I'll let you tell me if there's anyone you'd just as soon not have at the party."

"This isn't going to be one of those 'This Is Your Life' surprise deals, is it, where a lot of old chums from my checkered childhood pop out from behind the drapes off and on all evening?"

He was laughing at himself, but he was clearly tense, too.

"Not exactly, although it is Alumni Weekend, so I thought it a good chance to rope in some of your old college friends, at least. Your old roommate, for example, Mitch De Saulniers, who I now understand is famous under another name."

"Famous and probably too rich to bother coming back to OH. He's Michael De Soul now, didn't you know? I forgot for a minute, you haven't been watching American television the past year. Big TV star. He opened a chain of body-building shops in shopping malls all over California, and now he has a daytime TV show, the works. I predict that if he shows, he'll make a deal to broadcast from the local mall. Gay fitness. I gather the women, for some reason, are his greatest fans. He might show up at the house with autographed T-shirts to sell. They say *Body by De Soul*. Cute?"

"I was also going to invite the coach. Would you mind?"

"I gather you've learned that we stopped speaking in 1959. We actually haven't exchanged a single word since. It's okay with me if Coach is there, but I think he'll just tell you to get stuffed when you ask him. I'm a pariah to a lot of people at OH, you know, not the golden boy of legend." He thought a minute. "That Murphy girl has been going around interviewing people, hasn't she?"

"She wants to write a book, Dick. It's her father, after all. Who has the right to stop her?"

"I guess I was pretty short with her in my office. She scares me in a way . . ."

"She's a tough little lady, but *scares* you? Come on."

"I mean it. She has the gleam of the true fanatic who will not be deterred in her eye. I know the type. When she left I felt a frisson of doubt at my own capacity to look back now without again falling into that slough of despond I was once in, before God's grace opened my eyes. I just wish she'd leave all that ancient history buried."

"Your own book is all ancient history, my friend, but you wrote it."

"Touche." He pronounced it to rhyme with "ouch." "And I suppose I can't really cop a plea of my disinterested scholarship being one thing and her family passions being another. Damn."

11

MURPHY SAT AND tried for the hundredth time to remember the father she was seeking. It was not easy to recall a man who lived only on the edge of their lives when she was a girl. She and her sister Catherine and their mother had maintained an unspoken women's alliance against the shambling man who ate with them, stroked their heads sometimes with clumsy, hard hands, and spent a great deal of his time being elsewhere, as if ashamed. His daughter Margaret had, more than once, felt disloyal to the woman thing and yearned to go find him wherever he was in the town and just walk beside him. She loved his eyes, which were just like her dog Tippy's, but she could think of no way to explain that, to him or anybody.

She had, in the last year, written to their distant relatives in New Hampshire without getting back any word of his having been with them these past twenty-plus years. There were three or four sets of exiguously connected cousins who did not seem to care much, from their blunt postal card replies, whether that branch of themselves down in Massachusetts lived or died.

Murph had tried to make out a pattern of cunning deceit in their notes—always from a woman in the family—but they were transparently simple and plain, concealing nothing. No, they never did see Dan after he disappeared down there. Willie looks just like him through the eyes, Ma says. Sadie remembers that he liked to go to that shrine in Canada sometimes, maybe he went there. Josie says Dan owed Jerrold fourteen dollars, so he wasn't likely to show up in Glimanton. A pile of dead-end replies.

Her mother had died without revealing either her true feelings about her husband's disappearance or her shame at having a suspected moronic criminal in the family.

What Murphy needed to know now only Catherine might know. Catherine the quiet. Her sister lived just one town away, married to a real estate man and the mother of three children, but she and Margaret Mary rarely saw each other. Catherine does not change, except to get a little fatter each year. She wears her hair in a loose bun and she dresses like any Hadley housewife. Her house is neat, her kids are polite, if a little frail-looking, and her husband, a slight man with a soft mustache, coaches Little League and takes pride in his sales record. An unexceptionable life, if pure dullness doesn't count.

But Murph knew that when Catherine and Dickie Colrane were in high school together, they were close enough so that Catherine spent a frantic week clutching her sister's hand and worrying because her period was late. It was a false alarm, and they laughed hysterically about her panic afterward, never telling their mother, but that had been Margaret Mary's first inkling that Dickie Colrane and her big sister were actually having sex together and had, in the horrific term of the time, "gone all the way." For Oldhampton high school seniors in those days that was pretty unusual, but when it did happen, everybody including the couple just assumed that marriage would follow.

Murph knew that she had to ask Catherine now the kind of detailed, nosy question she had, out of sheer embarrassment and politeness, avoided asking before.

Like most of their talks in the past few years, this one amounted to only a ten-minute phone call.

Catherine had laughed at first when she heard her sister's question, but she quickly became angry and confused. She had often had the suspicion that Margaret Mary was making fun of her in some obscure way. Quirky people affect normal people in that way more than they know.

Catherine repeated what she had already said, exasperatedly. "Well, we just did. You know that. You know I was so scared I was pregnant it wasn't even funny."

"Kitcat, you know I'm not just nosy. I really have to know more than, you know, that. I *know* you and Dickie were making out, okay, but I really need to know if it was like one time or every Friday night or what."

There was a long silence down the line, then her sister's voice, suddenly indignant. "Are you writing a book about it for gosh sakes? What is this?"

Murph had hoped she wouldn't ask that. "Not the way you think."

"Are you?" Her sister's voice went up a frightened notch.

"Not about you. About Daddy. About his disappearance. Look, I wrote this article. About the mystery, how it was tied somehow to Dickie's accidental shooting that time, and this publisher up in Vermont wants to make it a chapter in a book about little unsolved New England mysteries . . ."

"Hey, hold on, Margaret. It's not as though Daddy got murdered or anything. He just ran off, for crying out loud. You call that a mystery? Why'd anyone in their right mind put that in a book? And what has it got to do with, you know, how many times Dickie and I like slept together? It's pretty ancient history. To tell the truth, I'm not even sure *I* remember. My God, if Lester was here and heard this, he'd have kittens."

He probably would, her sister thought unkindly. Little fluffy ones.

Murphy knew that when anybody dragged Telling the Truth into their conversation, something was up. "Well, trust me, will you? I am your sister, you know. I care about my own family."

The voice in Hadley was not coming down to a reassured level at all. "I'm not telling you anything until you give me one good reason why it matters to your book or whatever it is."

Murphy was sure that her sister was trying to defend something, but what? A personal myth of a high school romance with the school hero that had got all blown up out of proportion in her dreams? Here goes nothing, she thought.

"Somebody told me that Dickie was a homosexual in college."

She thought her sister would come out through the phone. "Are you kidding me?" she screeched. "Pardon my expression, sweetie, but that is the biggest bunch of bullshit I ever personally heard. I ought to know. If anyone tells you Dickie didn't like girls, they're nuts. N.U.T.S. Period."

Murph felt cruel pushing her new advantage, her sister's honest outrage. "So why not answer my one simple question, Cath? Did you guys do it just that once or not? Come on, kiddo, even I remember it was right after the prom, and you guys went over to Silver Pond with some other kids for a moonlight skinny-dip. Was that or wasn't that the only time you made it with him?"

"Yeah. I guess. If you mean going all the way." Her reluctance at saying it was palpable. "I swear, Margaret Mary, I'll kill you if you put that in any book and Lester ever sees it. I've got three kids, you know . . ."

"Calm down, will you? Jesus, Kitcat, you'd think you and Dickie Colrane screwing on prom night was the biggest news since I don't know what. It's just not exactly final evidence that he was an ardent heterosexual, is it?"

"I don't see how you get that from it, for crying out loud. Lester likes to say if a man steals just one car, you're entitled to call him a car thief. That's logical, isn't it? We dated a lot that year, you know, and even if we only, you know, once, I say Dick Colrane is as heterosexual as the next guy."

"Unless he and the next guy are caught making it in front of a witness, right?" Murph was sorry she'd said it, but she both wanted to give her smug sister a good shake and figured at the same time she deserved a little piece of gossip for her patience.

"Oh, my God, Margaret Mary, I just don't believe that. Never. I'd check the so-called witness if I were you. Dickie had a lot of people jealous of him, you know, who didn't have a nice word to say about him."

"I'm finding that out, Kitcat. Boy, am I ever."

She hung up not much less perplexed than she had been before. So much, though, for her big sister's fabled senior year romance with the star. One piece during a party on prom night and boom. Catherine loses her virginity, Dickie gets a reputation as a stud, a myth is born. It sure doesn't take much in a gossipy small town, one way or the other.

She wrote for two hours, barely looking up from the typewriter in time to see that something would have to be heated up for Dewi's dinner.

One thing about her nice unspoiled Welsh husband, he had never had any decent food in his life in Britain, and he didn't much care that their combined poverty and culinary ineptness made their general diet pretty awful.

He ate the heated-up leftovers she put in front of him and listened to her summary of the story up to date with equal appearance of pleasure. She even got a hint from the way he took an extra slug of red wine from the jug and settled back to listen without interrupting that he was getting really interested. She glowed with the storyteller's sense of power.

"What's your theme?" he asked her suddenly.

Her satisfaction at being taken seriously for a change was badly tempered by the realization that she had no answer.

"Who says I need a theme? I've got a plot, haven't I? Dammit, Neil said if I started with a metaphor, I'd be fine. Won't a theme just clutter things up?"

Dewi with a generous serving of wine in him was not to be denied the chance to dilate on his own theme. "There is only one fit theme for a murder story."

Jesus, who'd marry a teacher? "And what might that be, oh wise Welshman?"

"The imminence of spiritual danger." He belched with self-satisfaction.

Murph felt better. She was pretty sure she already had that.

"Christ, I've got danger enough, but who said it's a murder, come to think of it?"

"Your father was murdered. It's as plain as the freckles on your nose on your face."

"Are you the one who told me it's a good idea to have evidence before you jump to any conclusions?"

He waved away her objections airily. "I have been listening, and I have decided that whoever shot Colrane murdered your dad."

"So?" She might as well let him have his fun.

"So I think old Venuti was confessing. That *he* did it, not that one of his other ballplayers did. I'm sure of it."

"Now who's Lemuel Gullible?" she crowed. One of his favorite epithets for gullible her.

"You're not paying attention. Jasus, this is fun. I can see why people do this. Now listen. Venuti had his own motive. He said he'd gladly have strangled Colrane. Just for being bent. Letting down the side and so on. Then he admits later that what *really* bugged him about the incident in the locker room—"

"Rubdown room."

"Don't interrupt, I'm rolling now—in that room between the two boyfriends was that he compromised himself as a coach. Look at it from his point of view. He is just about to cap his first-ever winning season, champions of the valley, all that, after umpteen years. Then suddenly, he stands to lose it all if he does the natural, to him the right, thing, which is to can both of his quarterbacks. Now these people, if you have explained this silly game properly to me, are his scrum halves. Without them he has only some child who will lose the game for him, and the championship. So he swallows his principles, nearly chokes on them, but lets Colrane play and win his last game. Venuti is now compromised forever. The sin against the Holy Ghost from his point of view. His whole life is a mockery. Did that diminish his murderous rage at Colrane? Tell me another. It made it worse. And what did he say to you? 'I'm sorry about your father.' Didn't that strike you then, doesn't it strike you now as just the least bit unnecessary unless his conscience forced him to spit out an apology for something he felt *he'd* done? I think yes, he might have scared off your dad, but I like even better the idea that he caught the old man spying on him, grabbed him, and did what he'd really wanted to do to Dickie boy all along, wrung his neck."

He leaned his chair back against the kitchen wall licking his lips with satisfaction. "Eat your heart out, Neil Kelly, you amateur detective, Dewi Morgan-Evans is here, and this town isn't big enough for both of us."

Murph gave him a slow, large horselaugh. "Is this the same scholarly person who looked at poor me over his glasses, as I'm sure he does to all the fluttery young things who come to his office for petting, and said, 'Now Miss Gullible, you must remember not to get carried away by your hypothesis, eh?'"

He laughed her off breezily as they stacked their small collection of dirty plates and put them in the dishpan together. "Don't quote my good advice, it's a waste; just take it. Here I go showing you how to interpret your data—something I do only for the most promising cases involving the nubile nippers who flood my chambers seeking solace—and you show me only crass ingratitude."

She ran hot water and squirted detergent into the dishes and began arguing and washing. He, from established married habit, tucked a dish towel in his belt and took another to dry.

"I can't wait to get those people all together here at this party Neil is going to give," she said gleefully. "It will be like one of those grand old English murder mysteries where everyone is at this great country estate for the weekend, and this brilliant young woman detective unmasks the killer to everyone's total astonishment."

The full significance of what they were joking about passed quickly through her mind. "Do you really think it's probable Dad got murdered, not just ran off, Dew?"

"Yes, I do. And there might just be a second death in the family if Neil takes it unkindly that you decide to turn his party into a P. D. James thriller."

She dumped the dishwater out with a ceremonial gesture. "Oh, my old colleague Neil won't mind. I think. I hope. Dewi, do you think he'll be furious if I just sort of slink around and eavesdrop on people's conversations?"

He draped the towel he had been wearing for an apron around her head. "Some hostess. Here, have some more cheese. What was that you were just saying to him about shooting my father?"

"I hope I'll be subtler than that."

He kissed her hard suddenly, on the face, and held her. "Listen to me. It could get very unfunny. Guilty people aroused make for angry consequences."

"Why, I believe you're concerned for my little old safety, husband."

"Shut up," he said brusquely. They went into the living room together. "I'm only concerned for my own refined British sensibilities. Do you think I want to stand watching whilst they shovel you into your three square yards of consecrated hole, and all the Jesus perverts in your family wailing in a hushed hullaballoo of black umbrellas clustered over the wet gaping grave, half Our Town and half The August Bank Holiday Tragedy? Is that your real ambition, to be remembered around here as the late, daft, brave, wee Murphy girl, sob sob? I couldn't love you at all dead, Murph. It would ruin everything fine between us."

"You're not worried about me, you black Welshman. All you're worried about is who's going to take care of you and cook leftovers for you after I'm gone."

"That too, to a degree. Doesn't that alone move your stony heart?"

12

NEIL WALKED ALONG Williams Street, in no hurry to get to the house, and still, after several days back in Oldhampton, enjoying the flavor of his hometown. A white Ford with a Witches Heal bumper sticker waiting patiently at the light. A red Dodge with a Question Authority sticker edging around the corner, past the No Right Turn on Red sign. An apple-cheeked girl in pigtails eating yogurt with intense concentration. An unkempt, bearded, dirty young man with bare feet sitting on the curb reading a comic book.

Music of a particularly mindless, basic kind was blasting from speakers set in the open windows of the Knights fraternity house up the hill. William Oppeker, gentle, white-haired, genially childlike genius, who taught biochemistry and was drunk every minute of every day. Christine Rolfe, who looked like any no-nonsense housewife and was the sole prostitute in Oldhampton specializing in flagellation.

He knew them and he didn't know them. An excessively long bumper sticker: You Left Tracks on My Entrails When You Walked Out of My Heart. They were his neighbors, and they were strangers in whose midst he felt alien. He wondered if he had made himself, with his wanderings and his witness to too many terrors, a man without a hometown. He thought of Dolly in London.

He watched Vassily Petrovsky, who taught Russian, who had once been petted by Stalin before the defection, trotting briskly along the edge of the sidewalk, his roly-poly wife, Marika, two steps behind him as always, carrying the groceries for them both. "Was there a time when dancers with their fiddles/ In children's circuses could stay their troubles?" Dylan? Someone with the habit of asking mournful questions. He must ask Dewi.

Murphy had talked him into substituting for her to talk with Carl Parrish. He tried now, driving the car out of the garage, and marveling again that she had repaired his insoluble problem with so little difficulty, to remember exactly how she had let him volunteer for the job. He had promised himself that he would give her all the free advice she thought she needed, but under no circumstances would he let this feisty little heroine of her own melodrama con him into doing any of her legwork for her.

She had not only smiled like an angel (Could she have possibly imagined he was a bit nostalgic for the detective's role? Nonsense.) but had waved good-bye to him with a final word of advice about how to guarantee his entry into Parrish's house if they were reluctant to talk with him.

"Just tell them you want to talk to their two twins, Willie and Coker, about a blue Subaru Brat with a roll bar. They'll let you in quick enough if they think you know about that."

Actually, it was Carl Parrish's daughter's house he was looking for over in the wide open east side of Oldhampton.

Carl had been a cop in Oldhampton when the entire police force comprised the chief (then a rubicund toper named Downey, whom everyone cheered lustily and sarcastically when he marched with full gold braid and sword in the Fourth of July parade, but otherwise ignored), one other cop, a part-timer named Gil Saunders, who also ran the feedstore, and himself. The campus cops handled most of the drunk and disorderly calls then, and what was left amounted for the town force to perhaps one messy suicide a year (an astonishing number of academic suicides chose to bespatter their prime working capital on the living room ceiling with a shotgun applied to the tonsils, as though in revenge aimed directly at what had made them teachers in the first place) and three dozen traffic accidents. It had got more complicated in the sixties and seventies, but that was after Carl's time.

Carl had quit being a policeman for the simple reason that he couldn't stand Mrs. Chief Downey's crying jags every time she had to come down and help get the chief out the back door of the station into their truck to take him home, which was about twice a week in season. He said it just took too much of his time, listening to that damn woman weep. He had only become a cop because his asparagus farm had been the first in the town to go under to blight, and about the time he found he couldn't stand Marie Downey anymore, a developer bought up his acreage for forty-one thousand dollars. With that he turned in his badge and moved in which his daughter Lena, who was glad for the forty dollars a month he contributed ("I figure I can live with them for one thousand months at this rate," he had told the boys at the VFW, "until about two years after I'm going to be dead anyway.").

Neil's conviction that Murph was in possession of most, but not all of the pieces she needed for her puzzle had led him to spend an afternoon in the back room of the *Oldhampton Gazette* reading back issues from 1960.

Carl Parrish's name appeared three times in the stories, as the officer who had found Dickie Colrane on the road. But it had never been mentioned in any connection with the subsequent investigation. Chief Downey was roundly quoted in all stories, but it was obvious that he was dealing out generalities and police pieties (" 'We'll have the man who did this in irons within the week' says the Chief") and had done none of the brute work of rounding up evidence, chasing down leads, or interviewing suspects.

Neil parked the Volvo in the front yard and rang the bell of the Wisniewski front door about three in the afternoon.

Lena Parrish had married Stan Wisniewski while they were both still in high school and she was two-months pregnant. Their five sullen, short-necked boys, all blond, square versions of their farmer father, were all on sports teams and locally famous for their indestructible toughness. That meant, Neil knew, that on a fine afternoon they were all going to be out of the house playing ball somewhere or in the fields with their father. If Stan Wisniewski was like his Polish neighbors he thought that coming into the house before sunset was justified only by a medical emergency. Lena and her father were not likely to be close; few such living arrangements produced affectionate father-daughter ties. So at three in the afternoon, Neil was reasonably sure he would have the old retired cop to himself, his daughter glad to have him off her neck. He had a pint of Jack Daniel's in his coat if it came to outright priming the pump.

It took some three or four minutes of talking through a locked screen door to convince Mrs. Wisniewski that he was a professor from the college and not a developer after Stan's land.

It took another short, elliptical conversation to assure her that he wasn't an attorney come to harass old Carl about his pension. A lifetime close to the bone engenders paranoid expectations in the working class. He was considering playing his Subaru Brat card when she relaxed her pinched face and decided he could be let into the hall. Once she accepted his story that he just wanted to talk for an hour or so with her father about one of his old cases, she was so tickled that she made them instant coffee, whipped off her apron, and announced that she was going over to Luella's for a visit.

"You and Dad just have yourselves a nice old chat," she said, all homey warmth, and fled.

The cramped parlor he and Carl Parrish sat in was crowded with the furniture of perhaps three previous living rooms, all of it bargain hardwoods in a variety of fake finishes, all of it showing the stresses of putting up with the Wisniewski rough-and-ready style of daily living.

"She hates to stay home, that girl. But I told her good in 1975 that I wasn't here to be her housekeeper, and anytime she left, I left. Go sit out there on the stone wall if I have to, I won't sit here and answer her damn phone for her, sweep up, all that crap." He grinned, pleased with himself. "You can't let 'em think because you're old they can just boss you around. She'd have me doing the laundry, up to her. What can I do for you, Professor?"

Neil phrased his request with as much care as he could without lying. He knew old skinflints like this. If Parrish got any hint of a project afoot that was going to earn someone three hundred dollars, he'd claim half for allowing himself to be interviewed. Hating himself, Neil became as professorial and pedantic as he could. Everyone knew scholar's books didn't pay, and an astonishing number of otherwise sensible people will feel honored to be taken seriously by a professor.

The leathery old man, head half-turned to hear him with his good ear, listened and watched him.

"A colleague and I are writing a scholarly book, Mr. Parrish. About the history of Oldhampton around 1960. After World War Two. We're interviewing well-known people from the town back then to help us get the history straight. People in positions of authority, you understand."

"The Colrane shooting?" The washed-out blue eyes didn't budge from Neil's. No one was likely to be asking him about anything else. It was the most interesting thing that had ever happened to him.

"That," Neil nodded judiciously. "Among other things."

The old buzzard cleared his phlegmy throat and jerked his head back to indicate a humorous remark. "Nothing else worth writing about."

Neil decided to change tack and cut across the circumlocutions. He produced the Jack Daniel's and his host had them two water glasses before he had the cap off. The path to discourse seemed open.

They toasted each other and drank, one sparingly, one at a toss.

"You were the officer at the scene of the accident when Dick Colrane was shot, is that right?"

"Yup."

Neil quickly put the bottle on the table next to him and indicated that he should replenish himself at will.

"Did you also do the investigating afterward?"

The snort and the head jerk again. "Who else? Downey? He wasn't about to ruin his street shoes down there in that swamp, poking around in the brush."

"Was that land just wet, or was it polluted even then?"

"Full of that chemical crap if you got close to that dump DVR had down there. Just a little one then, but it stank to high heaven. Big mess now, according to the paper. Posted. All that land was posted against hunters, picnickers, you know. Trying to avoid lawsuits, I guess. I know I wrecked my best high tops. Damn soles fell right off. Acid or something."

"Did Saunders do any investigating at the scene of the crime?"

"Gil? You kidding? We wouldn't of let Gil investigate some kid showing his dick in the school yard. Gil just handled traffic, so on."

"So we can say you were the sole investigating officer from the Oldhampton police."

"Yeah, you can say that."

"But your reports were all in writing to Downey?"

"Well . . ." Carl Parrish scratched his throat and consulted his memory. " . . . until the state cops got into it. District attorney sent one of his so-called specialists in forensics down, a lieutenant named Stoller, wasn't worth the powder to blow him to hell, and he threw his weight around for about a week, then he decided there wasn't anything worth their trouble, so it all got filed. Downey was sure scared of that state cop. He stayed sober all but Friday that week, give you some idea."

"Would the police in Oldhampton have those records still?"

Parrish burst into bubbly, choking laughter, hawked, went to the wastebasket, spat, and sat down again.

"Hell no. You hafta remember, Professor, we weren't exactly a big-league force back then. We got by with about as little paperwork as we could, and the files were mostly for show, nothing in 'em. That state cop, Stoller, took one look and turned white as a sheet. He says to me then, 'Are you guys serious here?' I says to him, 'Hell no, Lieutenant, we're just small-town fellers who try to get along.' He just shook his head. Had a big round head, wore tight collars, one of them flattop haircuts, looked like a goddam bowling bowl was all I could think. Stick your thumb in his ear and bowl a strike with that head every time. Boom!"

It was clear to Neil that what Carl Parrish needed was what a lot of old men living on memories needed, to be allowed to ramble and tell his story in his own way.

It took nearly an hour, but four things emerged clearly from the undergrowth of incidental anecdotes and self-important reconstruction. First, Carl Parrish didn't believe that Dan Murphy did the shooting. Second, that he didn't believe Dan Murphy had been anywhere near the spot at the time. Third, that the squirrel carcasses found at the site had not been shot there, but had been brought there after being killed elsewhere. And fourth, that whoever had shot Dick Colrane had lain in ambush waiting for him to ride by.

It was like a cloudburst when Neil had been hoping at best for a few drops of rain. And there were enough bits and pieces of remembered fact in Parrish's story to make the whole plausible.

Every hunter in town—and Dan Murphy had been a hunter for his whole adult life—knew that there hadn't been any squirrels nesting in Milkwood since that dump started up there years before. The trees had started to die almost immediately, and he recalled that people had been asking what DVR was up to even then. Parrish was pretty sure himself it was some stuff they had tried out for the government in the Korean War, then got stuck with when the war ended, stuff to kill the trees in North Korea.

"That place was mostly still called Milliken's Woods then, the late fifties, but when that kind of white scum started forming on the ground there every time it rained, like soapsuds bubbling up from the ground, the paper started using the name Milkwood and pretty soon everybody called it that. Old Milliken, he gave that land to the college, but they sold it over to DVR, the way I heard.

"And anyway," he said, going off in a new direction while he rummaged in his nose and his memory at the same time, trying to get the feel of the event in his own way, "those squirrel bodies were cold."

"Frozen, seemed like to me. I walked right in there off the road, even before I put that boy in my car, and I seen them squirrels laid out. I thought it was kind of, you know, queer, them being there, being as how there wasn't any there to my knowledge, no cuttings under any of them trees, you know, like they always drop from the nests, so on. I just turned them over with my foot like, and they was hard as rock. I touched 'em, and those little fellers was stone-cold. Listen, I told Lieutenant Stoller that. Pitiful asshole he was, never hunted one damn day in his life. Grew up in Hartford, Connecticut, for Christ's sake."

He went over to the wastebasket and spat again, then covered it with crumpled paper. Neil's sympathies in the domestic war were tilting to his daughter. A snort of Jack Daniel's cleared his throat.

"Listen to me, Professor, them little suckers were *frozen* someplace and then brought there to Milkwood. They never nested there, that's God's truth. Ground underneath 'em was cold. I touched it. I thought at first, y'see, maybe it was like a fox we'd found down there two, three years before, when DVR filed a complaint some kids were camping in there. Damn fox was dead, see, stiff as a board, but like he was smoked or tanned or something. He didn't rot away, you see, just kinda got cured like by whatever it was in that groundwater there. So I said to Stoller, I seen a fox that looked like them squirrels, except so on and so on, explaining it to him. He looks me in the eye and says, 'Rigor mortis.' I says 'Bullshit' to him, but that's all he knew. 'If you knew any forensic science,' he says to me, 'you'd know what that means.' Old Fatso Downey meanwhile is sitting there in the office with us, sweating bullets because he hasn't had a drink all afternoon since lunch and his eyeballs are beginning to fry he's so dry. 'Let the lieutenant get his job done, Carl,' he's yelling at me, 'so's he can get back to Springfield and make his report. Don't interfere. Sure it's rigor mortis,' he says.

"He's dying, see, afraid I'm going to keep this asshole state cop around the station one minute longer than I have to and Downey waiting to run out back for a good belt before he starts seeing pink whatchamacallits coming out of the cells at him."

And Carl Parrish swore that whoever had brought those squirrel carcasses there had also put some kind of burlap sacking down and sat down or laid down on it. He claimed he could still remember the marks where they had tramped down the brush and put the sacking down.

"'Sure,' the hotshot from Springfield says, 'the chief here explained that to me. That was where this Murphy character sat down to shoot those squirrels.' In a pig's eye he did, I say to myself. Not three feet from the side of the road he didn't. But I knew Downey would crown me if I got him into an argument about it. You hafta realize, all that week while we was investigating this thing, Colrane was telling everybody he didn't blame anybody and he wasn't pressing any charges for negligence or anything. He got a lot of praise, so on, for that. Sports hero stuff.

"Anyways, that's the way she went into the file. Accidental discharge of firearms while hunting. Who cared if the kid didn't? You going to write what really happened after all this

140

time? If you do, you tell them what I just told you. Someone shot that boy deliberate."

Neil had jotted down two pages of notes as Parrish had talked and punished the pint of JD. Now he paused and drew a line under what he had scribbled.

He leaned forward, making sure he had the old cop's attention. "Every report—including Dick Colrane's statement— says that a squirrel ran across the road in front of his bike." He decided to leave it at that, just the flat fact, and let the statement hang out there for Parrish to rebut or explain if he could.

"I thought about that a lot." The throat was scratched again, and the lungs searched for effluvia which, hocked up, was swallowed again with much straining of the neck cords. "Funny. I dunno." He shook his head angrily, as if shaking off an insect. "Maybe he was imagining things. I dunno."

It was a hole in his theory that squirrels didn't at least live or play in Milkwood, and he shrugged helplessly. From informed source he was suddenly demoted to confused witness. Neil guessed that he had been confronted by the same question early and often, perhaps until he had stopped pestering his drinking cronies with his own side-of-the-mouth version of the event.

"One final question, Mr. Parrish. Do you think Dan Murphy really ran off that day?"

The old cop bunched his mouth as if tasting his answer before giving it. "Possible. If he did, though, it didn't have nothin' to do with that boy getting shot, I'll bet you on that. Dan was all kinds of a nut—religious nut, kind of a local history nut, all kinds of things—down at the VFW he could tell you more about World War Two battles than most of the guys who'd been in them. Read a lot in the library. Tell you one thing, too. He was utterly devoted, utterly devoted, to that daughter of his, the cripple girl. Dan wouldn't of left her for anything, except to go visit some shrine like he was always doing, to pray for one of them miracle cures the Catholics believe in. They're funny about that, y'know, no offense. My son-in-law Stan, he's a Catholic, but I'll bet you it was something like that. What I think, anyway," he concluded lamely. "Went off somewheres and just had an accident and fell out of sight. Commoner than you'd think, being I was a policeman, I know. Listen, you ask that father down at Holy Name Church in Fairfield. He used to always be leading them bus tours, what do the Catholics call 'em, pilgrimage things to this shrine and that shrine. He tried to run his own buses back years ago, but we clamped right down on him. No religious persecution, either, the way he claimed, the damn fool just didn't have the carrier's license. Claimed his Ford station wagon was a bus. Cripes . . ."

Neil took advantage of Parrish's last JD stop to get himself out of the musty, crammed house. He had obviously extracted as much from the man as he was going to.

He put his notes into the glove compartment of the car and sat looking out over the potato fields before driving away, thinking. "Utterly devoted" was the phrase that stuck in his mind. He took out his notes again and scribbled the phrase on the paper and looked at it.

13

"Utterly devoted? Was that what he said?" Murph asked. "It sounds weird when you say it that way. Let's just say Daddy was convinced I had a bad deal with this bum hip of mine and he had this private bug about curing me by the power of prayer."

They were taking a rest on the slatted bench in front of Town Hall. It was a Saturday morning to gladden the hearts of the merchants who sponsored the annual Spring Sidewalk Sales booming all around the center of town, cheery, sunny, and dry. Balloon sellers, juggling clowns from the high school Joey Club, a unicyclist, and assorted ticket sellers for the Lassie Team jacket fund circled the square and added to the festivity. The firemen's Oompah Band pumped away on the roofed bandstand near the war memorial.

Neil and Murphy had just come from the contest awards in front of the bank. Just before the crowning of Miss Downtown on the little platform strung with yellow bunting, they had announced the winner of the bumper sticker contest, and it had been Mrs. Margaret Mary Morgan-Evans. He and Murph and Dewi, who had bought an instant camera for three dollars at a sidewalk bin in front of the photo shop, and was snapping away like a madman with a new toy, had clapped and cheered and jumped up and down like everyone else.

Red in the face from excitement and embarrassment in equal parts, Murphy was hauled up onto the platform with plenty of whispered solicitude for her stiff leg from the burly fire chief to stand next to the three finalists for Miss Downtown, none of them smiling much for fear of cracking their makeup or dislocating their precarious hairdos. Someone with a real camera took her picture for *The Gazette*, and the president of the bank asked her what she planned to do with the thousand-dollar

143

check. Since the theme of the whole promotion was that every-one, incited by her slogan (she still didn't know which of the nine entries she had written was the one they chose, but eventually it would turn out to be: Oldhampton: A Glad Diversity and a Common Center, her own favorite) should truck on downtown to the business center (which wasn't what she had meant) and take advantage of the wide variety of consumer goods there (which wasn't what she had meant), the bank president hinted broadly as he asked the question that she might want to spend the whole thou right there at the sidewalk sales.

Murph smiled winningly and said that she was writing a book about her father's mysterious disappearance twenty-three years ago, and except for a twenty-dollar contribution she would make to SPEW, she was going to spend all the money on that.

Neil thought to himself, standing in the midst of the small crowd around the platform, most of whom couldn't understand a word she said through the buzzing loudspeaker, that if there was anyone in town who doesn't want that old event dug up again, they'll certainly know who must be stopped now.

The bank president, himself a member of the board of DVR, swallowed his grin, but stuck around bravely, long enough to pose for another picture with Murphy, the two of them holding up ends of the first red-and-white bumper sticker. The picture in the paper the next Monday caught their adjacent dilemmas exactly, Murphy looking cross-eyed because she was trying to read upside down which slogan had won, and her chum the president looking as if he had just wet his trousers.

"Yet," Neil said persistently, "several persons in town, when they speak at all of your father, seem to feel the need to add some remark about his being—forgive me, Murph, but this is the phrase that keeps cropping up—a religious nut of some kind. Why?"

"Pshaw." Neil hadn't heard that word in years, a good old country expression of mild disgust. "That's just a lot of exaggeration. Daddy wasn't any more of a religious nut than anyone else who goes to church regularly and makes a novena and says the rosary. He was just an old-fashioned country Catholic with a little superstition thrown in, was all."

They sat there, in the hullaballoo of the sidewalk fair, discussing Carl Parrish's recollections of her father for half an hour. She kept stubbornly denying that Dan Murphy had been anything like the way Carl Parrish described him, except for the part about him reading all the books in the library about World War II.

"Oh, he had a bottle of holy water from Lourdes that Aunt Mary brought him back years ago that he used to tell me to touch to my hip and say a prayer for Saint Bernadette to cure me." She snorted and punched herself softly in the hip. "Stuff like that. But you've got to realize, in his parish, down there at the Fairfield end, the old people are still all like that. That old pastor there still says the Mass in Latin whenever he feels like it. Crazy old bastard."

Neil made a connection that had eluded him before. "I thought that the date of this business, the day your father disappeared and Dick was shot, was connected with something, but since it was just two days before my own birthday I've been assuming that was it. But do you know what April sixteenth also is?"

"No. Spring? The beginning of daylight saving. I'm guessing, I'm guessing. The end of World War Two? What?"

"The Feast of Saint Bernadette of Lourdes. The miracle girl. The miraculous water, all that."

"Coincidence." She let him see that she didn't think much of his idea. "I'll tell you one thing, though. Daddy thought that movie—with Jennifer Jones?—was the greatest movie ever made. He saw it about ten times. But, I'll tell you, I think the idea that those animals' bodies were frozen and brought there is a lot more interesting."

"I shan't knock coincidence," Neil said. "It accounts for a lot of strange things in the world. But before I assign this to coincidence, I think I better go have a talk with the famous pilgrimage leader Father Sullivan over at Holy Name."

"Better you than me," Murphy groaned. "What a pain. He'll sell you two raffle tickets and a trip to La Salette before he lets you out, so watch it, and don't say I didn't warn you."

"Nancy Drew meets S. S. Van Dyne, hold it," Dewi ordered them, crouching to take their picture.

Holy Name parish church stood on the boundary between Oldhampton proper and Fairfield, an underpopulated village which had originally been part of Hatfield, but had been reincorporated in the nineteenth century as a district of the larger town when its population dwindled below two hundred and no taxes to speak of could be collected. The church itself, a white wooden strucure badly in need of paint, one story high with a truncated steeple, was almost obscured from the road by a billboard advertising both a raffle (for a Chevette Scooter) and a trip (to Epcot Center and the Shrines of Florida). The wonderful World of St. Walt.

The rectory was the sagging little farmhouse behind the church, the windows of its sun porch crammed with stacked boxes and furniture. The old man in slippers and black shirt sleeves, his rusty, shapeless black pants held up by red, white, and blue suspenders clipped on the front, regarded him from pouchy eyes.

Father James X. Sullivan was a throwback whose sheer inability to get along with the hierarchy, his parishioners, or his neighbors had condemned him to a grouchy exile in a church the bishop had all but written off anyway.

Holy Name offered one Sunday Mass (in Latin when the classical spirit moved Father Sullivan, who did not hold with the fancy shenanigans and language changes of Vatican II, or with Polish popes, or a great many other things his Church had seen fit to inflict on his poor suffering self), confessions by appointment, baptisms by appointment, a monthly bingo game in the rectory dining room (with prizes of vouchers for reduced rates on bus tours to favorite pilgrimage places, supplied gratis by Yankeeland Bus Tours), and scant hospitality to strangers who looked as if they might be some of the bishop's fancy legal hands from the Chancery.

But he was glad to talk to a book-writing professor about the late Dan Murphy, as he referred to him.

They settled in the parlor. A Sacred Heart portrait of particular anatomical savagery glared at Neil. Four crucifixes did not relieve the atmosphere created by the mad eyes of the portrait and the shrewd ones of the host. The furniture was the color of dried blood. In the feeble glow of the twenty-five-watt lamp burning on the end table against the wall it was hard to tell, but there were either a dozen statues standing in corners and on tables, some with red vigil candles burning in front of them, or just one statue and candle, but several mirrors.

Father Sullivan took his chair, the Barcalounger with the torn seat, folded his hands across his lap, tapped his thumbs together, and said, "Well, are you going to ask me about him?"

Neil had been pondering his options. How did you ask a religious nut about religious nuttery?

"I wonder exactly what your recollections of Dan Murphy are, Father. For the book," he added hastily. The first time the lumpy old priest had shown a spark of intelligent interest at the door was at the mention of a book being written. Neil hauled out his notebook and pen again to prod the memory.

"You say this woman is his daughter, the one you're working with?"

"Yes, Father. His daughter Margaret."

"Why didn't she come herself? Too busy marching for ERA or abortions on demand or some other crime against nature? God will punish these women horribly. Do you believe in hell, Professor Kelly? Kelly. Were you raised a Catholic or is that one of those Northern Ireland names with an 'e' in it? Kelley, is that it?"

Neil patiently established his credentials as a Mass-going Catholic, although he didn't expect that attendance at trendy St. Michaels with its guitar masses and women assistants on the altar would cut much ice with this old bastard. He was right.

"That joint. Casey over there is right up with the Polish and the Jesuits and the women serving Communion, the whole kettle of nonsense." He lapsed into sullen silence, his bitterness burning in him like a vigil flame. "So?" The eyes flew up. "You want to know what I remember about Dan Murphy? A finer man never lived than Daniel Murphy. The man was a living saint. You're not writing."

Neil thoughtfully nodded and wrote down several lines from John Donne.

"Daniel Murphy lived his religion, didn't just show up before Trinity Sunday to make his Easter duty. Lived his faith and loved his Church."

The care with which his listener wrote, even underlining some words, impressed the speaker. He began to speak more distinctly.

". . . great devotion to Our Lady." He indicated her picture on the wall behind Neil, who obediently craned to admire the insipid girl daintily crushing an impossibly large snake beneath her bare foot.

"Did Dan Murphy ever talk with you, Father, about making a pilgrimage to Lourdes?" Neil knew that if he didn't simply direct the interview where he wanted it to go, he was in for a long morning of tortured detours through the comic book iconography of the parlor.

The fierce old head snapped up. "Of course he did. Wouldn't you, if you had a baby daughter with a crippled hip? He worshipped the ground the baby walked on. Crawled, whatever. Terrible tragedy. She Margaret, the one working on this book?"

"Yes, Father. The same unlucky girl." Neil prayed privately for forgiveness, but his meretricious ploy got no sympathy anyway.

"I don't think I'd call her unlucky. I'd say the will of God. We can learn a lot about our Blessed Savior from our own small sufferings, offer them up. Source of inestimable graces and blessings."

The tag lines from uncounted sermons tumbled out. Nei accepted it as deserved punishment for his own low conduct

"Indeed," he mumbled penitently.

"Daniel Murphy wanted to take that poor tyke to Lourdes, France, with him. That was his dream. He'd been to Ste. Anne de Beaupré once, but that's not the same at all. Wonderful shrine, don't get me wrong. Wonderful hospitality there, marvelous shops. But it's not Lourdes, is it?"

He might have been one old wordly-wise gambler asking another rhetorically to accept the difference between Vegas and, say Reno.

"What is?"

There was another silence while the old terrapin sank into his shirt front and snoozed or meditated over the reply.

"You ever been there, Professor? To Lourdes? Where our Blessed Mother appeared to Bernadette Soubirous? Saint Bernadette?"

"No, no, Father. I've never had that chance."

"Wonderful place. Finest shrine in the world, you ask me. Do you know how many shrines I have personally visited in the last sixty-four years?"

God. "Dozens, I imagine."

A gleeful snort, the precipitation from which was then grandly wiped away from the stained black shirt front with an arthritic hand and deposited in the air. "Forty-one. Starting in 1919, when my mother, God rest her soul, took me to the graveside of Father Powers, the miraculous priest buried in Holy Cross Cemetery in Malden, Massachusetts, and we rubbed some of his dirt on my ear."

Neil wrote it down, trying not to spill a drop.

"Cured me like that of a painful inflammation of the ear. I've had a devotion to that man ever since. Crime he was never beatified. This Portugee cardinal they've got in Boston now probably never even heard of him. Cardinal O'Connell knew him, all right."

Neil, who had lived a part of his childhood not far from the place being discussed, recalled only that Cardinal O'Connell had a great belly and a matching fondness for having his picture taken in full red regalia surrounded by crooked Democratic politicians.

A modest inspiration struck him. Thank you, Lord. "Has it ever occurred to you, Father, that it's odd we do not have a really fine shrine right here in western Massachusetts?"

It was as if an unseen hand had banished all worry and concern from the collapsed countenance of the old priest. He lit up like the true nut whose nutty soul has been touched. Neil almost expected him to speak in tongues.

He leaned forward in the Barcalounger and pointed and whispered to emphasize the solemnity of his message. "I still have hopes, Professor. That we shall see in this remote part of the commonwealth one day—a grand shrine. Right here in Fairfield, no poorer place than Lourdes when they started out. That would be the glory of New England."

The old turtle eyes were seeing the illuminated billboards on every highway approaching Oldhampton, Neil was sure of it. The Glory of New England indeed.

Balanced now on the edge of his teetering chair, the barrel-shaped old priest looked like a dressed frog, his eyes bulging and his tongue darting uncertainly over his spotted lower lip, seeking unthinkable nourishment.

"Now you're an educated Catholic, Professor Kelly," he began, with an almost coquettish glance at Neil's eyes.

Neil knew he was being sized up for a sale. Was this where poor Dan Murphy had found himself once, half-hypnotized by the back-parlor mysticism and conversational tricks of this old huckster?

"Have you ever heard of the Devil's Well?" The priest blessed himself as he said it, raising his eyebrows importantly.

"The Devil's Well is it?" Neil wrote it down without answering.

"A well-known local legend. I've got a pamphlet on it here somewhere that I wrote myself years ago. A very old legend. Our earliest settlers hereabout were Calvinists, you know. Persecuted our kind in no uncertain terms. Puritans, you might say, although they were anything but pure in the eyes of Almighty God, you can be sure. Death on the Holy Mother Church, like that old devil J. C. himself. John Calvin," he added hastily.

"I see." Carefully writing J.C. = John Calvin.

"Two hundred years ago or more. They believed there was a well, some early farmer dug it, you know, unless the Indians themselves did. You know it's well proven that Catholic missionaries were in these parts years and years before the Calvinists, and they could easily have taught the Indians to dig wells. Up around Milliken's Wood there, that they call Milkwood now. These Calvinist girls, young girls, people of that sort, would go there at midnight and hold intercourse with Satan. Prince of Darkness didn't get his name because his worshippers practice their faith in the broad sunlight, did he? Terrible things happened, we know that. All hushed-up later of course by those old protestant pastors, all evidence destroyed. But one strange thing, like a miracle. Now I know how this

150

sounds coming from a Catholic priest, order of Melchisidech, all that." He crouched forward even farther, his head nearly severed by his short collar.

"They say one of those flibbertigibbet girls was caring for a small child, child with incurable epilepsy—some say dropsy, some say polio. You know and I know that they didn't know those names as medical terms in those days, but we may safely assume a gravely afflicted tyke. Well, whatever went on between that girl, may God forgive her, and the Prince of Darkness himself, one night after those frolics of theirs, that baby was put down into that well, then pulled back up washed as pure as snow of her disease. We have the testimony of many good people of that time. Cured. That put the wind up, you can bet, with that crowd. Miracles? Forget it." He slashed the air savagely with his hand, canceling all miracles as a Calvinist might wish he could. "Popish superstition, eh? The hand of God more like it, Professor, as you and I know in faith. And like our brethren the Jews, those early protestants spit in God's face and turned their backs on Him. What do you think of that?"

Neil considered several possible answers. "Incredible. What happened next?"

"What happened next was predictable. They stuffed a gigantic stone over that well. Ordered to by the ministers. Local people said for years that sounds of muffled cries, moans . . ." he blessed himself again, ". . . as if from souls in torment, could still be heard out there in the woods at certain times long after. They put a stone over it, Professor Kelly, just exactly the way our Roman brethren tried to put a stone over the tomb of Our Blessed Lord. Well, we know what happened that time, don't we?" He sat back triumphantly. Christ's resurrection proof enough of events in Oldhampton for him.

It was in there somewhere, Neil was sure, a dim outline seen in a cracked glass darkly, but an explanation connected however tenuously with where they had begun.

"What do you think, Father?" he asked in a hushed voice.

"Ah. What do *I* think? What do I think?" His voice went up as he tried the question out aloud. "Me? It's not up to me to think, Professor, is it? Prayer is my recourse at this point, not rationalistic thought à la Descartes or the rest of them."

A la Descartes. The shred of dessicated education fluttered in the dark air like disturbed dandruff, drifted through the stingy lamplight, and was lost in the crumbs on the carpet.

"Prayer."

"Prayer." The priest clasped his hands in front of him and shook them at Kelly to illustrate his point. "Now Dan Murphy, *he* was a searcher. *He* knew the story of the Devil's Well. And he believed, as I do until someone proves me wrong, that what we are dealing with here is one of those spots of holy ground God for His own mysterious purposes has put on the earth to lead men to salvation. The so-called Devil's Well, Professor, might well be a miraculous spring, given by God and His Blessed Mother for our betterment, right here in western Massachusetts, to make us, when discovered and revealed, the Lourdes of New England. I don't *think* that, Professor, I believe it on faith, which is to say I *know* it."

"Do you think—believe—that Dan Murphy was searching for this—well in the old abandoned DVR grounds that day, the day he disappeared?"

"Don't you?" The priest seemed incredulous, after his explanation of the facts, that this man before him remained dubious.

"Do you think he found it?" Neil asked.

"Don't you?" Father Sullivan answered portentously. "Do you happen to know what the date was that very day, Professor?" Big finale coming, clincher. Neil could see the crow of final triumph building in the old man.

"Yes. It was the Feast of Saint Bernadette, April sixteenth."

"You see! You see!" The priest glowed with the final proof.

Neil waited for Father Sullivan's ecstatic moment to abate. "What do you think, Father, about the shooting of the student that same day, down at the same place, on the road?"

The old priest sank back in his battered chair, feeling his back. "God Almighty, my back is killing me. Either, Professor," he said, probing his kidneys with stubby fingers and flexing his shoulders, "either it has no connection at all." He groaned and tried to reach his own shoulder blades. "Or. It is very directly connected indeed." He gave Neil a knowing look.

"How, Father?"

"How? How? Use your imagination, man. Do you think it would be beneath the devil to take a gun and shoot that boy to bring his athletic career into ruin and waste? Does that sound like the act of a rational person in the state of grace to you? Maybe you think the devil can't shoot?"

Neil tried to remember if Milton had conceded marksmanship to Satan in his catalogue of powers. "To be honest, Father, I never even thought of the devil in that connection."

The weary priest closed his eyes and rested back in the chair, to all appearances asleep. But as Neil rose to let himself out, the tongue darted out onto the lip again and the cracked voice croaked, "The man, woman, or child who finds that well and opens it up and brings the overdue blessing of Almighty God to this valley will live in the annals of the Church as a saint. A saint, think of it. It won't be poor old Father Sullivan. *Non sum dignus ut intres sub tectum meum*, so on. I am not worthy, Professor. With my back how can *I* be the looker? No, I'm the waiter and the watcher and the prayer. But what a power of grace and eternal glory awaits 'he who seeketh and findeth,' eh, Professor?"

He lasped back into silence, breathing heavily, almost snoring.

14

Sunday's chill rain had curtailed the pastel carnival, balloons, and sidewalk booths, in the center of town around the campus, even though the merchants, happy with the new state law that permitted them to open on Sunday, made a game indoor effort to attract the well-heeled alumni who poked glumly through the center waiting for the legal hour of one when the class tents could open their bars.

Neil attended late Mass at St. Michael's, and if there was an annoying air of breezy self-help humanistic psychology about the sermon (which explicated a text from Walker Percy) and a surplus of guitars (whose manipulators sang one song with a plot more intricate than *War and Peace*, but which apparently centered on a hero who left the phone booth dressed in miraculous garb and climbed up on a telephone pole to save the world, an allegory Neil found so alarming that he decided he hadn't followed it properly), at least there was no smell of soured piety.

By day's end he had dined with the Foster's sprawled at blessed, indolent ease on their sofa reading the *Times* for two hours, watched four innings of a game the Red Sox had apparently decided could not be won by such primitive means as the sacrifice or the stolen base, and made the few phone calls necessary to complete the guest list for Monday night's party.

Murphy had volunteered to do the shopping for the affair, and he had given her one hundred dollars and carte blanche to use his charge account at the package store. She had also extracted from him, with a diffidence so unusual for her that he had suspected her motives, an agreement that she might "spruce the house up a little" for the party. He hoped that the phrase didn't mean she was going to throw out his collection of *Massachusetts Reviews*, piled in the library on the floor, or move all the furniture around, but having said it he decided that he'd better just be ready to take whatever improvements she made.

There was an adaptation of D. H. Lawrence's *Sons and Lovers* on TV at nine, and all three of them, Liz, Vic, and himself, watched it inattentively until one scene about the miners, showing the hideous slag heaps of northern England, set Liz off about industrial dumping and toxic waste. Neil could hear Vic sigh softly and he sensed that the program was a lost cause. They ended the evening over coffee, stuffing envelopes with flyers to raise money for continuing the SPEW campaign against DVR. The meeting of the Selectmen was to be a closed session, over the howls of protest from SPEW, because of some technicality involving the personnel record of the assistant town manager, who was under review, and so all they could do was go on with their party plans and wait for their man on the Select Board, Felix Manning, to come over after the vote and tell them how it had gone. Felix was responsible for the SPEW motion, compelling the board to instruct the Board of Health to proceed with an investigation of the DVR dump and if possible to close it down.

Neil thought as he prepared for bed of how out of touch with this town he had been just one week ago, and how intricately he was entangled in its levels and problems now. He fell asleep thinking about how Lawrence had found it necessary to leave Nottinghampshire in order to see it plainly and write about it, and how different it was for him. While he was here the town and the college seemed to define and delimit his reality. Even Dolly back in London, who one week ago was the center of his world, seemed exiguous. Oldhampton the town, Old Hampton the college, Dewi and Murphy, Dick Colrane and Jill Purlie, all were part of a drama in which he had been given some role as a voice, or a link or catalyst. Twenty-three years ago here a terrible event had taken place, possibly involving another fatal event, and nothing had been done, no one had been punished. Now because of the passionate curiosity of a daughter, the routine academic politics of the college, and the ecology of a small town whose economics were implicated in the immunity of a chemical company from investigation, what had been buried and blurred over might very well now be brought

155

to light. Surely someone in Oldhampton stood to lose a great deal if the truth were fully revealed. Who? Neil was asleep before he could imagine the answer.

Lying on his bed five streets away, Dick Colrane dug his nails into the palms of his hands and arched his body against the waves of pure terror that went through him, to be followed by hard cramps in his left leg. He breathed deeply, he pinched his upper lip, an instant relaxer for cramp taught him by a swimmer, but this time it did nothing for him. His body was fighting his mind, the turmoil in his bones was rebelling against the calm faith in his spirit, and his spirit was losing. The black waves of convulsive cramp kept coming. He truly wanted to kill someone, and there was no forgiveness in him. He tried to pray. He prayed to be able to pray.

15

"WE ALL WANTED to be S. J. Perelman. All of us, me, my two brothers, and my old man."

"Ted Williams. I would have given ten years off my life to be Williams for one season. The year he hit .406."

"Spencer Tracy. Katherine Hepburn was like a queen to me. I wanted to wear trench coats and wisecrack with Katherine Hepburn, have her tuck in my scarf the way she did Tracy's on that roof where they had lunch in *Pat and Mike*."

"*Woman of The Year*."

"You sure? *Woman of The Year*?"

"You're nuts. Williams? When you could have been Di-Maggio?"

"Listen, with my luck people would have thought I was Vince. Or Dom. Williams was unique, unmistakable. I stood next to him once, at a sportsman's show. He was teaching fly casting. Big as a goddam house, like a building, huge. Intimidating, physically intimidating."

"There was my old man, he could speak English at about the level of a three-year-old. Half Yiddish, half Austro-Hungarian or Serbo-Croatian, whatever they spoke in Brno, Czechoslovakia in his day, and he says S. J. Perelman breaks him up, he should be able to write like that."

"I actually think it was Jimmy Stewart's scarf she tucked in, in *The Philadelphia Story*."

"*The Philadelphia Story* my ass. That's ridiculous. *Holiday*, maybe, in which case it was Cary Grant's scarf, but don't give me Jimmy Stewart."

"He actually started to take an evening course in creative writing at The New School when I was at NYU. The teacher committed suicide in the first month, a well-known short story writer, I forget his name. I'm not kidding. My father signs up for the course, bam, this guy shoots himself. They said he was depressed about his wife leaving him, but I know what I think."

"Who, the Red Sox? Would you mind telling me how, without any pitching?"
"What about this kid Brown?"
"What ever happened to that Dutchman they had, was supposed to have such an arm? Willander? Wilhelmina? What was his name?"
"It doesn't matter. Eckersley's dead, washed up."

"He wrote this: 'It is the rhythmic, inevitably narrative movement from overclothed blindness to a naked vision that depends in its intensity on the strength of the labor put into its creation.'"
"Well, sure, that's *his* definition, but what about ... ?"
"You're missing the point. It was his answer on a questionnaire. If I gave you a questionnaire to fill out and one of the questions was What's Poetry? would you produce anything like that? No. But a poet ..."

"Did your father think he was to blame for the guy killing himself?"
"Pop? He wrote a comic story about it and sent it to *The New Yorker*. Pop'll tell you his teacher was depressed about his wife. That poet who used to save his toenails in a glass jar, lived out on the Coast, but we knew it was my old man. Jesus, S. J. Perelman."
"I wanted to be a ballet dancer. Any ballet dancer. Or a modern dancer. José Limón, I suppose. Fiery, passionate, colored. 'Colored' was a very big word with me then. Or the president of France."
"De Gaulle? You wanted to be de Gaulle?"
"Any president of France. If they still had a king, I'd have wanted that. Just to be running France seemed wonderfully elegant, just the top of the tree. *Allons, mes enfants. Le déluge, c'est moi.*"
"I'm positive you're thinking of another deluge. 'Singin' in the Rain,' maybe."

J. A. G. Robinson looked at him coldly, grandly, from French and presidential heights, elevated by four scotches. "There was no *rhythm* or *singin'* or *dancin'* involved. I was a dignified chief executive."

"Fuck that. Funny. I wanted to be so goddam humorous that when I walked into a restaurant, even during the rush hour, people at all the tables would burst out laughing. I always imagined that S. J. Perelman simply couldn't go out to dinner anymore after a certain point. I know goddam well if he walked into this party right here, I'd burst out laughing."

"We need a woman."

"I haven't needed a woman since ten years. Twenty years. Moscow, 1963 was last time. What do we need a woman for?"

"To round out our survey. It's all one-sided. Hey, Mrs. Morgan-Evans, if you could've been anyone else when you were a kid growing up ..." He took Murph gently but firmly by the arm and wedged her into their circle—"who would you've been? I'm Spencer Tracy, Vic's S. J. Perelman, Jag here is either the president of France or José Feliciano, I forget ..."

"Limón, you idiot. No rhythm. Well, wait, if I was a ballet dancer rhythm was okay, I guess, but not if I was the president of France." He collapsed helplessly with laughter on the shoulder of the man next to him.

"... this is Ted Williams here, did I tell you I'm Spencer Tracy?"

Murph eased herself into a half-sitting position against the sideboard. When she drank red wine her hip ached for some stupid reason.

"Amelia Earhart."

Her husband joined them, putting his arm around her waist, and winked at her, massaging her hip. "I never knew you wanted to fly. You never told me. I'd have bought you a gas balloon. I saw one yesterday going over town at six in the morning, blasting away, red and gold."

"She could fix cars. Hey, it's true. Over in Northampton, there are still people who knew her. They said she could fix anything that had an engine in it."

"But," S. J. Perelman said solemnly, she had a tendency to get lost."

"That's not funny, Sidney."

"Hell, never mind. Look what happened to Williams after the forty-six all-star game."

"Tracy after Prune Face got through with him."

"Prune Face and that cockteaser Tess Trueheart."

"Junior. Didn't you want to kill Junior with your bare hands? What a little jerk."

"Listen, which little kid in the comics did you hate the most?"

The faculty party is the businessman's party is the truck driver's party is the perhaps only universal social situation still obtainable for the price of three hours of potable spirits. What was tight becomes loose, what was sober becomes tipsy, what was tipsy became tight, and foolishness puts on the garments of profundity without the usual daily accessories of discretion or inhibition. At parties we are all ourselves as we really are drunk, a drunk once said.

Neil, trying as host to stay just about three safe drinks behind his guests, eyed the guffawing group, which now included Dewi and Murph, and marveled. So far so good. No race war, no toxic waste jokes about the rum punch. If the guests of honor would show up, it would be fine.

On the sofa Grace Whittaker, a senior professor of astronomy and a bit of a tart, was holding court, George Purlie on her right and Carter Forsberry jauntily on the arm of the sofa to her left. She did not seem to mind being crowded between the two most distinguished men at the party.

Neil had forgotten how really small this room was when you crammed more than four or five people into it. Even after having lived in this house for twenty years, coming back to it now, it seemed darker than he remembered and smaller. His furniture was shabby in the arms and the books in the built-in shelves were stacked every which way, most of them with worn bindings, the personal books of a reading man. Murphy had obviously done some housekeeping. He wasn't happy to see his Rouault *St. Joan* missing from the wall above the sofa, though.

Did he want to come back here? How would Dolly see this room if she were here? Suddenly he experienced an honest ache of uncomplicated lust for her.

John Venuti glowered around the corner of the dining room door, as if scouting enemy territory. He caught Neil's eye and edged over to him, a bottle of Beck's in his hand. When the coach had gone to Fordham fifty years before, the Jesuits saw to it that all athletes wore blazers, blue ties, and white shirts on all public occasions when they were not holding a ball or bat. John Venuti still observed that tradition, and still expected his athletes to honor it, even if madras jackets and such alternative dress attire had crept in.

"He coming or not? You said the party was for him, where is he?"

The question was not unexpected by the host. He knew that it had taken a major effort of will for the coach to accept the invitation, and even suspected that the occasion had its own special significance for him. And it was already after ten, and the first guests had arrived at eight-thirty.

A small commotion of greeting at the front door translated itself into a stagy entrance, complete with sung fanfare, by the former Mitchell De Saulniers.

He threw his arms wide, smile gleaming. "Ta da! You lucky, flabby people. Okay, everybody, take comfortable positions on the floor and lift your left leg over your head. One, two. Hey, only kidding! Coach!"

He was brilliantly polished, handsome, white-suited. Some kind of California perfection in the imperfect New England group, like a figure in a TV ad who shows up wearing silver tails in a kitchen; Mr. Glitter, who had the magic formula to take away those daily chore blues. Michael De Soul was an exemplar of that supreme export commodity of California, a human being who had been cloned from an advertising concept.

He plowed through everyone and reached out two hands to John Venuti.

"Coach! Long, long time. Good, good to see you again. Except for me you look in the best shape of anyone here." He laughed and punched the coach in the pecs. "Wow. Like a rock."

"You're supposed to be a millionaire and you can't afford a necktie and a dark jacket?"

"You don't like my suit? Hey, tailored for me by my man in Beverly Hills, feel. Twelve hundred dollars. Look, double-vented, look, cut fourteen inches." He turned to Neil, shaking his hand, eyes shining. Insincere, hearty, magnificent meat, absolutely soulless.

"Michael De Soul. Professor Kelly, I'd know you anywhere, you haven't changed a bit. Thank you for thinking of me and getting in touch with my secretary. I love being here. I wouldn't have missed Dickie's party for gold."

He pointed a manicured finger playfully at Neil's chest and pulled the trigger. "Saw that TV series you wrote out on the Coast. Hey, like being back in school. God, really, I haven't enjoyed anything on the tube that much in years. John Donne was it? Elizabethan England, that whole shtick? Beautiful. I'm sitting there in the lounge at the club, see, and these seven or eight thousand people are hanging around waiting for me to say something wonderful, ha ha, we've been watching some piece of shit sitcom or something, and this intellivision comes on, like public broadcasting? It's your show, I'd heard of it, see, and Gabby is going to turn it off, but I said to her—she's Tommy Willow's whatsit, you know—'that guy was my teacher, for Chrissake.' Listen, not all of those lovely people out there have been to grade school, let alone, you know. So we watch it. Sensational. Half of them are coked up to their keesters, but I am on a culture high, it was like being back in school. John Donne. No man is Long Island, all that beautiful stuff. Loved it, really. Loved it."

Neil remembered his one visit to California. They really carried on like this on the freeway of the human mind, everyone firing out, no one really going anywhere except to another part of California.

"I didn't write it."

"Come on, modest. Your concept, right? Your book."

"The series was made from my book on Donne, but I didn't write a word of it."

"Hey, the same thing, right? Idea by ... and so on?"

Neil persisted. Some things have to be said right once. "As a matter of fact, I thought that they distorted almost everything I wrote about Donne into a cartoon of Elizabethan comic book simplifications."

De Soul rocked his head back and forth between his hands, grinning. "Wow, man. They really stuck it to you, huh? I'll bet you cried all the way to the Chase Manhattan Bank. Hey, listen, I swear, if that show had been any more elevated, those people I was with would have ascended into heaven and lost the channel. Those people knew what they were doing, believe me. It's called merchandising, Neilo." He made a money gesture with the tips of his fingers rubbed against his thumb. He liked you to see his hands. "Maybe if Richard Chamberlain had played Donne, huh?"

Venuti studied his former player sourly during this performance, then strolled away to another corner of the room.

"Coach hasn't cheered up much in twenty years, has he?" De Soul said. He shrugged. "Hey where's the guest and guestess of honor? Where's my old roomie, Cool Colrane?"

Neil wished he knew. "They're late. I expect they'll be here soon." It was beginning to sound lame even to him, but Neil couldn't think of anything else to say. He could see that Murphy was doing her best to encourage the party along, but Neil wished that for the moment he had a hostess skillful in dashing from group to group replenishing people's conversations and making the party move.

The white-coated student hired for the evening came through again from the kitchen with hot hors d'oeuvres, listening with continued amazement to his unbuttoned teachers.

"Ned, I'm not a wayward child. Are you warning me or something?"

"Connie, just cool the fun and games, okay? Let's just pretend you're not a nymphomaniac tonight, okay?"

"Phil? I haven't seen him. Larry says there's someone out in the side yard puking in the rhododendrons that sounds like Phil. Have you looked there?"

"When is Felix going to get here? The Selectmen never meet this late. God, I hope they vote to shut that damn dump down."

"I'll tell you who was the best football coach who ever lived, and you probably never heard of him. George Halas. Papa Bear."

"What about Chuck Fairbanks?"

"Chuck Fairbanks couldn't carry Halas's jockstrap. Sorry, ma'am."

"Is this supposed to be a party?"

"It would be a party if the happy goddam couple would show up. These shoes are killing me."

"It would be if I could be sure what water the ice cubes are made from."

"It would be if I could get Francisco to dance. Where's the record player in this house, do you know?"

"If I agree to lunch, will you promise me that's it? And not in Oldhampton. All I need is for someone to tell Phil we had lunch together."

"Absolutely. I swear. I know a place up in Buckland. We'll make an afternoon of it, drive around a little. Hey, have you ever seen the Chesterfield Gorge?"

"Cardinals maybe. Dodgers definitely."

"Did you see the wallpaper in the upstairs bathroom?"

"I heard no dice."

"What do you mean, they turned down our petition? I knew we should have made them hold an open meeting. That executive session stuff is pure bullshit."

"He says we framed our petition all wrong."

"Christ."

"It's only a rumor, but that's what I heard."

"They were all out of gin so I used vodka, all right?"

"Can't you do anything right?"

"What is it the woman on TV says about her laxative? I'm not thrilled with it? Well, I'm not thrilled with this dress, but it was marked down to forty-eight dollars. Is it too tight across the back?"

"If you just happen to go out to the kitchen for anything, you'll get an eyeful. I'm telling you, he has his hand halfway down her pants. I just hope poor Phil doesn't wander in on them."

"Who, the Red Sox? Without pitching?"
"Remember Wilbur Mills, the kid from Belmont with the wicked knuckleball?"
"His name wasn't Wilbur Mills. What was his name?"
"Wilbur Mills wrote *The Phantom Tollbooth*."
"Bullshit. That crazy Rumanian we met at Arnold's wrote it. The one with the sexy black wife, what's his name."

"So John says he's really interested in this job at Carleton College, so I told him, listen, buddy, if you go to the north pole, you go alone. Mona is not freezing her ass off through those nine-month Minnesota winters, department head or no department head."

"Who, Reagan? That clown?"
"Just give me a rational argument, not name-calling. Has he reduced inflation over ten percent or hasn't he?"
"Do you know how many unemployed steelworkers alone there are in Pennsylvania? Do you know what the *black* unemployment rate is in all industries?"

"I haven't bought a new dress that wasn't marked down since Sally was married. Who can afford a hundred fifty dollars for a little afternoon dress?"

"Wilbur Mills wrote something. Or was he the guy who cleaned out all the banks in Georgia for Carter? Burt What's his name. All I can think of now is Burt Lancaster, and I know it's not him."
"Fred, Fred, c'mere. No hints, now. Who wrote *The Phantom Tollbooth*? Wilbur Mills, right?"
"Hell no. Wilbur Mills was the pig in that E. B. White kids story about the spider web. Either that or the knuckleballer who used to pitch for the White Sox."
"I told you, I told you it was him. Wilbur Mills."

"Martha, I think you're missing the point. I'm not asking you to be unfaithful to Phil. All I'm asking is that you listen to me and let me explain why we'd be so good together. I'm talking about your growth as a person, this has nothing whatever to do with Phil. This is about you and your needs that go beyond Phil ..."

"Susan Sontag, Jacques Lacan, okay. Basically aren't they saying the same thing?"

"Has anyone even heard if they're coming to this party? I mean, it's supposed to be in their honor. Poor Neil looks like he's expecting bad news. I heard Dick wasn't all that well, you know. He had that weird born-again thing, you know ... you didn't know about that? I kid you not, he carries this miniature Bible around in his shirt pocket or something."

"That's what they said. All that stuff about they turned the petition down is a crock of cranberries. Ellie called, and she's posted right outside that door, and they are still in session, so nobody outside that room knows what they're deciding."

"Relax. If the Selectmen vote approval, then the Board of Health has to investigate, that's the law. Felix says we can get an injunction in one day to lay on DVR, and they have to stop dumping then and there and open up the site to investigators. We'll be in there tomorrow, I'll bet you five dollars. Ten."

"I just don't see them leaning on DVR, I'm sorry. There goes the tax base, there goes local unemployment if they do."

"And if they don't, there goes your drinking water, Larry. Milkwood equals Love Canal, sweetie. Times Beach. We're talking about the life and death of this town."

"Oh, for Christ's sake, Barb, what kind of excessive rhetoric is that? It just does more harm than good, all this SPEW raving about Love Canal and life and death. We're talking about a little local pollution."

"I'll tell you what, Larry, let me put just a little local pollution in your drink and you go ahead and drink it. You buy imported springwater by the jug, don't you? Do you know anyone in town anymore who doesn't? You're just being willfully dumb, Larry, if you don't think SPEW is talking facts when we talk about life and death.''

"You're writing a book, is that what you said?"
"Yes. A publisher has asked for a chapter about my father's disappearance for an anthology of New England mysteries, but I've decided to expand it into a whole book.''
"I think it's marvelous about you winning that bumper sticker thing. What was yours again?''

Michael De Soul was holding forth by the front windows. The waiter loitered.
"You think body styles don't change? Listen, I'll tell you about a certain Hollywood leading man who will be nameless because he would sue my ass off, but let's say he's short and not all that well-built, okay? So I said to him—we're spitballing some story ideas for a comedy set in a body-building shop, they call me in, 'creative consultant,' okay?—and he says, this little tiny person who gets two mill per effort, with final control—why? because he made a sensational four-hundred-million-dollar schlock pic the fifteen-year olds got off on all last summer, for something like a thirty-eight-mill investment. This midget says, 'I can play that.' We all look at him. I mean, Ziggy was there, Paul, Robbie—these are creative people— but they know what's bankable, so they listen to him. We're talking about the manager of this body shop. Muscle guys will be here, there, everywhere, lots of skin. Someone had to break the magic bubble, so I say, 'Body styles change, Star, but not that much.' I mean, it's my role, right? Jesus, he goes apeshit wild. Tells them to throw me off the project. Nobody moves, right. No. Body. I've done them all a favor. I mean. You take even Arnold Schwarzenegger, he's dead meat. He'll get up out of bed some morning, his fortieth birthday, all his muscles will be hanging over the side of the bed in a big tangle, he'll trip over them trying to get into his carpet slippers. I'm saying those two guys are the extremes. Puny is out. I don't care about the face. 'Your fans don't only see your face, Ace,' I told this other star out there. 'They are reading your body like a book, and frankly, yours is getting to be a comic book.' Bam, he signs a lifetime—did I say lifetime? Yes—contract with De

Soul studios for body work. Last month he signed tentatively for the new Harold Robbins? Am I telling industry secrets? Listen, we're talking one mill per week, six weeks' work for my friend Ace, plus a piece of the gross. What are we talking, twenty million dollars? The two hundred thou he paid De Soul is deductible, for Christ's sake. Body by De Soul took off to a new plateau when word got around. I got more stars than fucking Sam Goldwyn ever had, begging. Listen, listen, I've got *screen credits* in the new UA release with your favorite Itralian superstar, if it gets off the ground. You know what that means? Like Hairstyles by Dah dah dah, Makeup by Dee dee dee, right? Now, for the first time in motion picture history, a screen credit for body style? Hey, I'm a screen first! They'll have to give me the Oscar, won't they, I'm the only one?"

He paused long enough in his self paean to scan the faces around him. There had been ten, maybe twelve when he started. After all everyone likes to hear the dirt about Hollywood celebrities, even New England academics.

But when Michael De Soul wound down enough to check his audience ratings, he saw that three people had drifted away and at least two of those who remained were glazed over and stunned, unable to escape but obviously wondering how they had got into this.

The kid in the white jacket looked delicious. Of the remaining handful, one woman was opening her mouth to ask him, he was sure, something stupid about Richard Gere. He forestalled her by placing his hand across her tummy.

She automatically sucked it in, looking wide-eyed with shock. All questions about Richard Gere fled her mind. She turned crimson.

"Hold it in, sweetness, in, in, in. Always in. You've got a marvelous body style, basically. Essentially you're an ectomorph, a willowy woman with a natural style, but you've developed wicked poor posture. Honestly, do you want that?" He was just one of the girls now, hand on her tummy still, but somehow no threat. "If you were to restyle your posture alone, your whole image and carriage would be transformed. Try it, try it, love."

He leaned forward with a dazzling smile and kissed her cheek. The woman on his other side held in her stomach, but

168

waited trembling. He reached out to her and tenderly touched the tips of his fingers to her bottom. "We're going to have to do something about that, aren't we?" he whispered in her ear.

Across the room her husband, chairman of the philosophy department, who had not had an unconfused conversation with anyone but Immanuel Kant for ten years, wondered mildly why on earth that great pansy in the white suit was fingering his wife's bottom, but hoped in his amiable way that they were both enjoying it. Must ask her, he thought. Odd, though.

Dewi, drunk now on the rum punch, had just been asked by Jag Robinson if he would buy two tickets to support an Afro-American dance group scheduled to perform at graduation.

"*What* did you say they call themselves?" he asked, owlishly amazed.

"The Divine Iambic Dancers."

"They each have one foot shorter than the other, do they?"

"No, and they do not dance bare-breasted. This is not an exhibition from the *National Geographic*, but an expression of ethnic poetic joy."

"Sounds ghastly. Why no bare tits? I thought you people wallowed in bare tits, couldn't get enough of them."

"That is an image seared into your white imagination by years of brainwashing by media whose sole aim was to debase us."

"Well, why not at least Divine Dactylic Dancers? Acrylic Dancers? That certainly sounds better. Trochaic Trotters. Sonnet Steppers. Terrific Tetrameter Terpsichore ..."

"Eight dollars the pair. Faculty discount, five."

"Not until they change their name and take off their clothes," said Dewi firmly. "I made a religious vow when I was eighteen never to go see any dancing where they didn't end their act by twirling tassles with their tits."

"Hey, I saw that one." It was another political scientist. "In *The Graduate*, right? Dustin Hoffman and what's her name went to that roadhouse ... hey?" He realized that he was talking to a large black man, but he had been talking to a short Irishman about movies, something. Where have you gone, Joe DiMaggio? "Anne Bancroft," he said finally.

"Don't be an ass," the black man said and left him. He wanted to cry. This was some crummy party. Where the hell was Patty?

Neil saw Murphy alone for a minute, standing by the fireplace looking puzzled.

"You throw a nice party, hostess," he said, offering her some cashew nuts.

"I feel like an imposter."

"Well, Dewi seems to be having a good time. Phyllis Steckhouse certainly seems impressed." They both watched the portly lady who hung on Dewi's current outburst, wide-eyed.

"Are you mad I changed a few things around?" Murphy asked Neil.

"I did have a start when I realized my Rouault *St. Joan* was missing, but the Van Gogh looks good in that corner. Where did you unearth that?"

"Sorry, was that Joan of Arc? I couldn't figure out what it was, and I didn't like all that green there. I dug it out of your attic. You could furnish two more houses with the stuff up there."

Neil laughed. "That's why I never go up there anymore. Should I be looking around for other lost treasures from that trove up there?"

"I promise I'll put everything back when we leave. I just changed three or four pictures and brought down that straight-backed chair in the hall. I notice so far no one has sat in it, though."

"I'll bet you no one does, either. Are you getting lots of congratulations on winning the slogan contest?"

"Oh, that. I'm sick of it already. I promise you, I'll never put one on the Volvo." She crunched a nut. "Can I ask you something that might sound stupid?"

"Do you have to ask? Have you been listening to some of the conversations in this room? Fire away."

"Do you think everyone is a split personality down deep?"

"You don't mean schizophrenic."

"No, not split like in half. But really two or even three different people. And I don't mean geniuses, like Dewi. You, for example." She winced at her own temerity. "How do we know what the famous writer and professor of literature is really like when he's off somewhere? Maybe you're a real bastard." She realized what she was saying and held his arm, laughing at herself. "I mean you're nice to me and Dewi, but maybe when you're in England or somewhere, you're a real bastard to people."

She gritted her teeth. It had sounded like a great insight when it was in her head, but after listening to herself explain it, it sounded really dumb.

"Certainly we all wear masks—the Greeks coined the word *persona*, our personality, to mean the masks in a play. I think we do all have a variety of selves ticking away underneath our social masks, and some of them would probably surprise our closest friends, yes." He thought of Woody Allen's phrase, not for the first time, listening to his pedantic, tutorial tone.

"I sound like FM radio."

"Maybe you're the exception. I suppose teachers get in the habit of talking nicely to ignorant people, so they just learn to treat it as normal. Dewi hasn't got the hang of it yet, as you might have noticed."

"He does have some difficulty suffering fools gladly, doesn't he?"

"Junk food drive-ins for pets? That's your million-dollar idea?"

"Hey, think about it. People take their pets out for a drive, right? Okay, here we have a Dog McDonald's, a Cat Wendy's."

"You ask me, that's what you've got now."

"You telling me the average cat likes potato chips? French fries?"

"Tell me, son, what did you say your name is?"

"Tom, Michael."

"Tell me Tom, what year are you here at OH?"

"Basically, I'm a sophomore."

"Nice. What club, Tom?"

"I've been invited to join the Knights. Should I take them?"

"Hey, I'm Knights."

"Really. Fantastic. Like will you be coming up the hill to the open house?"

"I'm an alumnus, right? Hey, maybe you can advise me. I'd like to give a little something to the club for the house. What would you say they need, really need?"

"They need a new pool table, man. The cloth on the old one has grooves in it."

"Let's you and me go up there tomorrow and tell them they've got a new slate bed table coming. Hey, you're not a pool hustler, are you? You look more like a power lifter. I'll have to watch my step around you."

"Like I do a little lifting. I actually wish I was a little slimmer, especially my ass."

"Maybe I can give you a few tips. What do you press, Tom?"

"I told you, Connie, that's not funny."

"Take a joke?"

"Just leave my goddam zipper alone, okay?"

"George. How you doing? Have you thought about our earlier conversation?"

"James, let's have a truce at least until my daughter's engagement party is over, isn't that reasonable?"

"Just checking, George. Want to make sure everybody knows no new appointments going down without approval from my committee."

"Have I said I'm planning any new appointments? Do you have an FTE slot for me to fill in sociology that I haven't heard about?"

"Hey. 'Who de cap fits, let dem wear it' they say down where I come from. 'Who de cap fits, mon.'"

"I mean thin is fine, but anorexia nervosa?"

"I thought she looked good."

"Connie is doing her zipper trick again. Ned better grab her before she gets out of hand."

"Or gets it in hand."

"Larry doesn't know if he wants her to stop or get on with it."

"Say it again."

"Meirionnydd. In the county of Gwynedd. Canolbarth Cymru."

"Marvelous."

"Ned, how've you been?"

"Hi, Neddie. Larry and I were just talking about senses of humor."

"Honey, do you think maybe you should call the sitter, see if everything is okay?"

"Sorry, ma'am, the things wrapped in bacon are all gone. There are cheese things and fish things on crispy crackers, I think."

"It's called *The Only Tenor, Nimble and Crocus*."

"I guess I don't get it. I don't understand much poetry."

"Dylan once described himself as the only tenor surrounded by slim sopranos in the waterfalled valley. The other is his description of a spring morning."

"Marvelous."

"And I say if we wait for their permission, we're never going to get in there. The hell with them, why can't we just walk in there? Do they have it mined or something?"

"Don't ask."

"What about EPA? Haven't they got federal funds for cleaning up toxic waste? Does that make it an FBI case?"

"God, Lanie, where have you been? EPA is in bed with these people."

"Take those sardines away, anything oily turns my stomach."

"Neil, did you actually invite Jag Robinson?"

"I sent a sort of blanket invitation over to social science by phoning Millie."

"Christ but that guy gives me a pain."

"Say it again, slowly."

"Meirionnydd."

"Marvelous."

"Liz called the state. Twice. Environmental Quality Engineering says only local boards of health have authority over private water supplies. Nada, I'm telling you."

"Hey, ladies, this is supposed to be a party. You guys look like a lynch mob."
"Show me some DVR people, I'll show you a lynch mob."

"I just don't see how you can say that the Women's Movement has nothing to do with the pollution question."

"Isn't Susan Sontag rather irrelevant at this stage?"
"Passé maybe, but irrelevant?"

"As long as we've got Ronald McDonald for president, there's going to be no peace in the Middle East, it's as simple as that. And no low mortgage rates, either, to mention one more thing."
"Come on, at least admit he turned inflation around."
"Has he turned unemployment around?"
"I didn't say he's a miracle worker, just that he deserves credit for what he's realistically accomplished."

"Nora Ephron says he's been making it with this English bitch since they were married."
"Neil Kelly?"
"Read the book, Barbara. That hotshot Watergate husband of hers."
"Was he Redford in the movie or Hoffman?"
"Wilbur Mills? Wasn't he the one who claimed to be Howard Hughes's real heir? The Mormon?"

"Has anyone seen the guests of honor?"
"I haven't. Helen, were Dick and Jill here and left already or what?"

"Neil looks a bit fatter to me, does he to you?"
"Why not, he's a fat cat now. They say in England he gets invited to Ascot, the Royal Family, the whole bit."

174

"My, my. Still waters run deep. Sheila said that she heard he was making it with this English lady even when he was married to Georgia."

"Sly old Neil."

"Who is that dark little man who keeps trying to sing 'Who Threw the Overalls in Mrs. Murphy's Chowder'?"

"The little leprechaun of a feller who keeps getting drunker and drunker and putting his hand on Gertrude Annondale's leg when he talks to her?"

"My, he is, isn't he? Seth won't like that. Although it seems that Gertie does. Isn't he a funny little man? Does he teach here at OH?"

"Yes, he's taken Neil Kelly's place while he's away."

"Pity, really. What did you say his name is?"

"Dewi Morgan-Evans. He's my husband."

"I am sorry."

"I can see you are. Well, I'm not."

"Neil? Some English poetess?"

"That's what Terry said Sheila said."

"I'll believe it when I see it. He's just having a little fling. After you know. What happened with that student. Ugh, that was so awful. Poor Neil."

"Poor Neil."

"Yes, it's Jill all right, but I don't see Dick. You don't suppose they've, you know ..."

"Neil, I think Jill Purlie is trying to get your attention. Over in the hall."

Neil turned, ready to be relieved. But Jill was alone, and making those grimaces and head motions that can only mean *can I see you alone?*

"Where's Dick?"

Jill and he had eased into the tiny study and shut the door behind them, trying not to be too obvious, but attracting attention with their confidential manner. Jill was breathing shallowly, her face was drawn.

"He's upstairs. We came in the back, through the kitchen. God, it was bad enough sneaking into our own party, but did Martha and Earl have to be actually screwing in the back hall? Jesus, I could have killed both of them. I don't think Earl even noticed."

"Neil, he's really in bad shape. Dick, not that ass Earl. I've spent the last five hours just convincing him to come here and not take off in his car for Boston. He's in a real panic. Will you, please—God, will you talk him down?" She wept and wiped her face angrily. "I mean literally and otherwise."

Her tense composure broke and she buried her face in his coat, sagging against him helplessly, her big woman's body shuddering with her sobs.

"I'm really scared. He's never been this—" she held herself in and tried to get her composure back. "This—oh shit, I don't know—so goddam dark. It's scary. I'm ..." Her voice broke again and she wailed helplessly on his chest. "He had this born-again thing at Harvard, and I don't know what, he thinks he's possessed or something. I'm just so scared. I don't want to marry a man I don't even know ..." Her crying gradually lessened in intensity, but she clung harder to Neil's shoulders. He waited until it was all out. Then he asked her to sit in the study for a minute and went to get her a good stiff drink. He left her sipping it, then went upstairs to find Dick.

The bedroom to the left of the stairs had been Neil and Georgia's for many years, then Neil's. He had worked at the desk placed facing the Pelham Hills for a lot of contented hours, had, indeed, written all of the first draft of the now-famous life of Donne there.

Dick Colrane was lying face down on the bed, still in his topcoat, one arm folded back, grabbing himself by the back of the neck.

Neil entered quietly and shut the door on the downstairs party noises behind him. "It's Neil, Dick," he said softly. "Jill told me you were up here. I'm going to look out the window a minute or two."

Few things are harder for a man than showing another man how much he is hurting. He let Dick lie still on the bed and moved silently to the window and stood staring out at the distant hills to the east. Daniel Shays had taken shelter in the natural caves of those hills once, when the authorities were on his tail, and many a man since had probably lit out for those caves when something at home in the town was too much to bear. Neil had sometimes wondered, almost longing sometimes for the natural peace up in those hills, how many men had crouched there in the pines staring back at the lights from the town, longing for their peace. God help us all.

"I was praying." The voice from the bed was calm.

"So was I. For Daniel Shays and everyone who ever ran for the hills."

"Jill tell you I almost ran out today?"

"Yeah."

"I'm spooked, Neil."

"We all get spooked sometimes, Dick." He turned finally away from the hills and toward the man on the bed. Dick was sitting on the edge now. He extracted a cigarette from a crushed pack and lit it, shaking the match out carefully and placing it on the edge of the table for lack of an ashtray.

"I started to smoke last year. Me. Mr. Death-on-smoking all my life." He blew out a long breath of smoke. "Slow suicide, self-hatred, awful. I had to fight like a demon to keep it up, it made me sick to my stomach. Still does a little. I'll probably never really get the hang of it." He laughed dryly.

"Come on downstairs and have a drink. My own personal cure for the urge to set fire to your lungs. Cured many a man."

"Those people? I'm scared to death."

"You think they want to hurt you?"

"One of them did." He put the cigarette on the floor and crushed it thoroughly, then swept up the ashes into his palm and put them into his pocket. "Stupid. I'm split in two halves, Neil," he said, leaning back against the headboard and carefully lifting his left leg onto the bed out straight. "There's still a piece of me that's twenty years old and thinks I can conquer the world with a football in my hand. That half scares me the most."

Neil sat angled against the foot of the bed on the far side. The only light in the room came from the streetlight beyond the maple tree, just coming into red leaf.

"You are also entering into middle life, my friend. That old swamp in the trees where more than a few American males of all stripes of courage get moments of panic and want to turn back. Some chase teenage girls, some dress up in sandals and earrings, and I suppose some dream the old dreams of athletic glory again. What makes you think you're different?"

"That I've had. God, I can still run like a deer in my dreams, did you know that?" He paused. "This is something else. Not so much ..." he stopped and took a long breath. "I don't want so much to *be* Dickie Colrane, all-American again. It's more like I owe that kid something. For what he lost. To avenge him, I guess you'd say."

He almost mumbled the last phrase shamefully, and for the first time looked at Neil's eyes to see his reaction.

"You really mean 'avenge,' don't you?"

"You bet." His voice grated on hatred.

"How?"

He punched his knee softly. "Get the person who did this."

"What would that accomplish, assuming you could?"

"Nothing positive, I know that. Just flush me out. Catharsis, old and true."

"First you'd have to find out who did it? Have you always assumed it wasn't an accident?"

"Yes." He only whispered the word. "I couldn't hate anyone just for being stupid. Yes, it was no accident."

"The Murphy woman doesn't believe her father did it, although she says that if he did, she'd rather know the truth once and for all. If you leave Dan Murphy out, there are probably three or four ideas around town about who did it, accidentally or on purpose." Neil was trying to keep his voice even and not suggest that he believed any of it.

"Dan Murphy," Dick waved the name away disgustedly. "You can forget Dan Murphy."

"If not him, who?"

"That's the beginning of the hard part, isn't it?"

"When Mrs. Morgan-Evans is finished with her book, maybe it will all be easier to sort out. Are you afraid it will be someone you liked?"

"We're talking at cross-purposes, Neil. You've got to understand what I really mean. I don't want to hurt that woman, but I do want to keep her from writing that book."

"You don't want to know." He made it a flat statement.

"That's right. I'm afraid that if I know, I won't be able to resist what I have to do. If I never know I think I can live with my old devils. I think I can forgive." He put both hands over his face.

Neil waited for a long minute until he began to speak again.

"I told you I was born again when I was in graduate school. I really was. I may not be the enthusiastic convert now I was then, but I do truly believe that the Lord entered my life and took it over and guided me to a new way. I'm basically a happy man, Neil. My work, Jill, this college ... And I identify that happiness with my faith in Jesus. Now ..." he put his head back and stared at the ceiling, his eyes shining in the reflected light from the street. "Now I'm being tempted, and I'm scared to death, literally. I'm so scared that everything is going to come together and I'm going to find out what really happened to me, and that it will be that someone I trusted shot me and cut my life in half, and that I will kill that person and damn my own soul to hell. I have all that in me." He rubbed his knee slowly. "I lay in that hospital bed and brooded about my poor self for a long time, then that wonderful, kind woman gave me the Scriptures to read, and I felt the life flow back into me again, and I was truly reborn, and I left all that darkness and despair behind me. Now it's back."

"Does Jill know all this?"

"Part. Part of what I'm afraid for her to find out is what a savage I am down deep. She really believes I'm a nice person, and I'm not, not while I'm carrying this blood vengeance in my heart. Listen. I decided, when I was still in the hospital after the shooting, that I'd find out who did this to me, and I'd wait. I'd wait until some crucial stage in that person's life, then I'd wreck their life the way they did mine. I became like those unquenchable old Jews who were broken into rag dolls in the concentration camps. I wanted to spend the next forty years if necessary walking through the world looking at faces, until I recognized the face of my torturer, so that I could call in the vengeance squads. Except that I would be my own vengeance squad. And I've always known that whoever shot me lived in my town."

There was another interminable silence between them. Neil waited, because there was nothing more he could say or ask that was going to influence Dick now. What would come would come. His friend continued to grip and massage his knee. He would stop, then his hand would return to the old injury.

"I was determined to become the scholar they had always told me I could be. Once I knew that no surgery, no miracle—do I need to tell you that I prayed for a miracle?—was going to heal my leg, I studied as hard as I had ever played. I got my doctorate in four years flat, thesis later published, assistant professor at twenty-six. Now I've got tenure, and I'm going to chair my department, and I'm vice-president of my professional association, and now I'm to be married to a lady who is the only one I've ever really loved or wanted."

The hand gripped, stopped, folded itself into the other hand, then returned to the knee.

"Success is a great sweetener, as you must know. I really lost that black urge in me to go for my enemy. Really. I almost literally stopped thinking about it. Almost. That's the key word."

"And now it's back."

"I feel like a man whose cancer was in full remission for fifteen years who then learns that it's back. So my mid-life identity crisis has a few elements you don't usually read about in the self-help books. The rising scholar wants to get on with his teaching, put the past away, get the new book finished ... the whole, familiar generative ball of wax, including sons and daughters."

"So much for the rising scholar. The all-American boy?"

"That little bastard," Dick said blackly, "has come back with his dream of vengeance. He still wants his pound of flesh."

"It's really a war between you and him, isn't it?"

"Yes. Except that he *is* me and I *am* him. It's really not between me and my old enemy with the gun. I have become my own enemy. The me with the blood grudge against the me with all the normal, midcareer hopes of getting on with it ..."

"Who's going to win?"

Dick smiled grimly. "We're both very good. That kid—sometimes he comes back and takes possession of me—not just in dreams, but for a moment when I'm alone I can imagine I'm back in his body, cool, physically perfect and aimed like a gun. Then I wake up and realize I'm not a goddam jungle cat or anything else, just an aging teacher trying to live a useful life."

"Sounds to me as if the aging professional has it all over the angry young man."

"He has a lot of unexpected power, that young man. He's like an old thirst for booze, or an old, burned-out drug habit." He thought a minute. "I talked once with a man who had been a heroin addict for years, then went through detoxification and was completely rehabilitated. Once he admitted to me that every now and then, at completely unexpected moments, he'd feel a rush, and his palms would sweat, and he'd want to run somewhere and get a fix, start the whole thing over again, live in that insane high, even if only for twenty minutes. 'It never leaves you,' he said. Well, he was right. That kid with the rifle arm, Mr. Cool Colrane, Sugar Colrane, Smiling Assassin Colrane, he can come back and for a minute at a time I want to run back into my hate, put it on like a burning shirt, and go after my enemy."

"Have you ever talked with anyone else about this?"

Dick smiled wanly in the shadowed light. He took another bent cigarette from his pack and straightened it with his fingertips, then broke it in half and put it into his pocket.

"You mean my friendly local psychiatrist? My confessor? My bartender? No, none of them. This is the first time I've said this much to anyone, including Jill. She's the one I'm worried most about hurting."

"Don't you think she deserves to share in this before she marries you, Dick?"

"What's she ever done to deserve this, eh?" he wisecracked grimly. "Yes, of course. And also no. Neil, what if she says, 'Hey, you are a crazy man, and I have had a taste of that in my own life and I don't want any more?'" He frowned. "Jill went off the deep end badly with her first marriage, you know, and I wasn't exactly unimplicated in that. If she finds out now that I'm a potential basket case, she might just shy away from me so fast it will create a vacuum."

"But shouldn't it be resolved before you marry?"

Dick slid off the bed and walked to the window, his topcoat collar still up around his neck, and stood spread-legged, watching the hills. "That's what I'm afraid of. When it dawned on me that this party downstairs represented both things coming together, that's when the shakes started."

"Why afraid? Wouldn't it be a relief?"

"I'm afraid because resolving it in the first stage—finding out who shot me—might just be more destructive than living with it. Messy, ugly, and painful for a lot of people. And it's happening without any help from me because that Murphy woman is slowly digging the whole business up again, and you're the one who is going to show her how to put it together. Do you get it now?"

Neil realized what his friend had said and sat in stony silence. If Dick was right, only Neil Kelly could prevent the rekindling of Dick Colrane's gnawing passion to avenge himself on his unknown enemy. But if he did prevent that, by simply not helping Murphy make the connections in her search for her father, she could never have the answer to her question. And even if he did prevent that, his friend Dick Colrane would still be living with his own haunting.

As if echoing Neil's own thoughts, Dick said, "I've lived in a haunted soul for a long time, Neil. I think I can handle that. What I don't know is if I can handle the job of exorcising my own ghost."

Despite himself, and disliking himself for the egotism it betrayed, Neil thought again of his own dilemma, putting Dick's aside for a moment. If he did renege now on his word to Murphy and Dewi, and not help them while they tried to define a stable, creative life to be proud of, he must simply do it without any extenuating explanation. Dick's story to him was, in the deepest sense, a confession, and wholly sealed; a profound sense of personal evil had been shared and now must be protected or never cured.

Not for the first time he wished he were a priest, so that he could whisper the words of absolution now, forgive this man his sin if it existed at all, in the name of a higher power. Cast out the sense of raging hatred and build a bridge again between him and God. Pontifex, the ancient name: bridge builder.

But he was no pontifex, and he had no power to forgive anyone. No absolution to pass on for a thing not done to him personally. He could only sit mutely in this leaf-shadowed room, his mind racing through the bleak desert of his own sense of futility, and try to think of a useful thing to say.

"If it's there, Dick, you know that it will have to come out."

"Murder will out, eh?" The man at the window turned, his face lost in the shadow with the faint light behind him. "Didn't Chaucer or one of your English poets say that?"

"You haven't murdered anyone yet."

"Oh, I think someone was murdered. I always have, although I never said a word about it. Come on, Neil, do you really believe that Dan Murphy just coincidentally ran off? Isn't it far more likely that he was killed that day?"

"You think he witnessed the shooting and was then killed by whoever did it?"

"It's logical, isn't it? He was known to hunt around there, legally or not, posted ground or not. He must have seen something. Perhaps he tried to confront whoever it was, perhaps make a deal to keep his mouth shut. Maybe the poor old guy just tried to run away. Hell, maybe he had more guts than anyone has ever given him credit for and he tried to grab the shooter. But I think he was there, and I think it cost him his life. If he was, then finding out who crippled Dickie Colrane means uncovering a murderer, too. Knowing that was what gave me a big part of the pleasure in contemplating my revenge."

"Your hypothesis is pretty close to what his daughter thinks actually happened."

"She's brighter than I thought. But she also knew her father. I gather he wasn't the best provider in the world for his family, but that he wasn't the kind of man who just ups and leaves them on their own."

Neil stood beside him at the window and looked out. A single-engine plane picked its way along the spine of the Pelham Hills, picking up the beacon there and circling down slowly toward the private airport in Northampton, its wing lights blinking.

Downstairs there was a party in progress to celebrate the forthcoming marriage of this man next to him and Jill Purlie. Up here Neil was standing with an old student and friend who had clearly come near the edge tonight in some denial of a raging, destructive force in himself that might destory his and Jill's chances for happiness together.

He spoke slowly. "Dick, listen to me. No matter what follows, no matter what it costs anyone else, no matter how it must be done, you're going to have to walk through this fire. I will be here with you, and Jill should be, too.

"Whatever happened to you twenty-three years ago canceled half your life. It might also have cost another man his life, if your suspicions are right. Now listen to me, goddammit. You must do it. The truth is that important. You will never have any peace in your soul unless you unearth it now and face it. You have got to trust the people who love you enough to go through with this, or you're going to do to yourself what someone else did once, you're going to cut off your own second life. And nothing is worth that."

It seemed to him that his voice was a shrill whisper, unconvincing and hollow, a mockery of calm wisdom. He glanced at the bowed figure beside him, waiting for that big curly head to lift.

"You are a scholar of distinction, Dick, and a fine teacher, and you have a whole life ahead of you as a husband and father. That's who you are. You're not Dickie Cool, and if he is still inside you, screaming to be let out of his purgatory, let him out. Give him a solution to his pitiful half-death and a decent burial, or exorcism, or whatever it is that is needed."

The head came up. The eyes shone with tears. "What if someone else, no matter what he did to me, is badly hurt? By getting rid of this—thing in me—won't it be—irony, I used to think, was something writers invented—won't it be just a way of giving in to Dickie Colrane's hunger for vengeance, even if I do nothing?"

"It matters what you want from it. Intent matters. You're not seeking vengeance. I know that and you have to keep reminding yourself that you know that, too. You're not the judge of this world, God is. Do what you have to do, Dick, and leave the rest to heaven."

For the first time a small smile flickered across his friend's lips. "Where would you English teachers be without Shakespeare to quote?"

184

Neil could feel the sweat pouring down his sides under his jacket. Both men were breathing audibly, as if they had just finished a race side by side.

"Tomorrow," Dick said in a croaking, parched voice.

Neil waited.

"It will be easier this time. I'll take a bottle of wine and a loaf of bread and all that stuff and take Jilly out to the hills for a picnic, and I'll tell her all this. I promise."

Neil put his hand on his friend's shoulder. "Maybe by tomorrow events will take some of the responsibility out of your hands. Sometimes providence cooperates with our best intentions."

They turned unselfconsciously and hugged one another, then both made for the door.

At the top of the stairs they could hear Dewi's *a capella* voice narrating the epic tale of Mrs. Murphy's chowder once again, with appropriately raunchy lyrics.

Neil was about to open the study door looking for Jill when she emerged, tense and white, gasped to find Dick standing there, and hugged him joyously. The two lovers stared into each other's eyes for reassurance and found it and hugged again, then, arm in arm, waded into the living room.

Before Neil could make it past the phone table, Vic Foster waved the receiver at him and mouthed "overseas," and swooned to show how impressed he was. "Dolly couldn't get to sleep alone, do you suppose?" he whispered in Neil's ear as he glided away.

Neil huddled over the phone with his back to the living room to block out as much of the party racket as he could. Fifty ideas flashed through his mind as he waited for the connection, watched Dick and Jill be greeted, embraced, patted, and finally toasted in a bellow by Dewi Morgan-Evans.

It seemed to take an age to get the connection. He drummed his fingers on the table furiously, willing it. He was sure Dolly had been injured, or ill. Or there had been an accident. Dear God, what? He squeezed his eyes against the hilarity from the living room and finally got a perfectly clear Thomas Bowie, sounding as though he were calling from next door.

"Neil, you old faker, how are you? I hope I got you up. What is that awful row in the background?"

"It's a party. Too complicated to explain. Is everything all right?"

"Why shouldn't it be? I called the other number you gave me, no answer, fine waste of time, so I figured your own number might be worth a try. It's early morning here, chappie, and I wanted to get you at a time convenient for me, since I'm going off duty, and maximally upsetting to you. Sorry I didn't get you up. If you'd like to go to bed I'll call back in a few hours."

"Thomas, you moron, I thought it was Dolly."

"Ah, Sorry about that then. Last I saw her, two days ago to be typically precise, in front of the Tate, she was all alone and looking as smashing as usual. I tipped my hat like a real gent and offered to relieve her loneliness on the spot with an hour or two of high-class companionship, but she is true-blue, your girl, and turned me down."

They bantered for another minute, Neil so relieved that there was no calamity to report that he didn't mind the ribbing Thomas always gave him.

It suddenly occurred to him with the clarity of an idea long known but deeply suppressed from consciousness that Thomas Bowie was going to be his best man someday, and he was amazed at the sureness of his knowledge and also at his not having realized it before.

Then Thomas gave him the answers to the questions he had asked about Dewi's mother. She had died just six years previously, in Islington, but that was not the whole tale by a long shot.

By the time he had finished fencing with Thomas, his free hand over his right ear, and eliciting from him all the details of his investigation into the records of Dewi's family, the party had reorganized itself around the engaged couple. If some of the crowding around was motivated by curiosity about their late arrival or the rumors of a fight between them, most of it was simply inebriated high spirits and relief that they were there.

Dick was being embraced by the ebullient, white-suited Michael De Soul. Was it pure accident that he turned his head to see John Venuti, thin-lipped and cynical, watching the scene?

Vic handed him another glass of champagne and he tipped a wordless toast toward Jill, who was now surrounded across the room by Liz Foster and her committee.

Jill had immediately got herself into their argument about DVR and the Women's Movement, and brushed aside Lanie's embarrassed attempts to change the subject to weddings.

"Listen, Lanie, it's relevant. I'm getting married to settle here in this town and raise a family, even if we have to adopt one at our age," she said with emphatic frankness. "I don't know any wedding plans more important than planning how to stop Oldhampton from becoming another Love Canal because of those bastards at DVR."

Saying it, meaning it, she experienced an immense sense of relief to be yammering away about something real, leaving her fiancé's black depression of an hour ago behind her for now. She turned to Liz.

"Bring me up to date. What does Felix say? What did the Selectmen do? Do we know yet?"

There was instant gloom in her circle.

"Hey, did I say something obscene? What, they wouldn't vote it? What about Holbrook? They did it." She turned from one listener to another, mad and confused.

Liz shrugged and blew a stray lock of hair from her forehead, looking and sounding defeated. "For now forget it. Apparently we phrased our whole petition wrong. The board voted that since we claimed pollution of the drinking water supply, not just standing groundwater, we'd have to show that DVR had a working well or other connection with the aquifer to get an injunction. No well, no public inspection, and DVR sure as hell isn't going to invite us to tour its land."

"And there ain't no well," Barbara said bitterly. "Felix researched every page of the town lands book for that acreage, and there's no record of any well or pipeline there. He says there never was or the town records would show it. Oh, shit."

Murph, who had just joined them listening, crowed happily, her chipped-tooth laugh making them all stare at her.

"But there is."

"There is what?" Liz asked her.

"There's a well."

"Felix says not."

"Well, he's wrong."

"Margaret Mary honey," Lanie said wearily, "the town records say you're wrong."

"Well, the town records are wrong then. Do you want me to prove it?"

"Prove what?" Dick asked, shouldering his way past Murph to hand Jill a fresh glass of champagne and kiss her on the cheek.

"I can prove there's been a well on that DVR land for over a hundred years. Maybe it's blocked up, but it's there, and I know where there's a map showing it."

Liz was ecstatic. "Where, for God's sake? How can it, I mean? If the official town records ..."

"Dick," Jill said, "when you wrote your book, didn't you tell me you found whole batches of town records missing or incomplete, from back around the Civil War?"

"Yep. There was a fire in the basement of Town Hall in 1911, and they dumped enough water in the west wing where the records and land books were that a lot of stuff got ruined. Four or five hundred irreplaceable documents were destroyed."

"Well," Murphy announced to them almost smugly, "if they want to replace the surveyor's map of that old Milliken Wood land that DVR now owns, I can show them the original drawing."

She paused dramatically and extended her arm to point toward the front hall. "It's in the lav. I found it in the attic when I was cleaning and changing things around. It said *Milk Wood* on the border, and also *Milliken's Wood*, and I thought Dewi might get a kick out of it. That's the name of a play by Dylan Thomas, you see," she started to explain, but she was drowned out by an excited rush of her listeners toward the front hall lav, cheering and clapping.

"Good Lord," Neil said to Vic, realizing what Murphy had said. "I bought that old map at a yard sale about twenty years ago for a dollar. It's been in the attic ever since. I could never think of a place to hang it."

Someone was in the lav. The laughing mob, now augmented by everyone at the party who had picked up the tag ends of their discovery, pounded on the door and demanded that the hapless occupant come out instantly. It was, from the unmistakable boom of the reply, Dewi.

"Go away, I'm meditating."

"We want the picture"

"Hand out the map."

"Open the door, who cares about you?"

The ribald suggestions began piling up, a hilarious shivaree that puzzled and even alarmed the poor man pissing inside.

"You want my picture? Go away with you. Rude people. Off or I'll piss out the keyhole at you. Man's toilet is his castle!"

He finally emerged, zipping and benign. "I had no idea you all cared so much ..." he began, but he was swept aside by his tiny wife and her sister searchers and hurled against the wall.

"Glory be to God," he mumbled, "I never saw so many who had to go so bad so quickly." He began cheering for Murphy to win the race, and was blearily astonished when no one chose to use the toilet, but everyone grabbed at the picture off the wall and the winner brought it out into the hall.

The ink was brown and there was a water stain in the lower left-hand corner, but it was a wonderfully drawn surveyor's map, twenty by twenty-four inches, framed in narrow oak and labeled in exquisite italic lettering: "Parcel 3108 / Book 152 / Page 81 Oldhampton Town Records, 1837." There was a fanciful border of leafy plants and smiling fauna. The words "Milliken's Wood" and "Milk Wood (so called since 1761)" were printed across the bottom.

One third of the distance in from the east edge of the parcel there was a double circle outlined with a six-pointed star, to which Murph was triumphantly pointing with her little finger. The legend read: "Devill's Well."

"There it is. Whatever 'Devill's Well' means, there it is, plainly marked."

Pandemonium.

Felix Manning stood on the second stair and held his hands above his head for silence. "You will all be glad to know that I got an amendment into the motion to table our petition tonight so that it's tabled only *pending further research into the alleged existence of connection with the aquifer*. I promise you, we now have the evidence, and we will be on that land with digging equipment tomorrow."

The cheers and general hugging and dancing could be heard a block away.

As the party drifted back into the larger rooms toward the bars for one last round of celebratory drinks, Dewi, only partly sobered by the confusion surrounding his ejection from the lav, saw Neil coming toward him grinning.

"Look at him," he said, digging his elbow into Jag Robinson's ribs. "Your cannibal ancestors must have had that satisfied look on their mugs when they were about to polish off a Welsh Methodist for lunch. Kelly, my lad, you're either drunk at last or alight with lustful pleasure. Was that phone call from your dolly? He's got a bit of crumpet on the side over in London, calls him up seven or eight times a day," he confided in a stage whisper to Gertrude Annondale, squeezing her thigh and making her squeal and say, "Marvelous."

"Well, actually, Dewi," Neil said, smiling broadly down at his Welsh friend on the sofa, "there's good news and there's mixed news."

He explained to the seated Dewi briefly what he had earlier asked Thomas Bowie to do.

"Now let me understand this," Dewi growled, squinting up at him. "You employed some chum of yours at Scotland Yard to find *my* mother? And he succeeded?" He shook his head as if to clear it.

"Not 'employed' exactly. And not 'found' exactly. Do you want to hear the story or not, you ungrateful bastard?"

"No, of course not. I haven't the slightest interest."

"Oh, Dewi, shut up," his wife said, rapping her knuckles on his head from behind the sofa. "We all want to hear it, Neil."

Neil grinned at her, too. "Your mother died in Islington in 1977, apparently happy, with some old friends still around her. No disease or accident, she just apparently died in her sleep."

"Jesus, that's almost yesterday. Six years."

"God rest her poor soul," Margaret said heartily.

Neil continued. "She left a large collection of memorabilia from her days in the troupes to the *Victoria and Albert* theater collection, and also a letter to a firm of solicitors in Glamorgan

190

with instructions to pass it on to you. They have not exactly been diligent. There was no money involved, and they sort of let it sit in the files. Thomas stirred them up a bit, and they gave him the letter on your behalf. Nothing confidential, simply a statement that your father, Powys Morgan, was not actually your biological father."

"Good God, I'm a bastard," Dewi said.

"I never had the slightest doubt," Murphy said.

"Would you like to know who your real father is?"

"Should I? Good God, it's not the Prince of Wales or any of that lot, is it? If it is, don't tell me."

"No," Neil said, "your real father is—or rather was, he was assassinated in a political coup in Pakistan in 1956—Ejad Khan, who, before he changed his name, was Ganesh Francis Xavier, a former banjo player with the Glad Cadets Pierrot Troupe."

Dewi whooped and lammed Jag Robinson across the arm with his fist. "By God, I'm a wog! You hear that, James, you bastard, I'm one, too! Half counts, doesn't it? By God, it better. I'm a wog, James!"

James was grinning hugely, and embraced the little Welshman beside him. "Welcome, Brother Dewi," he said.

And so the party that had begun as an engagement celebration and almost dwindled to an embarrassed sort of welcome home for Neil Kelly, then brightened briefly toward its end with the appearance of the engaged couple, then erupted in wild excitement when the map was found, ended in a new scene of rambunctious hilarity as Dewi Morgan-Evans, son of a hero of the Pakistani revolution, was formally declared a Third World person.

16

A MASSIVE, JOINTED, orange machine with an encaged man in coveralls strapped in a black iron chair high above its caterpillar treads was extending its single arm over the spot, waiting for the signal to dig.

Its little high hat of a top exhaust was flipping its lid in a simmer of power throttled back, the engine burbling, petillant with urgency.

"Case 880-C" in bold black on its shoulder. Eight hundred eighty something. Neil wondered what. Cubic inches? Cubic yards? His sense of physical volume was primitive. The steel shovel, with its five thick-clawed fingers dropped suddenly in an arc and bit into the molasses thick earth.

The cold rain came down, darkening the scene, the group in oilskins, raincoats, hiking jackets, and assorted brim-down headgear, some clustered under shared umbrellas. The morning kept nearly canceling itself under the slant downpour, wet elemental space in the dead woodland took the sound of the relentless machine without gentling it.

Neil had been shivering since he and Murphy and Dewi had walked into Milkwood together, joining up with the others authorized and unauthorized but curious, who were gathering for the excavation of the well site marked on the map.

He thought, looking around them through the stripped trees over the milky, scummy ground, of the gentle war of survival underfoot in any healthy woodland; half of nature is quiet catastrophe which gives pleasure. Flowers, days of open delight in the sun, rain soft on hidden glades as kind as the speech of sweethearts. We work and make war to walk at home in the soft air. But this small moonscape was like a land after war.

"If we stand here much longer, they'll have to fish for us soon," Dewi said gloomily, trying to tuck his collar closer shut.

The man in the cage held a shift stick in each hand and played the four immense flat pedals before him with his yellow boots. Pistons beside his turret, behind him, above him shot out, telescoped in, slammed open, gleamed wider, inched shut as he played his vast instrument.

The thick, glutinous ground pulled apart stickily. Not earth, but some chemical abortion of earth, a humus of toxins, inspissate with evil.

Chief Scalli of the Oldhampton police, Neil's old friendly enemy, lifted his feet in the Oldhampton Fire Department boots covered with giant Baggies from the supermarket. There had been a row with the fire chief about outfitting the investigative party with OFD equipment, but the Selectmen had shut it off with a brusque phone call ordering the surplus fire boots to be loaned to the group. They had agreed with the angry fire department supply officer at least to pull giant Baggies over their boots while they were in the toxic marsh of Milkwood.

The injunction permitting the excavation had come from an emergency meeting of the Selectmen over coffee at Nina's Cafe at eight o'clock Tuesday morning. It ordered DVR Chemical Corp. to cease and desist in the practice of stockpiling, storing, and dumping chemicals and chemical containers on the site designated in the attachment, known as "Milkwood." The document was served by a town officer, accompanied by Scalli, on William J. Ruppert, plant manager for DVR Chemical, at the company office in the professional building at 10:00 A.M.

That gentleman, white shirt cuffs folded back twice, company blue tie with a tiny, stitched chemical symbol on it held in place by a silver tiepin, smiled and politely declined to accept the proferred injunction.

He expressed pleasure with the visit of the chief and Mr. Manning, and even with the gentlemen of the local press just outside the door, but pointed out to them that the parcel of land in question was not any longer the property of DVR Chemical Corp., but of Old Hampton College. He suggested that they redirect their injunctive efforts to the administrative offices of that institution.

It took twenty minutes of yelling on one side of the desk and bemused insistence on the other, then three phone calls, but the new documents, produced by the DVR secretary in multiple copies, were distributed, and they supported the DVR assertion.

The crucial document was a memorandum of agreement between Old Hampton College and DVR Chemical Corp., dated October 28, 1955. It described in some detail the elaborate, but essentially unilateral procedures by which DVR Chemical might, at will, return ownership of the Milkwood property to the college. That option had been exercised, the final clause showed, in the previous week and approved by the executive officer of DVR under authority of the board of directors.

The Milkwood toxic waste dump belonged to OH. George Purlie's committee, and its chairman, old Billionaire Howard, had been just a tad more clever than was desirable.

When, an hour later, the injunction was served on Chip Allen, the president of the college, he had already received the original of the transfer memorandum by special messenger. He had nearly wept with frustration and fury.

George Purlie had been summoned hastily, the file on the entire land transaction had been dug out, and the two men had determined between them, and with appropriate expressions of dismay, that the most recent grant of the land back to the college was irrevocable.

The president issued a statement assuring the SPEW committee and the town that the college would lend every facility to the town in the proposed investigation of the site. The Case 880-C earthmover leased to the college by O'Daniel Construction for a heart-stopping hourly rate to finish the landscaping and piping around the new gymnasium was waved momentously, ponderously down Keg Road to avoid the heavy morning traffic on the main highway. It created its own crushed path through the rotten vegetation of Milkwood and sat a foot deep in the fibrous muck of the dump site.

George Purlie had been designated by President Allen to represent the college at the inspection, and he was there with ill grace, but wearing Baggies over his L. L. Bean hiking boots. Jill and Dick stood next to him, silent, arms around each other's waists. Liz Foster and most of the SPEW executive committee were there, many of them with cameras. And the local press was there, even one minicam mounted on the shoulder of a student reporter from the university who was free-lancing a feature on environmental pollution.

The vast claw went down and down, to the underworld through the roots of things. Massive bucketfuls, one dripping load after another, sucked from the earth obscenely, the muck redder, blacker, the smell fouler each time. An acre of scattered, ruptured, and rusted barrels lay beyond the well site.

Then what a Frenchwoman once called God's mistress, death, showed up.

Jutting from the side of the scoop, like a comic, gangling uncle buried by nephews at the beach, they saw the brown, hideous, mummified face, fangs grinning through peeled-back lips, of Dan Murphy.

A piercing she-wolf scream burst from his daughter, who grabbed her husband's arm for support. Her cry had no words, only an old, old story of rage, triumph, and sorrow, an Irish sound.

The foreman waved frantically with both hands, signaling the operator in his cage to cut the power and set the last load down. Enormous groundsheets of polyethylene were spread by Scalli's men, and the grisly load was eased onto it.

Two men with short-handled shovels, wearing full protective clothing and gloves, set to work to lift off the dirt crusted and piled around the corpse. It was easier than they expected, because the body was hard as leather and stiff as wood, as if a skinny effigy of the man had been carved from rotten oak, an Egyptian filthy thing a thousand years old.

"He's pickled in that crap," Scalli said aside to the fire chief.

"Like that fox we found down here that time," Carl Parrish, who loomed up behind Neil, said.

"Like he was embalmed," one of the shovelers said.

"Like he was cured over a slow fire. I seen them heads in the museum, from South America, like that, all leathery," someone said.

Carl Parrish pointed over Neil's shoulder at the face. "You never saw any South American mummy with a bullet hole in his face. See? Right under his left eye."

Everyone looked. Scalli squatted and squinted. "I'll be damned."

17

THE AUTOPSY ON the partially decomposed, partially preserved corpse of Daniel Murphy was to become a piece of forensic medical history. DVR had dumped so many kinds of waste in the immediate area around the well site that it was eventually to prove impossible to sort out what chemical processes had taken place in the soil from their interaction. The body yielded traces of chlorinated hydrocarbons and organic phosphates, two large families of deadly pesticides, but also dioxin and decayed compounds of dichlorophenoxyacetic acid (apparently an early experimental form of Agent Orange) and some creosote derivative whose chemistry was a puzzle to the lab.

Impounded DVR records, which it took the town and the state more than a year to get their hands on, were finally used to trace the history of disposal at the site, and only then did the police learn that the very first containers of chemical waste mixed with construction site debris from the main DVR plant had been dumped into and around Devil's Well on April 18, 1960, just two days after Dick had been shot and therefore, theoretically, two days after Dan Murphy had been murdered.

But by the time that history was unraveled and reassembled to date the last possible time the body could have been hidden in the well, Neil Kelly was back in England, and many of the other centrally concerned persons in the case had also left Old-hampton forever, including the murderer.

John Venuti was always ashamed of what he had done that April Saturday morning twenty-three years before, and of what he had not done.

The coach ran every morning. Years later jogging would become a fad among the middle-aged duffers of the College, and almost everyone would turn up on the roads one or two mornings a week in a coordinated jogging suit and forty-dollar Adidas. But in 1960 no one jogged; a few athletes ran. John Venuti ran, in old suntans and topsider sneakers and gray sweatshirt with nothing printed on it.

That morning he was running up the hiking trail on the north slope of Teakettle Hill and thinking about the Boston Marathon coming up in a few days. He had wanted to run in the Boston Marathon since 1948, but he knew now that he never would. Teakettle was his own "Heartbreak Hill," the long slope outside Boston College in Newton, and he ran it once a week.

Near its seven-hundred-foot peak, where a gravel company had long ago mined away the knob, he paused for a blow and looked down over the maples just coming into red bud on the western side of the slope, over east across the main road and over the sickly gray stretch of Milkwood.

Except for Dan Murphy's crazy-looking green-and-gray truck, improbably assembled by mounting a dismantled Winnebago cabin onto a Dodge pickup, there was nothing moving on the scene. The bastard camper parked in a lay-by three hundred yards back, edging under the cover of overhanging brush.

The coach ran across the hill and back up it. When he was back at his original sighting point forty minutes later, he saw the camper drive out of its cover onto the main road and back in the direction of town. It was almost 9:00 A.M.

John Venuti wouldn't know for several hours, when he heard it from a student, that while he had been running Teakettle daydreaming about racing neck and neck with Johnny Kelly into Kenmore Square, Dick Colrane had been lying stunned and bleeding, with his leg shattered, almost directly beneath him, hidden from his sight by the angle of the hill.

When he heard that, and then heard several days afterward about Dan Murphy's disappearance and the suspicion that he had fired the shot crippling Colrane, he had said nothing.

He had felt a fierce rage of justice in his chest that now no one who had disgraced himself and football as Colrane had done would ever play for his New York Giants. If God had used poor dumb Dan Murphy to punish Colrane, why should John Venuti be the one to go to them with an explanation that might inevitably lead back to other things he wanted forgotten?

———————————————

Mitchell De Saulniers dreaded anyone finding out what he had been doing the April Saturday morning twenty-three years ago, and what he had not done.

Milkwood was still only a polluted two acres surrounded by a lot of stunted, but still passable woodland then. It had gradually become, for the seven or eight homosexuals at Old Hampton College who knew each other, a refuge and a meeting place. It was attractive because it was unused. It mattered little to the students whether it was unused because it was supposed to be poisonous near the dump or because the ghosts of old German farmers were said to haunt the place. No one else haunted the place, and it was still a hell of a lot safer in 1960 for gay encounters than anyplace on campus. By the moral and psychological standards of the college then, Mitch and Paul Pettinger and the few other practicing gays who actually belonged to the exotic Mattachine Society and shared a post office box to receive its newsletter, and went to New York once a year for some partying in Greenwich Village, were lepers.

Mitch had been in Milkwood that April morning for the simple pleasure of walking with Paul, holding hands and sharing an occasional kiss, like any young lovers strolling any woodland path.

If Milkwood looked entirely gray and forbidding from the hilltop across the road, within it the struggle of tough, small, natural things to grow was still going on. Deep roots that had not yet felt the acid sting of seeping herbicides kept sending nourishment to branches that would burgeon each spring with new leafage. It would be another ten years before the choirs were stripped and wholly silent.

That damp, mild morning in April the fiddlehead ferns were thrusting themselves up, tight musical scrolls as tender and sweet as asparagus to collectors, and the willows, always thriving on the wet, were yellow with new hanging leaves. The two lovers stopped by an enormous paper white birch springing with palest green foliage to touch foreheads and look into each other's eyes.

Both pairs of eyes widened with shock at the same instant. The shot the two men heard came from less than fifty feet away, just one second after a terrible smashing sound like a club hitting a skull. Frozen in their touching posture for a moment, they both swallowed hard, and without a word broke apart and ran at top speed toward Keg Lane, away from the main road. Athletes from the college doing roadwork along Keg Lane and back up Mill Lane to the athletic fields three miles north were not an unusual sight in Oldhampton.

Gillian Purlie saw the wounded, stiff brown face of the corpse they dug from the humus mound. Then she heard Neil Kelly's sotto voce comment to the old man standing just behind him, and she shuddered with the jarring shock of deadly recognition.

Something she had seen on an April morning just a day or two before the shooting that had crippled Dickie had puzzled her vaguely. Getting out of her car in the family garage, she had wondered if there was room enough in the freezer for more meat. Seltzer's Market was having a special on quarters of beef, and if there was space enough for three or four packages of special cuts, she would buy a butchered quarter when she shopped on Saturday.

There was a brown paper sack taking up the right side of the six-foot-long freezer, and when she flicked it open idly to see what it was, she glimpsed what appeared to be a couple of frozen squirrels, not yet skinned. She drew her hand back quickly and wondered if their handyman, Orin Emerson, an undependable old scalawag, had stashed them there. She made a mental note to ask her father about the package, then simply forgot about it in her need to study for next Monday's psych exam, an exam she was never going to take in the aftermath of Saturday's tragedy and dismay.

It was only weeks later when she recalled what she thought she had seen in the freezer chest. While she was shopping at Seltzer's she reached for a package of hot dogs in the cold chest and blinked, fixed in time and space for a second, remembered the brown paper bag in their freezer, and reminded herself again to ask her father.

Their meals had been mournings since Dick had been shot, and they both grasped at any other topic for conversation. When she mentioned the dead animals in the freezer, however, George Purlie had looked puzzled and shook his head.

"Are you sure, Jilly? That rascal Orin using our freezer chest for his game? I'd certainly like to know, too, let's take a look after dinner."

They had gone out into the garage together and lifted the lid on the long white chest. If there had been something there, it was gone now.

Standing in the soaking morass of Milkwood, watching the workers in their stiff white coveralls lift the rigid corpse of Dan Murphy onto a separate groundsheet, she heard Neil Kelly say, turning to the old farmer huddled under a poncho behind him, "Well, Carl, your notion that those dead squirrels were shot somewhere else and frozen before being dumped here now makes sense. I don't think Dan Murphy jumped down that well."

"I told that dumb-ass state cop. 'Rigor mortis,' he says," and the old man spit.

Chief Scalli, who was standing on the other side of Parrish, raised his eyebrows and shrugged.

The rifle, a clogged and rusted-bolt action .22, was eased out from a bucketful of fresh soil. Scalli moved in closer, motioning to Carl Parrish and one of his young cops who was a hunter. He held up a hand to stop the excavating team and crouched over the gun, then told his cop to get something from the police pack they had lugged in. The young cop came back and handed him a small tank like a fire extinguisher, with a short hose and nozzle attached. Scalli used the water to pressure wash the dirt off the rifle until it was at least identifiable, although it was going to take disassembly and an acid bath in the forensic lab to get all the details.

The young cop, who probably owned the largest collection of *Shooting Times Magazine* in the valley, and who was a part-time gunsmith, said with hesitation. "1902 Winchester, single-shot. Rear peep sight and that heavy barrel weren't on the original 1900 model. Probably a million of them around the country, no serial numbers."

"Single-shot" was what lodged in Neil's mind. Perhaps in the minds of several others standing there, too. If someone had lain in ambush that morning to shoot Dick Colrane on his routine morning bike ride down past Milkwood, then the rifle was probably not reloaded when the shooter turned away, left his faked evidence of squirrel hunting at the spot, and started back through the woods. If he had encountered the hapless Dan Murphy then, poking around in the brush in his goofy quest on Saint Bernadette's day for a magical mystery well that his crazy priest had told him had divine healing powers, he would have had to subdue Dan first, then cold-bloodly reload and shoot him. The obvious fact that the back of Murphy's head was caved in by a terrible blow couldn't prove that, but it added up circumstantially. Whatever had been done simply to injure Dick Colrane, Dan Murphy had been killed deliberately.

Neil looked across into Dick Colrane's eyes and saw how hard he was thinking, putting it all together, his mind racing, trying to reason against the tide of his own emotions. They both knew that along with the obscenely preserved body of old Dan Murphy the excavation team was invisibly disinterring the dead all-American boy too.

Jill stared into the eyes of her father, standing across from her beyond the figure rigid on the groundsheet, listening intently, head bowed, to the college attorney. He watched her somberly for a moment, then detached himself from his companion and walked around to her side.

"You're crying, Gillian." He handed her an old-fashioned white cotton handkerchief. "You mustn't be so upset, it's all ancient history." He put a hand lightly on her shoulder and spoke quietly in her ear. "You're still very much a little girl in many ways, aren't you, Gillian?"

Jill was ashamed of the hot wave of childish humiliation his mocking tone could still evoke in her. The last thing he had ever said to her, in his study, just before her breakdown, had been a gentle admonition to grow up and face reality and stop pretending life was playing with dolls. She had, in fact, clutched a rag doll to her breast for weeks in therapy, and on his frequent visits her father was always patient with that, only smiling knowingly at her, talking to her as he would to a sick little girl.

"Those squirrels were dead," was all she could whisper at him, trembling with adrenaline, Daddy's little sweetie, dry-mouthed with shame and fear.

"Oh dear, you are upset," George Purlie said, hugging her to him with one bearish arm. "You're not making any sense, Jilly. The squirrels are dead and so is everything else in this awful place." He was imitating her wide-eyed look and making it a mirror for her foolishness. He released his hug and carefully lit a match, screening it from the rain, and sucked the flame into his pipe bowl, watching her over the gesture.

Jill broke the hypnotic thrall of his stare and took a step toward Neil Kelly, her hand half-extended, her mouth open to speak, but no words coming. Neil instinctively reached out to help her step through the mud and heard only the end of a phrase.

"What did you say, Jill?"

She blinked and swallowed and made her lips move again. "I'm not a little girl. I'm a grown woman, Neil."

He turned away from Murphy and Dewi and held Jill's hand, which was cold as ice. A few yards behind her, Dick and George Purlie were conversing anxiously, heads together, looking toward Jill.

"Neil," she began to cry. "Those frozen squirrels were from our freezer. In our freezer, I mean. I saw them."

The work crew hauled the groundsheets into a clearing and wrapped their contents and tied the bundles. The digger had hit heavy stone wall construction down below land level in the well and they were moving it back with hand signals to examine the well itself. Scalli's men and the two firemen formed a squad around the evidence. It rained harder. The crewmen paid no attention to the little knots of people from the college talking together on the edge of the action.

Neil could see that Jill was distraught, and he grasped immediately both what she had said and what it might mean. And it fit together perfectly with the one elusive piece of evidence that he had never been able to make fit before. It had never been the dead and frozen animals at the shooting site that had concerned him, but the one lively animal that had scampered across the road in front of Dick Colrane's bike.

Now that quick detail made sense. Someone good at planning and careful about detail had prepared the site to look like a hunting place, and had left the squirrels, already shot elsewhere, there to create an illusion that the police had accepted.

202

Not all the police, but those responsible for the official record. But it took more than someone just good and careful as a planner to add the touch of a live squirrel, both a distraction to slow the cyclist and a proof that live animals still nested and foraged in Milkwood. To take an additional animal there in a sack or a cardboard box to be released at the crucial moment when Dick was coasting down the long hill, knowing that instinct alone would direct the creature's feet away from the poisoned soil of the dump and across the road to safe woods.

Neil realized that what had been set up long ago that spring day in this dying wood was a tiny military maneuver of classical delicacy and thoroughness, tactics and strategy, all thought out ahead. And like every military plan in history, it had been flawed by simple unpredictable chance, in this case the unexpected appearance at the site of old Dan Murphy.

And he knew also, as he moved away from Jill up the slope toward George Purlie that his whole hypothesis could probably never be proven. There was too much that was circumstantial about the evidence, too much time had passed, and to a skillful defendant there were just too many ways of turning aside any direct accusation and blunting it, too much unwillingness in decent people to accept cold-blooded evil as an ordinary component of a neighbor's, a colleague's makeup.

Neil stepped cautiously through the mud and around the great sunken tracks made by the prehistoric bulk of the earth eater that had spit out their murdered boy, watching George Purlie.

George had been to military school. He had won, he liked to boast, every damn award they gave there except sports trophies. Neil stepped over a thick length of tow chain. Math, science, debating, marksmanship, field problems . . . he remembered George reciting the list of firsts. And he had been faculty chairman of the committee that had investigated the conduct of poor old Willard Skink, who had tried to prove that you could train animals to act against instinct. By running in front of moving vehicles, for example.

Neil made his progress deliberately slow, keeping his eyes on his old colleague's face. There would never be, he felt, not even hearing the clank of the machinery and the exchanges of the workers, another minute so fraught with potential revelation, so dangerous for George as this. He made himself into a nemesis, plodding up the slope of George Purlie's fears, by the simple act of staring at him and walking a few steps toward him through the rain and mud with that corpse on the ground behind him.

"You can never be president of the college now, George," was all Neil could make himself say. "You can never play God with anyone's life again."

"Hey, Neil, what? You talking about this whole mess with the pollution and DVR? This—" he seemed at a loss for words and grinned ruefully—"this goddam Gothic incident, digging up some old bum's corpse?"

Neil almost had to admire his gutty actor's style, a battlefield company commander waving aside an unfortunate loss of a few platoons. Man of the world stuff.

"Skink's poor psychotic squirrels, George. Your committee had the responsibility for turning all those laboratory animals of his loose again. I'll go back over every inch of it, George, all the way back to 1960 and you and that committee and past that to you and military school and your sheer envy of Dick's athletic skills—"

Purlie stared at him as though he, Neil, were crazy. "What in hell are you talking about, Neil?"

"—your sheer envy, George, your poisonous, fatal envy of that boy you shot. And those dead animals your daughter found in your garage freezer . . . all of it. And do you know what, George?" The two of them stood side by side, watching the cleanup operation proceed, two old chums huddled together chatting in the rain. "Do you know what?" Neil repeated, shaking his head sadly. "I can never in a million years prove one bit of it. Never. I shall end up looking like a complete fool, and you will be acquitted. I haven't the slightest doubt of that. Do you?"

George Purlie looked at him sourly, sucking his wet pipe. What he saw was the rarest of sights, a man willing to sacrifice his own dignity and reputation to tell what he believed was the truth, even if he couldn't prove it.

"No, Neil, you're right. No matter what kind of wild fantasy you weave out of thin air and half-forgotten facts, you never could prove it."

"But they'll never make you president of the college, will they, George? You'll always be that slightly suspect, tainted figure Neil Kelly, the famous if marginally crazy amateur detective, accused of murder down in that poisoned wood."

Neil had not taken his eyes off George Purlie's face. His old friend broke first, taking his pipe from his mouth to spit to the side, a thin, cottony spit.

"I'm going to file a letter with the police and the trustees tomorrow, George."

He did not say good-bye. He walked back to the Volvo through the dense mud and sat in the car until Murphy and Dewi came to drive back.

When George Purlie shot himself in the roof of the mouth with a long-barreled .22 caliber pistol that evening in his study, everyone was surprised. He left all of his books and papers to the college he truly if imperfectly loved and had wanted to fashion into something perfect.

He also left a short note for Dick Colrane in which he said only: "I gave you your career as a wedding present. You are a scholar and I made you a scholar, even though you were too damnfool slow to get married before. Take care of my little girl."

Dick never showed it to his wife.

George left a brief note for Neil: "It takes one to know one. I knew you had a gift for tactics, you bastard, as Lee said to Grant."

Neil never told anyone what it said and no one asked.

Dick Colrane took the appointment offered by Yale, and a week after their wedding he and Jill moved into a heavy old brick monstrosity of a New Haven town house they both loved.

The college and the public accepted the simple conclusion that the affair of the toxic land reverting to the college, a transaction for which George Purlie was implicitly taking responsibility by his suicide, was the precipitating factor in the event. The brief duel of wills between George Purlie and Neil Kelly was part of no history, might never have happened.

The mystery of Dan Murphy's murder was left unsolved in the police records. His daughter saw him provided with a grand gravestone, on it the words, "ghost to ghost . . . the heart gives up its dead." People walked by to read it and photograph it for a long time afterward, but if they knew the Welsh poem from which the words came, none said.

Coda

A DISCALCED LAITY, *their feet loud in commemorative bed socks the colors of the college (except for the donor's wife, icily unwilling to wear* that *with her eight hundred and eighty dollar magenta suit), huddle at midcourt of the virgin floor.*

Students in gym shorts, cutoffs, and sneakers line the walls, basketballs cradled, silent and waiting. Through massive sliding-glass doors the blue pool steams in the thrifty, unheated air, its waters still to be broken by the first diver from the Olympic three-meter board. An unidentified man in a blue suit, standing spread-legged, like a security guard, which he is, commands the sliding doors, arms folded. The college will not know it for an hour yet, but he conceals in the pocket of his double-knit suit a court order forbidding the use of the pool because its water is supplied through the new campus piping complex which draws from an aquifer now determined to be dangerously polluted. Coliform bacteria will enjoy and multiply in the new facility beyond the glass doors, but no one else will benefit. It will eventually cost OH $800,000, enough for one thousand new dresses for the donor's wife, to install and maintain a water purification system.

But for now, big with ambiguity, the great central hall of the gymnasium waits to become what it was built to be, ceremonies in abeyance, play begun.

Possible geometries conceived by unknown thinkers mark the floor, illustrating unimaginable axioms. Black sidelines, giant green keyholes, and a green dividing line where nets will stretch.

A vaguely religious service is concluding, in the tradition of the American consecration of leisure. Rightfully reverent, shoeless and buskinned, the donor dissembles his pride and his wife her bitterness. She has flat feet.

207

The Frank Valpi Sports Complex is blessed, hailed, and declared officially open to the college.

From inside the vast lapel of his bespoke suit the donor, who once, one hundred and twenty pounds lighter, played second-string soccer for the college, and whose parent Frank Valpi was (and who, because long ago, when one hundred dollars was a fortune to him, won a bet, and thus got a friend of his a job as coach at this college), produces three pages of typed text.

The fidgeting basketball players sigh and the dignitaries hunker back down in their pad-footed chairs; one final speech is about to be made. It is neither too long nor too painful, although, like the suit, it was made by a specialist to the suggestions of the speaker. There is a sudden passage of spontaneous words at its end.

". . . because sports have a musical and a liturgical structure to them," the donor says. "I think we all have to agree with that. My good friend Professor Neil Kelly said that to me in a conversation yesterday, and I thought it was so apropos, with the chaplain here and all, that hopefully it fits in as a final amen. In fact I have asked the trustees and they have agreed to have it added on the bronze plaque by the door under the name of my late father, Frank Valpi. Amen."

The second amendment, President Chip Allen thought, and the building wasn't open yet. That morning, by hasty rump caucus of the trustee committee, the college had accepted a codicil to the dedication plaque outside the new weight-training wing. Alumnus Michael De Soul, OH '60, having learned that the wing had unexpectedly created a quarter-million dollar overrun to furnish it, had gallantly donated that sum to his alma mater, asking only the condition that it be designated The John Venuti Fitness Wing, and modestly allowing only his undergraduate identification, Mitchell De Saulniers '60, to be printed on the new sign. The honoree had unfortunately not shown up for the dedication and would resign his post as athletic director an hour later.

The applause is short, but spirited. The donor sits down satisfied. The beneficiaries who wait in shorts and sneakers join the applause if they are not holding basketballs or balloons. The college officials, who will never scuff this floor again, and the members of the trustee committee, each member of which privately entertains a vision of another scheme by which he can nick the donor for another memorial, mime enthusiasm.

The college anthem announces itself from on high and all rise. Above the shiny court the muses of all such occasions, a quartet consisting of three white girls and one black, visible only to the pure of heart, hover as in an apotheosis scene.

They sing a single long chord, which lifts every face to the lights of the scoreboard clock, their spirit and the college spirit (which also cannot be seen except by the few) infecting every eye and ear. And more than one nose and throat. Their sequined jogging suits are slit to the knee, and give the onlookers one tantalizing glimpse of the crucial interosseus ligaments when, in tasteful finale, they dip together and harmonize a sustained, melodious "Doo Wah!"

If you have enjoyed this book and would like to receive details of other Walker mystery titles, please write to:

Mystery Editor
Walker and Company
720 Fifth Avenue
New York, NY 10019